THE FIRST LIE

After studying literature, linguistics and Spanish at university, A.J. Park trained as an English teacher and actor. He has edited magazines, and taught English, media studies and drama in secondary schools across England. He was also a competitive fencer for seven years.

THE FIRST LIE

A.J. Park

ORION

First published in Great Britain in 2019 by Orion Fiction,
an imprint of The Orion Publishing Group Ltd.,
Carmelite House, 50 Victoria Embankment
London EC4Y 0DZ

An Hachette UK Company

1 3 5 7 9 10 8 6 4 2

A CIP catalogue record for this book is
available from the British Library.

ISBN (Trade Paperback) 9781409187424

Typeset by BORN Group

Printed and bound in Great Britain by Clays Ltd, Elcograf S.p.A.

www.orionbooks.co.uk

Wiola

Maya

Max

'False face must hide what the false heart doth know.'

Macbeth, William Shakespeare

2 October

P

When I see the front door is open, I slam on the brakes.

Six missed calls.

I grab my mobile from the passenger seat and leap out of the car.

Why didn't Alice answer any of the times I tried calling her back? Why the hell is the front door open? Why is the house pitch-black inside?

It's 9 p.m. and just as dark outside.

As I charge towards the front door, passing Alice's soft-top Mercedes, everything replays in my mind: I'm returning late from work, I've had six missed calls from my wife, I haven't been able to reach her since noticing them, and I've arrived to find the house completely dark with the front door open.

Alice would have been expecting me three hours ago, but I was called back to work. I should have let her know I'd been delayed, but work is busy and things got the better of me again; I was putting the finishing touches on what will hopefully be my final case as a barrister for Blacksmith's, one of London's leading law firms, before the committee interviews and then the panel's final decision about who will be named the UK's next Circuit Judge. If I'm chosen, at thirty-seven, I'll make UK history by becoming the youngest ever, and I'll be based in part at the High Court, or the Old Bailey as it's more commonly known, and in other courts around the south-east of the country.

Alice is patient with me; she knows the pressure I'm under, so she never calls to badger me if I get held up. Which is why six missed calls means something's very wrong. And now I find myself at the edge of a black hole, not knowing what I'm about to encounter.

I leap into the house, barely able to discern any of the objects in the reception area, even though I know the location of every item and feature. I call out Alice's name, trying to contain my alarm, but failing I'm sure. My heart skips a beat when there isn't a response. I flick on the corridor lights and barge into the toilet, which is on the right. Then the kitchen, which is straight ahead. And then around the corner to the lounge, and to the right beyond that, the spacious dining room.

Nothing, no sign of Alice.

The house would normally be lit up like Christmas. Alice would normally be in the lounge, a glass of red wine in her hand. The television would normally be on.

She'd normally walk towards me as I enter. We'd normally share a kiss, my hands on her hips, her hands tracing my face, sensuous as the day we first met thirteen years ago.

Normally, but not today.

I take the stairs two at a time, moving too quickly to catch the light switch on my way up. Reaching the landing, there's a wall of silence, so I stop, every door before me closed. 'Alice?' I repeat, more tentatively this time. Something doesn't feel right.

I try the two nearest doors. Nothing. Then the third, my office. As my head's in it, a sound, something muffled, emanates from our bedroom at the far end of the corridor. I move towards it, passing the bathroom on the left-hand side. 'Alice?' I repeat, almost in a whisper.

Reaching the door, I breathe in deeply, clasp the handle and turn it, opening the door onto thick darkness. Suddenly, without much thought, I shoulder-barge my way in, fists clenched, body tense. Expecting something, but I don't know what.

It takes a moment for my eyes to adjust to the black cloud. Something comes into focus.

Someone's sitting on the bed.

'Alice,' I say softly. I can tell it's her because of the shape of her silhouette. She's facing the built-in wardrobe, her head in profile to me. She hasn't seen me, or if she has she doesn't react to my presence.

'Alice?' I say, now at normal volume, no longer as alarmed.

She turns slowly.

When she doesn't reply, I reach for the light switch.

'No!' she screams suddenly, a painful sound. 'Don't switch on the—'

I step back, but my hand remains outstretched and touches the switch. The room lights up.

Her face is pale, her cheekbones and eyes moist. Her white shirt, which is undone, is covered in blood, her exposed skin also smeared red. There's blood on her hands, in her hair.

Specks of it are on her face. She looks like Lady Macbeth after Duncan's murder.

The sight of her shocks me and I struggle to catch a breath. 'Alice, what's hap—'

'The bathroom,' she sobs. I try to reach out to cradle her, but she swipes a hand at me. 'Please, the bathroom!'

I leave her there and rush to the bathroom. Pushing open the door, I switch on the light, and double over at what I find.

There's a man draped over the edge of the bath, his face in its water. There are bubbles in the bath, and blood. The back of his neck has been torn to pieces. Protruding from it is my letter opener, whose design is the shape of a dagger. It's normally on my office desk, but this morning, after opening yesterday's post while in the bedroom, I left it on Alice's dressing table.

I want to call out but, struggling to take in what I've walked into, am without voice. Then, suddenly, hands are pulling me away from the mess. In the doorway, Alice presses me up against the wall.

'Paul,' she says, squeezing my shoulders.

All I can see is the blood that layers her skin and clothing.

'It's not what it looks like,' she says in a panic, sensing my concern and confusion. She looks me deep in the eyes, making sure I see her. 'You know me. I'm your wife. Please believe me.'

I try to hold her gaze, even though my mind is wandering and it's difficult. 'Alice,' I say, 'what have you done?' Then more slowly: 'What have you done?'

A

'It's not what it looks like. You know me. I'm your wife. Please believe me.'

There's a period of time when he stares at me without saying a word. I can tell he's in shock.

Then, finally, he whispers, as if we might be overheard, 'Alice, what have you done? What have you done?'

'I didn't have a choice.' I clutch the lapels of his jacket and uselessly hit his chest with my fists. 'I didn't have a choice.'

He hugs me. 'How? Why?'

'He was in our house!'

Releasing me, he glances back into the room where a strange man's body lies half in, half out of the bath. A place where I normally relax, soothing candles lit, soft music playing in the background.

'What happened?' Paul asks, breathless.

I draw him back towards the bedroom and speak as quickly and clearly as I can, despite what feels like a stabbing pain in my chest. 'I was running a bath. There was music. I had music on . . . Music coming through the Bluetooth speakers, in there. I was about to come out of the bedroom and saw him – he came, he was just there, from nowhere – but he didn't see me, somehow, God knows how. Some kind of, some kind of wire in his hands, I could see it, and he was walking towards me, where he thought I was, I saw him going into the bathroom. He was . . . oh Paul, I knew he was coming for me, I just knew it.'

He looks confused. 'But why?'

'I don't know,' I cry. 'All I know is, I thought he was going to . . . he was going to kill me, Paul. I've never been so scared in all my life. Oh God, I'm so scared now. I didn't know what to do. I saw the letter opener on the dressing table and grabbed it. I didn't think. I barely knew what I was doing and then I was in there and it was over so quickly. I hit him in the back of his neck. Then again and again, I didn't stop. Couldn't, Paul, I thought he was going to kill me. There was a man in our fucking house! We're supposed to be safe here.' I stare at my blood-soaked hands and my body shakes uncontrollably. 'Why, Paul, why? Why was he here? Why did he have to come into our home?' I sob and he once again cradles me in his arms, trying to shush me. 'Why our home? Why me? Oh my God, what have I done, Paul, what have I done?'

He squeezes. I want the pressure to be reassuring, but it isn't. I fear nothing will ever be able to change how I'm feeling.

Nothing will be able to make this better.

'It's okay. Sshhh. It's okay, sweetheart. I'm here for you.'

I press myself deeper into his shoulder, wishing I could be absorbed and taken far from this place. Away from what I've done.

He's breathing heavily, but there's a calmness about him. It should be soothing. I want it to be. 'Kiss me, please,' I murmur into his jacket.

He tries to lead me out of the crevasse I'm hiding in, but my body resists.

'Please,' I repeat, fighting my body's resistance, 'kiss me.'

He strokes my hair. His touch makes my body tingle and my head tilts backwards. I gaze into his eyes. He brings his lips to mine and, for a moment, I'm uplifted, like I'm on a cloud and looking down on a happier time, some other time, like when we shared our first kiss, or our first kiss as Mr and Mrs Reeve, which we shared on the makeshift altar on the Caribbean beach where we were married. His kisses, the feel of his touch, have the power to make all my fears disappear. Now he's pulling me away from a tragedy I fear will ruin the rest of our lives. And thank God it's working.

'Oh Paul,' I sigh, sinking.

He holds the kiss until I'm ready to let go. I place my head against his chest, my arms around his back, his around my shoulders. We hold on for dear life.

'Life will never be the same again,' I whisper.

He says softly, 'Yes, it will. We'll figure it out. Everything will be all right.'

After several minutes, he gently leads me into the bedroom and onto the bed. 'Stay here,' he says and he disappears downstairs. Without him, the shivering increases and I mouth his name, tears welling up in my eyes. He's back in a few moments and I'm overwhelmed by relief. He's carrying a large bowl and a cloth. 'Let's clean you up,' he says, crouching down beside the bed. Slowly, delicately, he dips the cloth into the water and traces it across my face, its warmth penetrating my body's resistance. I look down into the water. Each time he puts the cloth into it and squeezes it, a red waterfall drips down and a deeper red puddle appears.

'Don't look,' he urges. 'Just let me do this. You'll feel better when I'm finished and it's all gone.' My body shudders and I shed more tears. 'We'll work everything out.'

'How?' I say, the sound barely coming out.

'I just need time to think. I'll help us make this right.' He wipes my face, my neck, my chest, then my stomach.

'I've killed a man, Paul.'

'He broke into our house, Alice. You had no choice.'

'But I've killed a man! These hands' – I hold them up, watch as they shake – 'I've killed.'

Stopping what he's doing, Paul looks me in the eye and then brings his lips to mine. He puts the bowl on the floor and I feel his hands in my hair, massaging my scalp. Then he kisses me on each cheek. 'You're not alone here. I'm with you. I will help you. We'll get through this together.'

He lifts up the bowl and starts drawing the cloth along my forearms.

'What'll happen to me?'

He puts down the bowl again and runs the back of his fingers across my right cheek. I know he has an answer, but he doesn't want to say it.

'Will I go to jail?' I ask.

He smiles at me. It looks like a happy smile, but it masks a wistfulness. And still he doesn't speak.

'Should we call the police, Paul?'

When he remains silent, only offering a smile that's beginning to look pathetic and unhelpful and full of doubt, I repeat, now with some force, 'Shall we, Paul?' My tears have stopped.

I can see he wants to say yes, that he's thinking how to. He starts to nod his head, but lowers it and then shakes it. 'No,' he says, his eyes facing the ground. 'No, we shouldn't call the police.'

'Because you know what will happen? Because you're a barrister?'

'Because I know.' He shakes his head forcefully, winces and places his hands on my knees, squeezing too tightly. 'Of course we should call the police, Alice. We should call them and tell them exactly what's happened.' He looks devastated, like he's been given some awful news and has only partly digested the reality of it.

'But I've killed a man, Paul.'

'I know—'

'And you know better than most people what that must mean.'

He squeezes his eyes shut and slowly nods his head.

'What does it mean, Paul?'

He places his forehead in the palm of his hand. I look down into my lap, where my hands are. He hasn't washed the blood off my palms. I bring them closer to my eyes, so that I can really see the proof of what I've done, and then I turn them towards him.

'Look,' I say pitifully, holding them up. He looks up. 'Look and tell me, what do you see?' I think I can see moisture building up in his eyes. 'Tell me, what do I look like to you?'

An explosion of air comes out of his mouth and he lifts his hand, once again, to my cheek. 'You were only defending yourself.'

'It doesn't look like that, does it?'

He shakes his head as he says, 'No, it doesn't, but you were defending yourself. He was in our home.'

'Yes, our house.'

Paul, normally so confident, so sure about everything, looks lost. I've ruined everything.

'I'm so sorry.'

'Oh Alice—'

'I'm sorry. I've destroyed . . . everything.'

'You have nothing to be sorry about. You had to defend yourself. You'd be dead otherwise. I couldn't lose you, Alice.'

'You can still lose me. I'll end up in prison.'

'You had no choice.'

'I can see it in your eyes, Paul. You know what will happen to me. And you'll be ruined. Everything you've worked for. There's no way they'll give you the promotion if your wife's a convicted murderer.'

'No choice,' he says more forcefully, and suddenly he's up on his feet. I'm taken aback by the alteration in his movement and tone.

He becomes still. He looks down at me. 'You had no choice,' he says clinically, professionally. 'He was going to kill you. So now we have no choice.'

I lean forwards. 'What do you mean?'

'Do you trust me, Alice?' he asks.

'With every breath in my body.'

'If I'd only been here . . .'

I nod.

'Now I'm here for you.' And then he says quickly, suddenly, as if he doesn't want to hear the words himself, 'We're going to get rid of the body.'

4 September –
Four Weeks Ago

I

Detective Sergeant Katherine Wright and Detective Constable Ryan Hillier of the Major Investigation Team, or MIT, part of the Specialist Crime and Operations Directorate's Homicide Command North-West, arrived in Kendall Green. She parked the car and they got out. Hers was one of many police cars, both marked and, like hers, unmarked, in the street and neighbourhood surrounding the apartment block. She was there to take charge of the scene and collate information from the current investigators and officers in preparation for the arrival of her boss, Detective Superintendent Jonathan Lange, who led the MIT.

Wright looked across the bleak panorama that made Kendall Green the eyesore it was. The apartment block was designed in the shape of an L, very wide, very brown, very neglected, and only four storeys high, yet it housed over one hundred homes and five hundred people. It was rundown and wholly unappealing, yet its properties could fetch mid-six figures. Its postcode was NW5, making it close enough to central London to warrant extortionate purchase prices and even more exorbitant monthly rents.

Wright and Hillier made their way past the police cordon after showing their ID cards and found themselves at the block's entrance. Their destination: number 74. They had already been briefed on what they would encounter, but advance warning could do little to quell the unsettling stomach sensations that were a natural part of the job. Despite eight years of experience as a detective, the reactions were an intrinsic part of what made Wright who she was. And police officers, she maintained, were human, despite what movies conveyed, despite what kids thought. *You never get used to it; you just find a way to compartmentalise what you see and deal with it.*

Or you get out.

Which she'd thought about doing for a long time now.

As was usual in such circumstances, the two detectives stopped speaking as soon as they left their car. They needed, and were thankful for, time to prepare. They took the lift to the third floor and made their way along the corridor. An officer guarded the door to number 74. The front door was an immaculate, vibrant blue, the antithesis of the building's exterior.

Wright and Hillier produced their ID cards and the officer on duty immediately stepped aside, nodding his head. Both detectives placed protective gloves on their hands and paper shoe covers on their feet, all of which would be returned at the end of their time here for careful inspection in case any evidence was inadvertently taken from the scene. Wright led the way in.

Inside, the décor was in keeping with the front door: flawless, bright, contemporary and expensive. The apartment felt completely out of place from the shell that housed it.

The hallway was empty, bar the occasional framed photograph on the wall. Wright and Hillier passed the kitchen on the right and a bedroom on the left. The bathroom was also on the right, sans people, and the lounge was at the end of the hallway, opening up into a spacious, light area. A dining table and chairs were directly ahead, a corner sofa to the left and a television on the wall in front of it.

Various scene investigators, dressed in white body suits, were dusting for fingerprints, bagging items, photographing and busy completing countless other tasks.

In the middle of the large sofa sat the property's owner, its sole occupant, Richard Dollard. He was upright and his hands were in his lap. His head was tilted back against the headrest. His neck has been sliced through. A deep wound. So deep that from afar it looked as if his head was only held on by the skin at the back of the neck. Dried blood caked his white shirt, the top button open, and a significant proportion of the cream-coloured sofa.

Wright and Hillier walked round to the front of the sofa and stood next to a middle-aged man, who was the lead crime scene investigator. Heavily balding, Daniel Emerson was someone whom Wright knew all too well. Even though they got on, his presence was always a difficult reminder to her that death brought along countless mysteries, some too difficult to ever solve.

'Dan,' she said.

'Katie.' He was the only one of her colleagues who called her that. Although they weren't friends outside of work, they were on friendly terms. Given what they had seen together, there was no other option. Every arm was needed for support, and friendliness and familiarity helped.

'What have you found?'

'Some kind of wire. Very sharp. Sliced right through. He didn't even put up a fight. Wouldn't have had the chance to, poor bugger. He was watching TV and probably didn't even see it coming. Whoever it was, was behind him, leant over and pulled right back. It went through with ease.'

'How did he get in?' she asked.

'Front door lock was picked. We haven't found anything that looks out of place yet. Picking up lots of prints, but they could belong to him or any number of previous visitors. Probably do, if I'm honest. Will take ages to tell, maybe we never will. Not many people could pick that kind of lock and leave everything so clean. All this blood, not one footprint. Don't know about you, but I couldn't sneak up on someone as young as this and get away with it so easily. This one has confidence. Buckets of it.'

'Tell me more about the weapon.'

'Sharp wire, nothing more than that at the moment. But if I had to guess, based on the slice and how easily it seemed to go through the skin, how cleanly, I'd say piano wire. You want to use the technical term, or the old word, he's been garrotted.'

'Garrotted? Piano wire?' she repeated.

'Will do the trick every time,' he nodded. 'Effortlessly.'

The method was a first in Wright's experience, even though she had almost a decade with a London MIT. 'Not something just anyone would have lying around.'

'Indeed not.'

'Not something just anyone would think to use.'

'You took the words right out of my mouth.'

'Ryan,' she said to Hillier, 'find out where they sell piano wire locally and throughout the city.'

'Lots of places, I'd imagine.'

'Me too. But let's try. You never know, there might be a local place that can connect us to someone from around here,' she kidded herself, not believing it for a second. 'And let's see if method gets us anywhere. Find out if there are any unsolved or solved murders involving piano wire in the past, I don't know, let's say five years.'

'Just five?'

'Start with five, see what you get. Go to ten if you don't get anywhere.'

'May I?' she said to Emerson, indicating the body.

'With pleasure,' he replied, stepping back, removing his gloves. 'Needed a coffee and a pee anyway.' He made his way out of the apartment without another word.

'I'll see you back at the station?' Hillier asked.

'Sure, Ryan. When Lange arrives, I'll brief him and then make my way back. You take the car.' She handed him the keys.

He gave her a friendly tap on the arm as he took the keys and left.

Wright returned her attention to the body. Not a person any more. Not Richard Dollard. She tried not to look too closely inside the wound – didn't want to take that image with her, although she suspected the memory of this scene would be with her for a long time to come. Another image to join the stream of others that she couldn't flush away.

She leant forwards and looked deep into a pair of dead eyes, hoping for clues, hoping for a sign, hoping for some kind of help. Dead eyes, eyes that would haunt her, like all the others.

She swallowed down the bile that worked its way up. She wanted to cry. Another life extinguished. More waste and devastation. More lives ruined.

She was human, after all.

Dead eyes.

2 October

P

'I need to think. We've got to do this the right way.'

We have to turn the house back into our house. There can be no trace of that man having been here. And there can be no trace of anything untoward having happened here this evening.

'We have to be precise,' I tell Alice. 'We have to get rid of him and make the house spotless. I've tried cases in which the smallest piece of DNA, even a microscopic speck, has led to a conviction.'

It's hard to think of us in the criminal sense, but by doing this that's what we're about to become. I won't call us that in front of Alice; she's alarmed enough and I'm worried I could push her over the edge.

'Anything from a hair to a clothing fibre could place him here. That'd be enough if the police come looking.'

But what could possibly lead them to turn up on our doorstep?

'Are you ready to do this?' I ask.

She breathes deeply and nods her head. 'I'll do whatever you think we have to do to get our lives back.'

'Once we've started, we won't be able to change our minds.'

'I know that.'

'Then let's take our lives back. Fetch two pairs of rubber gloves, some masking tape and black bags.' She moves off quickly. While she's doing that, I grab an old duvet from the airing cupboard and lie it flat in the hallway right outside the bathroom. I grab Alice a freshly washed jumper, then I run downstairs and put on a pair of old boots, at which point she comes out of the kitchen. 'Have you got anything like this? Something you can get rid of after we're finished?'

She grabs some dirty trainers from the shoe cupboard that's next to the staircase. I hand her the jumper, which she puts on. Booted, we each step into a black bag, making leg holes in them. 'Now make a hole in that and pull it over your head,' I say, handing her another black bag. 'Then prise your arms through.' I use the masking tape to secure the black bag on her body. 'Tape this to me, in the same way.' While she's doing that, I ask, 'Do you have any hair covers, the kind of thing you can wear in the shower?'

'Disposable shower caps, yes.'

'Get two. Unused. We have to cover up every part of ourselves that we possibly can. Our hair mustn't fall out on him. The floor, the house, we'll sort out later, we can control that, but we don't want someone digging him up and finding bits of us on him.'

Noticing the masking tape is running low, I go into the kitchen, not worrying about the bits of dried mud my boots leave on the polished tiles, and search for more. As I find a new reel and go back into the hall, Alice comes back down from the en suite, saying, 'I've only got one shower cap.'

26

'Shit,' I say. 'Okay, you're the one with the longer hair, you use it. Tie your hair up really tight and high and pull that down as far as you can so that everything's covered.'

We go upstairs, where Alice gets some hairbands and hair clips, while I grab a hoodie from the bedroom wardrobe. I've got one with hood strings that tighten, which will have to do.

'Who on earth could he be?' she asks, reappearing.

'Probably some drugged-up psychopath. I wonder if he has an ID on him.'

'I've already checked. He doesn't.'

'You checked?' I say suddenly, alert to her error and frustrated by the move. 'You've risked DNA contamination, Alice. You shouldn't have done that.'

She brings her hands to her face. 'I didn't know, Paul, I didn't know.'

'We really should burn the body,' I say quietly to myself, but Alice hears.

There's alarm in her voice. 'Burn it?'

I close my eyes and groan. 'No, it's just . . . Oh, forget it, I shouldn't have. I'm sorry, I didn't mean it.'

We step into the hallway. I check Alice's shower cap. 'Snug fit,' I say. 'Good. Hold out your hands.' I pull the rubber gloves over them and use more masking tape to stick them to her jumper sleeves, and then I wrap it round several times. 'Tight?'

'Almost too tight.'

'Perfect. Do the same to me. As tight as you can.'

After she applies the final piece of tape, I ask her, 'Ready?' I don't say for what; she instinctively knows

27

what I mean. I lead the way into the bathroom. We don't approach him straightaway; we linger by the door, our hands clinging together and it's clear that neither of us wishes to let go.

I'm the first to move forward. Alice remains by the door. I take tentative steps towards the bath, towards my target. The dead body in my bathroom. This man, whoever he is. First thick-soled boots. Then dark jeans. Then a black jumper. Then a torn, blood-covered neck.

I try to pull him away from the bath, but nothing happens when I attempt to drag him backwards. He's huge, like a lead weight. Dead weight.

Seeing me struggle, Alice comes to me. Clinging onto my right arm, she shelters behind me, as if she's unwilling to look at what she has done.

'Try pulling that arm and I'll take this one,' I say.

She edges round me and does so but with squinted eyes.

'It's okay,' I try to reassure her.

Several heaves later, he starts to move out of the water, his head connecting with the enamel of the bath as we pull him to the floor. Water follows him, soaking the floor and our footwear. After a moment to regain our breath, we each take a leg and pull. We manage to drag him out of the bathroom, his neck twisting awkwardly because of the missing section of skin. In the hallway, I try to lift him under his shoulders so that I can position him on the duvet. 'Jesus, help me, would you,' I groan, unable to get him on it properly. Alice does her best to push and pull whatever part of his body she can clamp hold of. 'It's okay,' I repeat, expelling air, as much for my own benefit as for

28

hers. When he's finally on the duvet, I straighten my back and stretch, groaning from the discomfort I feel.

His eyes stare up at the ceiling. Now is the first time I take a long, hard look at his features. His wide-open eyes bore into me when I lean over him; he looks full of rage, or at least he was full of rage when he died. A visage of fury. His forehead is wrinkled, his head close-shaved. He's got a mole on his right cheek and a wide jaw. The front of his neck is intact and it's short, tucked awkwardly to one side, deep into his burly shoulders.

'Oh God,' Alice cries.

'Don't look at him,' I say, knowing immediately how ridiculous that sounds; the lure is impossible to resist. 'Just look at me instead.' I indicate my eyes with a forefinger. 'Look at me and forget about him. It's all about us now.'

She heaves a sob. I take hold of her wrist, squeeze perhaps a little too hard, but I have only one objective in doing so: I need her to keep it together and remain composed; God knows I can't do this alone.

'We have no choice, Alice. We're not the criminals here. He is.'

She nods. I reach forward and wipe away the beginning of a tear from under her eye.

'Fuck him.' Then I kiss her. 'We'll be okay. I've thought this through. We're being careful. We'll make it.'

'I believe you,' she says.

'Okay, let's try to wrap this around him.' Alice takes one end, I grab the other, and we pull the duvet around his bulk. Then, struggling, we turn him onto his side and try to roll the duvet around his body. We're partially successful, the duvet seems tight and snug enough. 'Where's the masking tape?' I ask, unable to see it. She scans the floor and finds it. I tape the duvet in place, using up reams of the stuff. 'Hopefully that will hold.'

I stand up, stretching again and breathing heavily. The package looks like a soft coffin. 'Okay, let's get him downstairs and out of the way. Then the real work will begin.'

We try to lift the duvet-wrapped body but can't manage. 'Drag it,' I say, taking the head end, Alice pushing from the butt end. Finding and then maintaining a grip is hard; the duvet keeps falling flat on the ground, but we encourage one another and persevere. Reaching the staircase, I say, 'Almost there. We'll put him at the bottom of the stairs and then we can start cleaning up here.'

Switching sides so that I can better control the rate of descent, Alice takes the first step onto the staircase. She's five steps down, the purchase of the floor lost as half the body is over the edge of the top step, when I recognise we've made a mistake. I see her balance waver. She stumbles and falls, tumbling down a few steps, and I call out her name, instinctively lurching towards her, dropping the duvet, which slides down several steps until it collides with the fallen Alice. 'Are you all right?' I ask as I reach her.

She winces, clutching her hip. 'Fine, fine,' she says. She tries to stand but doesn't manage to get up. 'Shit,' she says.

'Oh no, oh God,' I say as I manoeuvre round the body, which has come partly unwrapped. I can see an arm hanging out.

Please don't let anything be broken. I help Alice up. 'Can you put any weight on it?' My heart is pounding as I await an answer. If she can't, we're screwed.

She applies some pressure on it, winces, but manages to hold her weight. 'I'll be okay,' she grimaces. Momentary relief overwhelms me, but then a stark realisation hits: we have a long way to go before we're safe.

Swapping positions again, I pull and she pushes, and we eventually leave him in a bundle on the hallway floor. We go into the kitchen and pull from the cupboards everything I think we will or might need. 'Fill a bucket with hot soapy water,' I say, as I put into the laundry basket a bottle of bleach, more rubber gloves, paper towels, kitchen and bathroom cleaners, and black bags – everything that looks like it has the power to scrub and clean and conceal what we're doing here.

'Okay, side by side,' I tell her, 'we're going to do everything together. You watch every move I make, I'll watch every move you make. Don't blink. Everything has to be spotless. We have to make every mark, every sign that he's been here, disappear, and there'll be so many we can't even see. Watch and clean. I'll clean and then you re-clean the exact same surface.'

I put on the shower and rinse away as much of the blood as possible. It drains away in one long red stream. The sight of it makes me wince. We rinse the shower curtain, then I remove it and bag it, the same with the bath mat and toilet mat. What remains on the bath's surface, I blitz with bleach. I put on a second pair of rubber gloves, Alice does the same, and I scrub with a washing-up scrubber. Splashes of water, mixed with blood, hit my face and clothing. I pause momentarily and close my eyes, trying to ignore that I'm wearing his blood, wishing the moment away, but I don't have time to waste; I continue. I rinse away the bleach, and the bath looks clean, shiny, but I step aside so that Alice can do it all over again. She pours in a lot of bleach, too much, and there's a suction sound from the bottle before she says, 'It's run out.' The scent is unbearable.

The rest of the bathroom is filled with tiles and the corridor outside is a parquet floor. 'We'll need more,' I say. 'Do we have any more anywhere? I only found the one bottle.'

She shakes her head. 'No, I don't think so.'

'Shit.' The last thing we need is to stop right now.

I dash downstairs and open the cupboard under the sink. No more bleach. I look down at what I'm wearing. It's going to have to come off.

Back upstairs, Alice helps me undress and I put on some fresh clothes. 'I'll be back quickly,' I tell her, snatching a glance at the alarm clock. 21:45. 'Fifteen minutes and the supermarket shuts. I'll be quick.' I charge from the room and head downstairs.

'Paul!' There's panic in Alice's voice.

I stop. 'I've got to go! What's the matter?'

She appears at the top of the staircase. Dressed like that and staring down at me, she reminds me of Annie Wilkes. I shudder. 'The blood,' she says. 'You've got blood on your face. Wash it off.'

My hand touches my cheek. Nodding, I breathe a sigh of relief. I go back into the bathroom and scrub as vigorously as I can, all too conscious of the time I'm losing.

'Lock the door and don't answer it to anyone,' I call as I run downstairs. 'I'll knock three times to be let back in. Only open when you're certain it's me. Switch off the lights.'

'Uh-uh, not with him here.' Her voice is quivering.

Standing next to the corpse and with one hand on the front door, I turn to face Alice. I don't know what else to say.

'Paul, please don't leave me,' she says.

'Alice, there isn't time. We haven't got a choice. If I don't get more bleach, we won't be able to clean everything properly.'

'But he's there and you're asking me to sit here in the dark.'

I don't have time for this. My jaw tenses. 'He's dead, Alice. He can't hurt you any more.'

'He can,' she nods vehemently, 'oh, yes he can.'

'I have to go. Stop it. You have to be strong. Hold it together.'

'Paul—'

I take either the brave, or foolish, decision to leave. If I don't, we'll be stuck. 'I'll be really fast. Please.' And I don't wait for an answer, shutting the front door behind me.

Thankfully, the supermarket is only a couple of streets from our home, so I arrive just in time. I grab five bottles of bleach, just in case, and a range of other cleaning products. I'm aware that I'm being filmed on CCTV, but I don't have an alternative option. I have to be here and have to hope no one ever has reason to try to establish my whereabouts this evening. I make sure to use the self-service checkouts in the hope that no staff will see me buying an unusual amount of cleaning product. I add a sturdy material bag and quickly carry my purchases from the shop.

I rush back, worried about what kind of state I'll find Alice in. The lights are on. I park the car and get out of it as casually as I can.

A light is shining in the near distance, but I barely register it until I've heard a voice call out, 'Everything all right, Paul?'

I stop, realising there's nowhere to hide. I turn to my right. I've been seen. I lift up a hand in greeting and, noticing the supermarket bag, call back, 'Ran out of bloody milk, Bob, that's all.' Our neighbour is partly cut off from view by the thick and long row of trees and bushes that separates our houses and driveways, but I can see the boot of his car is open and he's rooting around in it.

'I'm a black coffee man myself, this time of night,' he says. 'That might make me an anomaly, but it knocks me out every time. Mark my words, you try it if ever you can't get some shut-eye.'

'Thanks, Bob, will do.' I feign a cheerful smile.

He offers a thumbs-up and says, 'Sleep well.'

'Goodnight, Bob.'

I knock on the door, slowly, three distinct times. Through the frosted glass, I see a figure coming down the staircase and approaching. She opens the door. I push through and close it as quickly as I can. Immediately, it's obvious that Alice has been crying. I don't say anything, just hug her, hoping that'll be enough. Her body is trembling and I instantly forget about Bob. We're moving forwards one step at a time, but I can tell she's fallen several metres back while I've been gone. I stroke her hair. 'I had to go, darling. We needed all this.' I indicate the bag.

'You left me with him,' she whispers and, for a moment, there's a trace of menace in her voice.

I pull back. 'Alice, please—'

'You're supposed to protect me.'

'I am.'

'By leaving me with a corpse!'

'Alice,' I snap, 'it was that or get stuck. DNA is used to catch people out every single day. For the rest of my career, many of the convictions I witness will be based around DNA findings. We have to decontaminate this house. You have to be strong and we have to do this. I'm sorry, but I am protecting you and this is for your own good. Hate me later if you wish, but right now, be with me and let's get this done together.'

She stares me deep in the eye and then, after what seems like an age, solemnly nods.

I redress in the bedroom, Alice helping me to apply fresh tape, and I check that her covering is still firmly in place, patching her up where I think is necessary. We put the bleach to good use, covering every tile in the bathroom, scrubbing it, rinsing it and then repeating. The stink in the room is rancid and I see Alice clutching her head. 'What's up?' I ask.

'My head feels so thick and heavy. We need fresh air.'

'We can't open the windows. We can't risk anyone seeing in.'

'This time of night? No one's going to see in, Paul. Besides, no one lives close enough.'

'I don't want to risk it. This place remains sealed off.' I can see she's about to cry. 'I'm sorry,' I say. 'Not much longer, okay.'

It's not long before my head also starts to hurt. The room reeks, we both feel ill and dizzy, but we don't relent. Won't and can't.

I stand over the hallway parquet floor with a bottle of bleach in my hand.

'It'll ruin it,' Alice says.

'Then we'll replace it.' I pour the bleach, get on my knees and start scrubbing. 'Follow me,' I say to Alice, handing her the bottle. When I get to the end of the hallway, I turn around and watch her as she approaches me, scrubbing every inch of the floor I've just cleaned. There's perspiration on her forehead and, seeing it, I realise how sweaty I am too. I also realise I've been working on autopilot, my attention focused on what I've been doing and not on how I'm feeling. Which is exhausted.

My eyes zoom in to a patch of flooring. 'Gap,' I say through gritted teeth, and I crawl towards part of the parquet outside the bathroom door where I find a hairline crack between two planks of wood. 'Shit,' I say.

'What's the matter?' Alice peers over me.

'Here.' I put my gloved finger on the crack. 'Anything could have fallen down here. We've walked over it several times. Anything, a hair, anything. He was lying just above it on the duvet.'

'So what do we do?'

I sit up, without an answer. 'I don't know. It's got to come up.'

'You can't be serious, Paul. How would you do that?'

'I don't know. Shit.' I see the bottle of bleach that Alice is holding. 'Let me have that.' I take it and open the lid. Slowly, I pour the entire contents over the crack. It slowly seeps through. 'This is going to have to be pulled up and replaced. Hopefully that will help for now.'

'Why, Paul?'

'A single hair will be enough for a conviction. If a single hair has fallen in there and they somehow place him here, we're finished. This floor needs to be replaced and quickly.' Then suddenly: 'Fuck it, I want to take it up now.'

'Now?'

'I'm going to get a wrench.'

'Really?'

'Yes, Alice. Yes.'

I return a few minutes later, wrench in hand, and get on my knees. Bending down, I pry into the floorboards, picking, scraping, frustrating, until eventually something gives, the wrench catches fully and a bit of wood rips up. I hit, catch and pull, hit, catch and pull, until I break away a large section of flooring. 'Give me something to scrub with,' I say.

As I'm scrubbing on the board beneath where the flooring was, I ask, 'Do you know if he went in any of the other rooms?' My body is aching, the sweat intense.

'I've no idea,' Alice says, her hands out to her sides.

'Think,' I snap, unexpectedly, unwantedly angry. This physical work, it's so hard, it's getting to me. 'I have to know where he was. I need to know. Think, damn it. Think. It has to be clean.'

Panicking, she says, 'I don't know, I don't know. Please, Paul, don't do this, don't be so angry with me.' Her body is shaking again.

Realising what I've done, how I've lost control, I stop scrubbing and get up. 'I'm sorry,' I say, stepping to her. I take her in my arms. 'I'm sorry. I just want to do this right.' She tries to smile. 'For you.' This time, she kisses me.

'I understand.'

We hoover the bedroom, moving every item of furniture, and remove the bedding, which Alice puts in the washing machine. We hoover the staircase, spray it with floor cleaner and scrub.

We still have downstairs to do, but the body's lying in the hallway and it's gone 1 a.m. We have to dispose of him somewhere far from the house, and we have to do it while most people are asleep, so we don't have much more time before we have to leave.

'Well done,' I say, although Alice looks anything but proud. 'Now the car.'

I poke my head outside before fully stepping out, checking whether Bob is still in his driveway, even though I know he almost certainly won't be at this hour. The driveway slopes down towards the house, so I'm able to let the car roll, and I bring it to a stop right next to the front door.

Back inside, I apply even more masking tape to the duvet and we drag the package, struggling much more than before because we're so exhausted, to the front door. I don't have anything to use as a cover in the car boot, so I'll have to have the car fully valeted in the morning.

I go as quietly as I can to the garden shed, from which I remove two spades. Only one is a proper metal garden spade; the other is made from some kind of thick plastic.

The Outlander's boot is spacious and the rear windows are tinted black. We move the body towards it in stages and we lift it in even more disjointed stages. Lugging the parcel upward, I thrust my body in the same direction, striking my head against the boot door. 'Shit!'

Before I know what's going on, Alice grabs me and applies pressure to my forehead with her gloved hand. I quickly see blood dripping. 'The toilet,' she says and she leads me into it.

I lean over the sink. 'The boot,' I say sharply.

She runs back outside to close it and I wet some toilet paper, applying it to my forehead. Releasing it, I take a look in the mirror at the damage. There's a nasty gash.

Rejoining me, Alice asks, 'Are you all right?'

'I'll survive. Can you grab me some plasters?'

After maintaining pressure and once Alice has applied a couple of plasters to the wound, we remove the black bags and gloves. I grab some more gloves and we jump into the car.

I haven't plugged in the Outlander, but I'm hopeful there's enough charge left in its battery to get us out of the driveway and down the road before the engine kicks in. I didn't think to look when I dashed to the supermarket.

I press the 'start' button, hopefully. Alice looks on nervously.

The dashboard lights up, but the engine remains off, which means the batteries have some charge in them. I quickly put the car into reverse, switch off the headlights, and pull out of the long driveway, letting the car roll as much as possible to preserve, and charge, the battery.

The driveway is about fifteen metres long and surrounded by trees on both sides, so I'm not sure of the value of killing the lights, but it feels necessary, or appropriate, given the circumstances. Plus, I want us to be inconspicuous once we're in the street.

I pull out of the driveway and turn left. My eyes dart between the rear-view mirror and wing mirrors. I switch on the headlights when we reach the end of the street, which is filled with large, set-back detached houses, most lined at the front with trees to shelter them from the gaze of anyone passing by. Privacy is important around here. Even though I can't see any signs of nocturnal life, I keep scanning until we're several roads away.

It's about a mile before the engine ignites and I verbalise my relief and appreciation for having purchased the petrol hybrid electric vehicle. Despite some everyday reservations, I couldn't be happier with it than I am right now.

'Thank God,' Alice says, even though she hasn't believed for eight years, not since her parents turned their backs on her. I know she means it, because I do too. She leans her head back against the headrest and closes her eyes. She looks like she's praying. I know she isn't.

'Thank God,' I repeat. I thank Him, thank Him from the bottom of my soul. Which right now feels blackened and buried in the pits of hell. But relieved. 'Thank God.'

12 September –
Three Weeks Ago

2

Detective Sergeant Katherine Wright, who was heading to the crime scene in Mitre Street, had received the call twenty-five minutes earlier. She was lying in bed, her eyes fixed on the ceiling, familiar with the early morning darkness. Her mind was filled with pictures, stills that had been collecting over a career already too long, despite her youthful thirty-eight years: images of the dead, of all whom she had failed to help and protect.

Her nocturnal mind-wanderings were interrupted by her mobile phone ringing. She glanced at its screen.

5.00.

With her mind swirling amid memories of fifteen years of victims, she answered the call to hear the grumbling voice of Detective Superintendent Jonathan Lange. He relayed the instructions: attend an unidentified male who had been discovered in his apartment in Mitre Street, NW3. Throat slit. A lot of blood. Assess the scene. Prepare to report.

She sighed. Another image to bank in the ever-expanding library. How long could she keep doing this?

Wright had started her career in the East End, a street copper for eight years, then a promotion to detective came, first as a DC, and five years later she made it to DS. That was two years ago. She was proud to have made it this far, but what she had to see and the responsibility she bore came at a heavy cost. She had to live with it all, which she struggled to do.

Stabbings, recently more than she could count, shootings, poisonings, stranglings, hit and runs. Throw someone off a bridge or from a building. Suffocate them.

Whatever the means, none brought killer and victim so close as slicing a throat. They would touch while it happened, like intimates. The second hand might support the chin, much like a lifeguard pulls a drowning victim to safety. There was something especially obscene about an intimacy such as this. And piano wire – to garrotte. That's what it was again this time, the second in two weeks.

Wright lived in a studio flat a ten-minute journey from the station. She'd never married – came close once, though – so she saw no need for more than the minimum. To her, home was merely somewhere to sleep, and she usually didn't get much. She was married to her work, even though it often made her sick to the stomach.

She knew her work was intensely important, so she believed that her suffering was a small price to pay.

In the bathroom, she stared into the mirror. Her eyes, the bags, the dark tiredness. The worry lines. The unhappiness, for every wrong she righted couldn't make up for all the wrongs she'd failed to make right.

Quickly dressed, she opened the front door, fresh air flooding the room. Inhaling deeply, she headed to her car.

Arriving in Mitre Street, she got out of the car, approached the police cordon, showed her ID card, ducked under the police tape, and made her way to the apartment block entrance. A quiet place, she registered, and noticeably more opulent in appearance than Kendall Green. This block was more like a small skyscraper, twenty-three floors of wealth. All the décor was fresh and the foyer was bright and airy.

Detective Constable Ryan Hillier was waiting for her outside the apartment's front door. Number 134.

'Have you taken a look?' she asked.

He answered grimly. 'Worse than the last one, if that's possible.'

The apartment was open plan, the front door revealing a large lounge-diner. The kitchen unit, which included a spacious island, was finished in a sleek glossy white. The floor and walls were tiled a shiny black, and the neighbouring lounge floor was a dark parquet. A cream leather sofa had been placed in the centre of the room facing an enormous wall-mounted widescreen television.

Booted and gloved, Wright and Hillier moved further in. The bathroom came off the area to the right. This was where the activity was. Wright looked in over the scene investigators who were busy at work, Daniel Emerson in the centre of them.

A room-centred, oval-shaped tub, facing a far-side opaque window, was filled with blood-red water. In it lay the corpse of a man who appeared to be in his thirties.

As Wright peered in, no one said a word to her, but they knew she was there. They knew who she was. She was always called in to deal with the messy ones. She was the one who pursued things relentlessly, with blood, sweat and tears. Her colleagues, however, including Hillier, had no idea of the toll it took on her.

There was a lot of blood here, not just in the water, but on the cream floor tiles. A lot of pain.

Wright stepped in, standing near the sink, giving the scene investigators space. She winced at what she saw. She moved closer and crouched down so that her eyes lined up with the top of the bath. She looked into his open gaze. She shook her head. Another waste of life. She didn't have children, but she visualised herself as a parent upon hearing about the death of a child. Or as a wife, being given the news about a husband gone forever.

'Any witnesses?' she asked Hillier, who remained in the doorway.

'No one.'

'Just like last time,' she said. 'He's good.'

'That he is.'

'Any prints?' she asked the technicians who were working on their hands and knees and facing walls.

One answered, 'A lot, as you'd expect, but nothing that stands out as abnormal.'

'Nothing odd with the front door, either,' Emerson called out.

'Clean,' she said to herself. 'Prepared and thorough.'

Hiller took a step in. 'Do you think this is the start of something?'

She stood up, but without turning to look at him, and said, gazing down at the ground, 'Maybe.'

'A serial?'

'Maybe,' she repeated, unsure, shaking her head. Thinking. 'Maybe.'

A

I've never seen a dead body before. When we turned him over and I saw his face, I thought . . . I don't know, I just wanted to run and never turn back.

Is it possible to escape a life? I wish it were.

By the time we got him downstairs and into the car, my head was pounding, I felt ready to gag, but I knew we had no choice. I believed Paul when he said it was him or us, and we chose to save ourselves. Or rather, Paul has chosen to save me. I need his help. We've got far too much to live for.

We haven't spoken about where we're going and we're sitting in silence as Paul is driving along the quiet roads, and then I speak up. 'What have you planned?'

'Berryhill Woods,' he replies and says no more. It's about twenty minutes, or fifteen miles, away. We discovered it quite accidentally when we had a dog. Tufty died three years ago. She loved it there. That is, until she was run over and taken from us. She used to love travelling in the back of the car – we used to have an estate – and she'd gaze out of the rear window, occasionally licking off the condensation that her heavy breath created, thanks to her excitement for going somewhere she could be free. Now, a dead body lies where our dog used to eagerly sit. She was the greatest companion we could hope for, especially when we realised children wouldn't be coming. God, how I miss Tufty.

'What are we doing, Paul?'

'We're going to go deep into the woods, we're going to dig a big hole and we're going to bury him. That's it.'

'That's not what I mean. I mean, why are we here and why are we about to do that?' Now that we're finally away from home, I've only really clocked for the first time exactly what we've chosen to do.

'Because a man broke into our house and you defended yourself,' Paul says casually, 'and I know what happens to people who defend themselves but can't prove it was self-defence when they stand in a courtroom in front of twelve members of a jury.'

'But we're making ourselves criminals in order to prove our innocence.'

'We're not trying to prove anything, Alice. We're trying to hide everything. We're getting rid of the evidence and then hoping like hell that we've done enough to remove any proof connecting us with him. Hopefully the only people who will ever know about this are you and me. If anyone else ever finds out, that means we've failed.'

'You're willing to risk everything for this?'

He turns towards me. 'No. For you.'

'The promotion to judge, it's everything you've worked so hard for, everything you've dreamed of.'

He nods his head. 'For you,' he says again, sounding confident and determined.

The windscreen wipers come on automatically, catching my attention. I sit in silence, staring at the rubber swiping one way and then back, squeaking softly against the glass.

Without taking my eyes off the windscreen, the black wipers a blur, I ask, 'Have you ever dug a hole that big?'

'I think you know the answer to that.'

'I doubt it'll be easy.'

'There are two of us, Alice. And when you have no choice, you'll see you can do almost anything.'

I put the radio on but can find nothing of interest. There are words in my head, questions I can't keep myself from asking. I switch it off. 'What about afterwards? How do we go back to normal?'

'You're asking a question with a thousand answers. We have to try. You have to find a way to move on. Try to blank it, forget. I'm here for you and I'll help. If you find it hard, I'll be there and I'll do everything I can to make things better.' He reaches for my hand and rests his atop it. They both sit still on my lap. 'Everything.'

I swallow deeply. The sound seems to echo off the car's roof. 'And what if I can't forget? What then?'

'We'll deal with that if we come to it.' He squeezes my hand. 'You're strong, Alice. You already saved yourself. That means you can do anything.'

'I'm afraid I won't be able to.'

'People respond to trauma in different ways, Alice. Some cope, some don't. You'll be the former. I know your strength. I experienced it every day when we were trying—'

He stops himself, but I know what he's going to say. He doesn't want to upset me, yet now he feels awkward. Stopping means he realises mentioning our desire to have a child will be difficult for me and might make me even more upset. I'm fragile enough, is what I suppose he's thinking.

'That's okay,' I say to reassure him and move my hand so that it's on top of his.

'Just brace yourself for this,' he says. 'This is going to be the hardest part. But after this, it's almost over.' Then more to himself: 'I just hope we can find some softer earth.'

'And what do we do afterwards?'

'We're going to have to come up with a watertight way of explaining these couple of days in case anyone comes asking.'

'Why can't we just pretend we weren't home? That we were away?'

'First, we'd have to prove we were away. Hotel booking confirmations, travel tickets, that sort of thing, which will be impossible. But even if we could, we can't. Bob saw me.'

'Bob?' She sounds alarmed.

'It's okay, calm down. He saw me coming back from the supermarket.'

'Did he see what you were carrying?'

'He didn't see anything, Alice. It's fine. He was more preoccupied with whatever he had in his boot. I told him I'd been out for some milk. All it means is we can't have been anywhere else. Or, at least, *I* can't have been anywhere else. But if he saw me, he would have seen your car in the driveway, too, so it's better that whatever plan we come up with includes both of us being safely and warmly tucked up in bed tonight.'

'So long as you're not worried?'

'I'm not. And remember, it's only got to be decided in case someone comes asking. At the moment, I can't imagine why anyone would ever come asking. This is all just as a precaution. We have to be ready, in case.'

He moves his hand back to the steering wheel and turns the car to the right. He reverses towards a space close to the dense woodland.

As we step out of the car, the rain intensifies as if it's conspiring against us. 'Shit,' I hear Paul mumble. I guess that means he didn't bring something suitable under which to shelter from the rain. I know I didn't.

He's about to close the door when he hesitates and then leans in and takes something from the glove box.

'What's that?'

'Torch. I forgot to bring the camping torch. This'll have to do.'

He opens the boot and we both stand there looking down towards the contents inside. 'How are we going to manage this?' I say. 'It was hard enough at home.'

'We'll find a way,' Paul says. 'It's called adrenaline. Hopefully it'll kick in straightaway. Come on.' He leans forwards and I can hear the strain in his voice as he exhales a groan that suggests he's in pain. 'Pull,' he hisses.

I do all I can to help. After the boot is shut, each with a spade hooked on our arms and the torch in Paul's mouth, we try to carry him upright and manage several feet when one of us stumbles and we both trip. The duvet falls heavily to the ground. I shriek. 'He deserves it,' Paul says, taking the torch from his mouth. 'Look, let's try pulling, both from the same end.

51

We each take hold of the duvet at one end, lift and drag. He's so heavy and with each step we take it feels like we're adding a small pile of bricks to the load we're already attempting to shift. Breathing heavily, sweating and covered in rain, but desperate not to stop, we don't let go. Each time our fingers slide down the material, we reclutch and heave with even more effort, to the point when I fear we're going to collapse. We're determined, working together, and the further we get to the entrance of the woodland, then the deeper we get into the woodland, the less we want to stop, the more we want to reach a suitable burial location, the more we want to finish this.

When I can pull no more, I fall to my knees, which forces Paul to drop the body. He leans against a tree. 'Well done,' he says, flashing his torch around. 'A bit more, though. We've got to go in deeper.'

'I can't,' I say. 'I'm sorry, I can't, my fingers feel like they're raw bone.'

'Okay,' he says, wiping the rainwater from his forehead and attempting to squeeze it from his hair, 'like this instead. You take these' – he hands me his spade and the torch – 'and I'll try to drag him. We'll bury him wherever we are when I can't pull any more. As far as we can manage.'

He thinks about pulling by the duvet but when it's once again in his hands he changes his mind. He feels, trying to locate the head, and then positions himself behind it. Awkwardly and without balance, he tries to lift up the corpse by placing his hands under the man's arms. 'The duvet's in the way,' he says. 'Okay, sod it, let's get him out.'

'Out?' I ask, alarmed. *Surely not!*

'I can't get a good grip and I won't be able to go much further if I have to pull the duvet. My hands are aching and I'm shattered.'

We lie the body flat and I start to pull open the masking tape.

Paul suddenly reaches out to me. 'Carefully,' he says quickly. 'I haven't brought the masking tape. We need to keep it in place and hope it has enough stick left to wrap him back up again properly.'

We carefully unpack the man. Seeing his face again is horrific. His jaw is wide open and stiff. I turn away.

I hear Paul curse as he pulls the man up, taking hold under his arms and dragging. He lugs the man along the mud. I try to stare at Paul's face, ignoring the man below it. I can see he's struggling, his cheeks puffing and his eyes wincing. His breathing intensifies, his shoulders slope further forwards and he moves his feet even faster. Pretty soon, he's moving as if both legs have poles inside his trousers and then his body comes further forward and then he drops down, the man's head landing in his lap. His own body instinctively wants to fall forwards, but when he sees the eyes staring up at him he lurches back and the man's head slides to the ground.

Paul looks relieved when they aren't touching any more.

Wrapping him up again is much more difficult than the first time, and that was hard enough. Neither of us has any energy left. 'Paul,' I say, 'how are we going to manage to dig?'

As he tries to tuck the duvet behind the man's back, he says slowly, not for emphasis but because he can barely speak, 'We have no choice.'

I try to reseal all the masking tape to give Paul a rest, knowing he'll have to take a lead with the digging. I don't even know if I'll be able to lift any of the earth out. Most of the tape sticks. Just a few bits are left dangling. It looks like it's holding okay.

'Thanks,' he mumbles, and he reaches for the spades, which I've leant against a tree. He kicks his foot into the ground. 'Doesn't feel too hard. Thank God for the rain. Okay, push in, step on, push down and then lift out. Which one do you want?'

'The plastic one.'

'You sure? That could be harder to use. The other will be heavier but might be easy to get the mud out.'

'I don't know,' I say despairingly. The rain hasn't eased up and I want to cry. 'How are we going to do this, Paul?'

'Alice, we have to try.' He hands me the plastic spade, flicks his head in a futile attempt at shaking off some of the water and perspiration, and pushes the metal spade into the earth. Using his upper body, he presses down, the spade lowers and then he pulls back, bringing with him a huge lump of mud. He tosses it to the side. 'Create a pile,' he says. 'Something near you but not so close it prevents you from digging the hole as it gets bigger.'

Digging for an hour feels like all night. Paul's much faster than me, but he's flagging. As we reach the halfway point, the rain starts to slow, but just as we're about to feel some semblance of relief it intensifies again. Soaked to the skin, soaked to the soul in fact, I reach the point when I can't go on any more, the hole ankle deep, and I sit on the original level of earth as if I'm on a step.

Paul doesn't stop and he doesn't speak to me. All his concentration is on getting this finished. Each step, each push and each lift require so much effort from him; I can see how hard he's trying and I can see even more clearly how much he's struggling.

Watching Paul, I feel almost certain that the sun will soon rise, illuminating us and revealing our deep, dark secret. But, no, it doesn't come up and I glance at my watch, which shows it's approaching half-past two.

After a short rest, I get up again and move closer to where Paul is. I line up the spade, push against it with my foot and press down. There's a loud snap, like the largest twig in the woods being stepped on, and my body tumbles forwards. I find myself face down in the hole, the arm of the spade having snapped, and I roll over. Paul is peering down at me, the rain is falling from above him and I feel like I'm under attack. I want to curl up, a baby in the womb, innocent and ignorant of everything and anything in this fucked-up world.

Remaining wordless, Paul leans down and helps me up. As I rise, I sob and he strokes my arm. He leans forwards, placing his forehead on my shoulder, and I understand what he's trying to tell me. He feels it too.

He takes me by the hand and leads me to the edge of the hole, where I sit again.

He digs for another half an hour and when the final piece of earth is scooped out he drops to his knees, holding onto the spade as if for dear life. His chest leans against it and he tries to draw in large lungfuls of air.

I want to tell him he's done so well, but the words seem inappropriate, hollow and wrong. I don't know what would be right, so I remain quiet, but I get up and stand behind him, bending down and gently rubbing his shoulders. A massage isn't appropriate either, but I want him to know I'm here for him. And that I appreciate every single thing he's doing for me.

Kneeling on the ground, we manage to roll the blanketed body over until it drops into the hole. Then, slowly but surely, we scoop the earth from the pile and start to cover him, using our hands at first, then our arms, and finally Paul retrieves the spade. The sloppy brown muck and the beautiful flower patterns of the duvet seem sinisterly at odds with each other, and I'm worried the combination is an image, along with the man's face, that I'll never be able to forget.

After I don't know how much longer, it's done. We sit on the ground, side by side, leaning against one another, our clothing drenched, our bodies exhausted, our minds even more so.

Paul eventually has the energy to lift his arm around me. He moves his hand forward so that I can see his watch. It's gone 4 a.m. 'Have to get back,' he says, struggling to speak.

We help each other up and, arm in arm, stumble back the way we came. I hope Paul remembers the route because I don't and I'm afraid we might spend the rest of the night wandering in search of an exit.

But Paul is Paul and we find the car in about five minutes. So fast, in fact, that I start to worry we didn't drag the body deep enough into the woods.

The fairly minimal step up into the Outlander is an effort, but its seat feels heavenly. My body sinks into it and I could fall asleep right here, right now. But I need to stay awake for Paul; exhausted, he has to drive us home. Getting this far and then falling asleep behind the wheel and crashing . . . it doesn't bear thinking about.

The whole journey home, I keep my hand on his thigh, squeezing every now and then. He holds the steering wheel with both hands, his eyes glued to the road and moist, from tiredness I suspect. After a while, I join him in staring at the windscreen. I see each raindrop as they fall. And I hear each raindrop as they fall. My senses seem to have been awakened.

We leave the car in a quiet street a short distance from the house and walk the rest of the way, leaning against one another, moving slowly, like a couple of drunks coming back from a night at a party, something fun, anything other than where we've actually been and what we've actually experienced.

We step onto our driveway and reach the front door. We step inside our dark house and don't switch on the light. It must be approaching five in the morning. Mud and filth and water, it all comes in with us. We drop our coats on the floor, the rest of our clothes too. I'll clean it later. Right now, first and foremost, a shower, a warm shower. I need to soak, I need to be clean.

20 September –
Two Weeks Ago

3

Detective Sergeant Katherine Wright's mobile phone started to vibrate in her jacket pocket. Reluctantly, she withdrew it; she didn't want to disrupt the hour she'd set aside to spend with the special person who could no longer answer the words she said to him.

It was Hillier. 'There's been another,' he said, excitement in his voice.

Silence as she looked at the ground.

'Hello? Katherine, are you there?'

'Yeah,' she said, disconnected, 'I'm here.'

'Where are you?'

She brushed a tear from her cheek. 'I . . . I had an appointment. Nothing to worry about. I can . . . cancel it. Tell me the address, I'm just leaving.' And once he revealed it: 'Meet me there in half an hour.'

She wanted to spend the full hour here, with the only man she'd ever felt she could trust and rely on. The man she missed so much.

She knelt down and placed the palm of her hand on the gravestone, tracing her fingers along the lettering. *A much loved husband and father, forever remembered, forever cherished.*

'Oh Dad,' she sighed and she slowly shook her head. 'Help me,' she mouthed. 'Help me find a way through this.'

Over two weeks had gone by and the Piano Wire Killer, as he'd been dubbed by the press, hadn't resurfaced, yet the expectation of his return remained like static. The search for him had so far led nowhere. National databases had provided no leads. Exploring the piano wire angle, both in past-crime records and the places where they could be purchased, had turned up nothing of consequence.

Wright placed her hand flat on top of the word 'father' and spoke silently to the dad she'd lost five years ago today, the man she wished she could see again, if only once, just to say a proper goodbye. Work had kept her away from him when he was suddenly taken ill and by the time she reached the hospital he was in a coma. He never awoke from it. She was by his side during his last moments, something she wished to God he knew.

Her faith was weak, but if there were a God she prayed to Him that her father understood it was the job and not her own will that delayed her arrival at the hospital.

Mournfully and regretfully, she said goodbye and made her way to her car. She jumped in and headed to the address Hillier had given her: 1C Marston Mansions, Hillingdon. She thought of her father the whole way there.

The time since his passing had gone so quickly.

As it was early morning, traffic was light, so Wright made it there in a little over twenty minutes. She parked amid a hive of activity, police units moving in and out, cordons in place and others being erected. Even though she recognised the uniformed officers guarding the scene, she showed her ID card.

The name Marston Mansions wasn't hyperbolic. The three-storey building, which was once a manor house, was surrounded by fields, despite being in a busy part of north London; somehow the fields were so deep they cut the building off from everything else, creating the façade of countryside.

Wright pushed open an entrance door of dark lacquered wood and ornate glass panels. A lavish foyer and the kind of staircase that features in wedding-day photographs were beyond it. She moved up the thick cream carpet, portraits adorning the wall as it spiralled to the first floor. There were only three apartments through this entrance, 1C the furthest along the corridor.

A uniformed officer stood outside the front door, staring at his mobile phone. Wright cleared her throat and he quickly pocketed it when he realised she was approaching, ID card in hand. She entered, immediately finding herself in the large lounge-diner, so vast it was larger than her studio three times over. The left side was the lounge: corner settee that could seat eight, gold and glass coffee table, huge television on the wall, an elaborate speaker system, a multi-tiered stereo complete with turntable. Shelves were filled with vinyls and CDs. The other end was the dining area: a long oval dining table, eight chairs around it, display units to both sides filled with plates and cutlery.

Hillier appeared from the corridor that came off the main space at the far end. 'Oh, you're here,' he said.

'What am I looking at?'

'Simon Michael Ryman, thirty-five years old, a solicitor.'

'Looks clean in here.'

'Completely, but not anywhere else. Chaos is the only word I can think of to describe what it looks like. He put up a hell of a fight.'

'Where?'

'The bedroom. At least that's where it ended.'

'Show me.'

They headed along the corridor. The first thing Wright noticed was the smashed door at the far end. 'What's there?' she asked, pointing.

'Bathroom. It looks like it started in there. We think he was in the shower. Perhaps caught by surprise, but he was fit and strong. They fought. It's a mess but not like the bedroom.'

He showed her. Puddles of water covered the floor, a soaked towel on one side, bottles on the floor, what looked like shampoo splashed like a Pollock.

'No blood?' she quizzed.

'None. From here, somehow they ended up in the bedroom.'

He led the way out. The paint at that end of the corridor was heavily scuffed. She looked at it. 'I imagine the piano wire around his neck at this point?' she thought aloud. 'He was fighting him off.'

'That's what it looks like. That's what we think.'

'Yet no water marks on the hallway floor.'

'Sorry?'

'No water on the floor, yet he was freshly out of the shower.' She pointed. 'Look.'

'None.'

'Where's Emerson?' she asked, moving forwards.

'Everyone's in there,' he said, indicating the next door along.

They stood in the bedroom doorway. The room was filled with scene investigators, Emerson in the thick of it. He saw Wright.

'Katie, this one's messy,' he said, lifting up gloved hands that were coloured a dark red.

Wright scanned the room. Chaos was an understatement. The contents of drawers were everywhere, the wooden drawers themselves smashed on the floor. Whatever had been on top of a chest of drawers – framed pictures, keepsakes – was on the floor, most items shattered, some no longer identifiable. The bedding was also on the floor, the mattress partly hanging off the base of the bed. One pillow remained on the bed, right next to Simon Michael Ryman's head, his body lying sloppily, half on the mattress and half hanging off it, his wrist limp on a muffled rug. He was face down and the mattress was blood-red. Further patches of blood were in random places around the room: on the wall, on the wardrobe, on the door. The mirror that had been built into the wardrobe door was shattered, some of the pieces on the floor. Shards of glass were sticking out of Ryman's body.

'Good,' she heard Emerson say to one of his colleagues. Then he said to Wright, 'We're ready to turn him over.'

She didn't respond, just watched intently.

As the body was carefully turned over, Ryman's head tilted back. A gaping hole was where his neck used to be. Wright could see the back wall of the throat. She swallowed hard and looked away.

Hillier stepped closer. 'Fuck,' he said.

'Yes, fuck,' repeated Emerson. 'He was vicious this time. Tried to take his head off. Almost did. You know, there's a photo of one of the Ripper's victims – Mary Kelly, I think it is – the same kind of wound, a huge gaping hole. It almost looks like an intricate spider's web at the back in there.'

'Which Ripper?' asked Hillier.

'Jack,' Wright answered.

'You are correct,' Emerson said and mimed a tentative round of applause. 'You know your serial killers.'

'I have no hobbies,' she said, deadpan. 'But while he did cut Mary Kelly's neck right through to the vertebrae, I believe the picture you're referring to is actually of Emily Dimmock, who is loosely suspected of being a potential Ripper victim but in 1907. Long after he supposedly stopped killing.'

'I'm impressed,' Hillier said, smiling.

'There are all kinds of theories about Jack the Ripper, of course. Take them with a pinch of salt.' Wright leant forward and looked as closely as her stomach would permit. 'What's the likelihood that our guy will have been hurt in here?'

'How could he not have been? It's likely there are bits of him in here. There's no way he could have avoided leaving something behind, not after this. There's too much mess, too many sharp bits. He's here, somewhere. The problem is going to be deciphering which bits are actually him.'

'Do it,' she said. 'Find him.' She stepped away, Hillier following. 'How'd he get in?'

'We don't know yet. No sign of forced entry on the front door or windows.'

'How do visitors get into the building?'

'Intercom entry. There's an on-site security officer who controls it.'

'Did he let anyone in today, or even last night?'

'He says no.'

'And no sign of forced entry anywhere on the building?'

'He's checking.'

'Fine. And once he's checked, you double check. Don't rely on minimum-wage night security.' She walked around the lounge, scanning the pictures and paintings on the wall. 'What went wrong?' she asked, as much to herself as to Hillier who stood at the side of the room. 'Because getting in certainly seemed to go right.'

'Maybe he picked the wrong person. Or the catch-him-by-surprise moment wasn't such a surprise.'

Wright stopped moving and stared into the television screen. It wasn't on.

'What are you thinking?'

'He's been able to kill two young, fit men without them lifting so much as a finger against him. And both times he's slipped off unseen and without disturbance. No trace of him anywhere. Then today, this one goes off like the others – a perfect entry – but then things change at the point of murder. Suddenly, he's caught off-guard or he messes up. That doesn't make sense. The others were so neat and tidy. So perfect.'

'Anyone can cock up, Katherine.'

With a beat, she turned to him. 'True. Even Jack the Ripper did, if you listen to the experts. But *how* did he cock up exactly?'

'What do you mean?'

'Exactly how did he cock up? What went wrong? What exactly do you see that is so wrong?'

He shrugged his shoulders, thinking the answer was obvious. 'Well, the guy fought back.'

'That's right,' she said, clicking her fingers. 'Exactly that. He fought and it's so clear to us that that's precisely what he did. Straight from the minute we walked in, we knew it.'

'Yes.'

'But what about what we didn't see?'

'I'm not following you.'

'Look.' She took him by the arm and led him to the end of the corridor where the bedroom was. 'How'd he get out?'

'Same way he got in presumably. The front door, I suppose.'

'You'd think, wouldn't you?'

'Yes.'

'And he had a huge fight, a scuffle that must have left a mark. Furniture everywhere, smashed glass all over the place, blood splashed all over the walls. It looks like anyone who was in here could only have come out bloodied and bruised.'

'Looks like it. Ryman put up a good fight.'

'That's what it looks like, yes.'

'What are you getting at?'

'Look closer. Look at this apartment. Inside the two rooms, there's every indication of a fight and injury. But outside the rooms?'

Hillier moved his eyes along the corridor, from the bedroom door towards the bathroom and then back towards where he stood and then to the front door. 'Nothing,' he said.

'Exactly. Not one speck of blood, not one drop.'

'Not a single mark. Not even water tracing the journey from bath to bedroom.'

'That's right. So we have a fight, or what appears to be a fight.'

'Where are you going with this?'

'What if it actually was exactly like the others? What if it went off perfectly, just what he planned? He got out and we can't see how. What if everything we can see is for our benefit? What if he's toying with us?'

'Are you serious?'

'This is staged.' She nodded her head. 'This isn't what it seems. I want the swab results urgently. Any trace of him, I want it, but something tells me we won't find anything.'

She stood silently, so long that Hillier started to feel uncomfortable. 'What are you thinking, Katherine?'

'I don't think this is a serial. I think we may have been wrong.'

'How can you tell?'

'He's too good for this to have happened the way it looks. It's too neat, too obvious. A serial killer can make a mistake, but then escape into the night with not a shred of evidence left behind when he's been in the middle of chaos, when surely he'd be nursing some wounds. No, not a serial.'

'If not a serial, what then?'

She said the words slowly, 'I think he's a professional.'

A

With a towel tied tightly around my head, I'm sitting at the kitchen table with a mug of tea clutched firmly between both hands, its heat penetrating my skin. I want the warmth and the comfort that comes with it. Fortunately, I don't have a job to go to in an hour's time; Paul's salary is more than enough to keep the two of us very comfortably. He likes to be able to look after me like that.

I'm still shivering, I'm not sure whether from the cold or the adrenaline rush, or if it's the fear I'm consumed by. I'm awaiting the impending knock on the front door, the police arriving to arrest us.

Paul is in the shower; he got in right after me and has been in it for almost half an hour. The only sound in the house is the water moving along the pipes above my head. The shower's force is particularly strong today; he must have the massage mode switched on, urging the water to cleanse him of the sins we share, which right now I fear I'll never be able to escape.

I can't stop thinking about what we've done. About what I have done.

I did this to us.

I have killed a man. I've buried his body and concealed my crime. I'm going to have to live with what I've done for the rest of my life. The thought fills me with dread. Being alone down here makes it even worse.

I'll have to live with it. Somehow.

Paul is in the shower for almost an hour. When he appears in the kitchen, it's nearly 6.30 a.m.

'I'm sorry,' he says, picking up the mug of tea I left for him on the sideboard and placing it in the microwave.

'I need you,' I say, a mix of annoyance and desperation. 'I feel so alone.'

'I needed to think. I didn't mean to leave you.' He walks over to me and places his hands on the back of the chair on which I'm sitting. He leans around to kiss me. First on the cheek, which I try to move away from. Then he twists his head further round and kisses me on the lips. The depth of his kiss makes me feel warm inside, even though outside I'm freezing. It gives me some much-needed comfort and I find myself slipping back in the chair, my hand reaching up to his cheek as the kiss lingers.

The ping of the microwave interrupts us and I pull away. 'Oh Paul,' I sigh, 'how are we going to live with what we've done?'

'This is day one,' he says. 'It's going to be a journey. We're going to take it together, one day at a time.'

'Don't ever leave me alone again.' The words are weak, my tone soft. I sound like I'm pleading with him.

'I won't,' he says, unconvincingly. Then more forcefully: 'I'm here for you. It'll be all right.'

71

I stand up and hug him. He runs his hands through my hair and I'm back to our honeymoon, a waterfall in the Caribbean, the water up to our waists, his hands running through my dripping hair, my head leaning back, and his hands and the falling water give me the most sensual massage I've ever experienced.

I tilt my head further back, imagining that water, imagining that all these years haven't passed and that we're still there, still young and fresh and inexperienced. I reach out to him, run my hands down the sides of his face and whisper, 'I want you.'

'Now?' He's surprised.

I open my eyes and bring my lips to his ear. 'Now,' I whisper.

Passing the microwave and mug of tea in it, we head upstairs, holding hands. We take each step slowly. I savour each moment as we approach the opportunity to make ourselves feel better. I want to feel that. I need to feel it.

I lie on my back on the bed. He leans over me, kissing me on the neck. I clutch hold of the back of his head, pulling him closer, desperate to never let go. 'Paul,' I moan. My eyes are closed and for a moment I'm not here, I'm somewhere else, a happier place, a happier time, years ago, way back when things were perfect, when we were miles away from the other man in our house.

And that's when he comes into our bed. I see him clearly and shudder. I pull back, mumbling, 'Sorry, I can't.' I sit up too quickly, for I see stars. 'I just can't. It's too soon.'

'That's okay,' Paul says.

'I want you, just not right now. I'm sorry. I feel so stupid, especially when I was the one who asked you up here.'

'I understand.' But he looks away.

A dead man was in my hands. I dug his fucking grave.

'I need to be strong, Paul. I know I do.'

'You will be,' he says. He looks at me and adds, 'You just need a bit of time.'

'I love you, Paul.'

'And I love you, Alice.'

'Will I ever feel safe again?' I ask.

'We have to give it time. We will both need time.'

'He's here in my head, I can't get him out.'

He takes me in his arms and we sit together on the edge of the bed. 'Me, too. But that's to be expected, Alice. It's not going to be easy to forget, but we've got to move on. We have to find a way. So long as we're here for each other, that's what matters.' He turns and we're face to face. 'Us. That's all that matters. We made the right choice. You're the innocent one in this, not him. I'm here for you and we're going to be okay. We'll still be a family.'

Family. The word starts off my tears. He's used the wrong word. He realises his mistake straightaway, but it's too late.

'We're just a husband and wife, Paul, not a family.'

'Come on,' he says softly, 'let's not go down that road again. We – you and I – *we are* a family.'

'A family has a ch—'

'I know.' As I sob, he pulls me towards his chest. I sense the pain in him, too. 'I know.'

I know.

'We mustn't go back, Alice. We have to find a way to go forwards. Again. Never look back after last night.'

'I don't know if I can.'

'You will,' he says, shushing me. '*We* will. We have to.' He kisses the top of my head. 'And we'll start right now, downstairs. We have to clean everything. It has to be like he was never here.'

'What about work?'

'Forget about it. I've sent them a message to say I'll be working from home today. I promise, I won't leave your side.' He squeezes me tighter. I hope he'll never let go.

10 February –
Four Months Later

P

'Court will rise.'

I get up from my throne-like chair, having delivered the sentence, briefly eye those in attendance and stare directly at the convicted man who sits on the cushionless wooden chair in the dock opposite me. I want him to understand the gravity of what's happened.

After bowing, I walk along the dais and exit through a heavy-duty door that's covered in a green material, much like that on an Elizabethan sofa. I walk down the corridor and head to my chambers at the Central Criminal Court in London. The Old Bailey.

After I unlock the door and enter, I take off the wig, which I'm required to wear while presiding over cases, remove my black robe and go into the bathroom, where I splash water onto my face and look into the mirror that's on the wall above the sink.

I see myself, the youngest Circuit Judge this court, indeed the whole of the UK, has ever seen, and I know I should be pleased with myself. I should be satisfied with my achievement. I am, to an extent, but thoughts of Alice are always lurking in the back of my mind and I can never fully forget them.

Without Alice, I couldn't have done it, but with her, I can't fully enjoy it; I'm worried about what's happening to her.

I go into the main chambers space, which acts as my office while I work here; at the moment, I expect to be here for just over four months before a tour of other southern English courts will begin. A large mahogany desk has been placed in the centre of the room and a leather sofa is on the far right. Next to that is a small fridge, from which I remove a can of Coke. I pour it into a glass cup that's on a side unit and then go behind the desk. From its bottom drawer, I extract a bottle of Woodford Reserve. I mix it with the Coke and take three large gulps, emptying the glass.

Feeling refreshed, I lean against the back of the chair and stare at the wall on which there are several framed newspaper articles. I glance from headline to headline. *UK's Youngest-Ever Judge. The Newest Law in the Land. Young Judge Makes History.*

The words mean so much and remind me how desperate I was to win this position. Three of the newspapers are national titles: two broadsheets and a tabloid. In addition to appearing in them, I've been written about all over the country by local presses. I beat the previous youngest by almost two years and did it against stiff competition.

The day I got the call, three months ago, telling me I'd been chosen, that I was the successful one, was the greatest day of my professional life. My own feelings should have mirrored that, but by then Alice was having difficulty with the day-to-day, so it was hard to disconnect myself from our home life when front and centre of my attention should have been my professional achievement.

Alice is always there, in my mind and right in front of me. She was by my side during the whole journey to this point, supporting me, but, now, concern keeps her clinging there. She won't let go.

In one frame, together we fill half the front page of our local newspaper. We're smiling for the camera, the picture taken at the naming ceremony, but I know Alice's smile hides horrors and secrets and desperation. *Our* horrors and secrets and desperation. Even though she hid it then, she had struggled much more in the previous weeks, and from the day after we buried his body I had felt, even smelt, her shame and her fear.

She hasn't been able to rest and be herself since that evening last October. The evening that changed everything. And because she hasn't been able to be the Alice I fell in love with, the Alice I truly know, I haven't been able to be me, either. I haven't been able to fully celebrate being the UK's youngest-ever Circuit Judge – we haven't been able to celebrate what I've striven for for so long. After learning of my appointment, the thing I most wanted was to return home, bottle of champagne in hand, toast together, share. But when I arrived at the house, she was already asleep; she took to early nights within a couple of weeks of it happening. She said the earlier she could fall asleep, the better, that it meant there was less time for her to relive those moments and that the true depths of darkness couldn't appear if she was fast asleep.

I should get a particular thrill when young and bright-eyed law students want to speak to me, fight to speak to me actually, and, when they do, gush over me as though I'm something special and important and unique. As if I'm a celebrity, which in the law world, I guess I am. I don't, though, and I can't, if I'm honest, because all I can think of, all I can see, no matter who is standing before me, is Alice. My beautiful Alice, the woman I fell in love with over a decade ago, the woman I would do anything for, the one I said I *would* do anything for and *did* do anything for.

Doing just that has changed so, so much.

She can't forget and she can't pretend to ignore. I've tried, and struggled, and some days I almost feel normal. But not Alice, and I'm worried about her. I want the Alice I knew to come back. I want to help her find a way out of the darkness.

I refill my glass with more bourbon and Coke and sit on the sofa. Rush-hour traffic has started, so I should leave if I'm to get home at a reasonable hour – afternoon sessions at the Old Bailey end at 5 p.m. I'd like to get home and spend some quality time with Alice before she goes to sleep.

I finish draining my glass as there's a knock at the door. Reluctantly, I open it.

'John,' I say, shaking hands with Judge John Fletcher-Smythe, who's both my mentor and a High Court Judge, one of the most prestigious legal positions in the land. He sometimes helps out at the Old Bailey.

'Well done,' he says, stepping in. 'A highly successful first trial, I'd say, and a great end to it.'

'Thank you,' I answer. 'I saw you watching a couple of times. I wasn't sure whether to expect you there. Thank you for being interested.'

'I was there every day, Paul,' he reveals.'

'Really?'

'When I mentor a judge, I like to see how things turn out.'

'And?' I ask.

'And I must say, I'm pleased. You did well, which must mean I've done a good job.'

'You have. Indeed, you have.' We shake hands again. 'I appreciate everything you've done for me.'

'A celebratory drink?' he asks, a mischievous grin on his face. For a man of over sixty, he looks surprisingly young and he's unexpectedly light on his feet.

I glance at my watch, even though I know the time, and hesitate. I wanted to see Alice. I should see Alice. But I know it would be rude not to. He's the most important man I know.

I decide to send Alice a text message. Now I always make sure to text if something delays me.

'Absolutely,' I say with a smile, which might be a bit forced.

He's heading out of the door as he says, 'Give me ten minutes. I've got a few things to pick up. I'll meet you outside.'

I start to type the message to Alice but stop, deciding to call her instead. After a few rings, she picks up.

'Darling, how's your day been?' I ask.

She sighs. 'The usual, Paul. Not too bad.'

'How are you feeling?'

81

'Not too bad.'

'What are you up to?'

'Reading a bit. Watching a bit of telly.'

'Listen, honey, John's asked me for a drink to celebrate the end of my first trial.'

'Oh, was that today?'

'Yes, I thought I said.'

'You probably did. I must have forgotten. How did it go?'

'Perfectly.'

'I'm glad for you.'

'Would you mind?'

'Of course, you go ahead. Don't worry about me. Have a good time.'

'Will you be up when I get back?'

'Will you be late?'

'I hope not.'

'Well, I hope so then.'

I'm about to say goodbye when Alice says, 'Thank you for calling me, darling.'

'Just wanted to make sure you were okay.'

'I'm fine.' I don't believe her. Then she adds, softly, 'Thank you.'

'I love you.'

'See you later.'

As I come out of the staff exit, I walk through the barrier and into Warwick Square. John isn't here, so I shelter from the rain in a doorway.

'The Waldorf?' he asks, appearing behind me.

He doesn't wait for my response, making his way towards Warwick Lane. There, he hails a cab.

'Sounds good,' I say, as I duck into the cab he's already sitting in.

Thanks to the traffic, the drive takes almost as long as the twenty-minute walk would have taken. John presses buttons on his phone the whole way there and, as soon as we're inside, with a scotch on the rocks in front of each of us, he says, 'I always had a good feeling about you, Reeve. I'm very pleased. You've done me proud.'

'I'm pleased, too, John. Thank you again.'

'You'll go far, I know that. You'll see.'

'I have a lot to learn, but I hope so. There's a lot I want to do.'

Three drinks later, John says, 'Dinner?', although it's not really a question. The answer is inevitable, even though I'm conscious of what I told Alice. We move to the main restaurant and order a starter and main course, the time and my waiting wife constantly in the back of my mind, but my thoughts slowly becoming freed up as I drink more alcohol. Wine that John selects flows and we finish the meal with the cheese cart, accompanied by a glass of port.

It's almost nine and I'm worried about arriving home really late when John says, 'Coffee?'

'A quick one,' I answer.

As the waitress comes to take away our empty coffee cups and I think John will ask for the bill, he suggests one more scotch on the rocks. 'For the road,' he says, mischievously. Even though my head is somewhat dizzy and I'm full and will no doubt be rocky on my feet, I'm aware of Alice at home. And now there's no way I can drive back, which means the train, which likely means even more delay to my return.

I type Alice a quick text message. I can't see the words clearly on the screen and hope they make sense to her and sound apologetic enough. She's good to me – she always has been – so I'm sure she'll understand, but that doesn't mean I won't feel neglectful for leaving her alone for an even longer period of time than is absolutely necessary, or than I'd hoped.

We shake hands when we're on the Strand. I'm absolutely stuffed, and drunk. John hails the first cab that approaches, barely a hesitation in his step despite the amount of booze he's consumed – the rich know how to live the good life – yet I stumble towards the next taxi, unsure whether it'll stop or even if the driver will be able to see me.

He does and takes me to Euston, from where I catch a train home. Another taxi takes me to my front door. The whole journey lasts just over an hour, through which I drift in and out of sleep.

The taxi departs and I look up at our dark house. I don't have good memories of this place being dark. It makes me hesitate. Then, aiming my key towards the lock, I struggle to open the door and, once I'm in, I press it shut, my body collapsing against it. I drag myself up the stairs, attempting to be quiet but still hopeful that Alice will be awake, waiting for me. Entering the room that we both hate, I drop my clothes on the bathroom floor, brush my teeth and then exit and fall into bed.

The bedroom light comes on sharply as my head hits the soft pillow. I open my eyes, angling my head towards the bedroom door. Alice is standing there, but her outline is blurred. I can't see her features clearly.

'I'm sorry,' I slur.

'It's okay,' she says, quietly, but I can hear anger in her voice. I can't see clearly enough to tell whether that anger is visible on her face.

'It was John, I just couldn't say no to the man who has helped me so . . .' I don't know if I'm making much sense, and pretty soon what I say drifts off into unintelligible sounds.

'I know,' I hear Alice say. 'Like always, I know.'

I sleep.

A

I eventually went to sleep at half-past two, two hours after Paul started snoring. I looked at him asleep on the bed, envy coursing through my veins. I want to sleep, but I can't. I want to relax. I just want peaceful sleep.

Alcohol works for Paul. I've tried it; it doesn't work for me. Too much and I see the things I desperately want to keep out of my vision. I'm jealous because I wish I could ignore what happened like he can. And every time he comes home late, I'm left to remember and suffer alone. I still need him, how he soothes me.

After it happened, for a few days while keeping busy and sorting out the house, I was able to shut it out of my mind. Paul was with me all the time and we didn't stop tidying and fixing. Activity kept the memories at bay. Exhaustion after a hard day's labour then sent me to sleep.

But when we stopped, everything I had tried to keep away came back, and more intensely than I could possibly have imagined. I don't work, after all, so I had little in the way of routine with which to distract myself. I haven't had to work for seven years; Paul's salary more than takes care

of us both. It's always been fun – living a life of leisure has
been a pleasure – but now I feel trapped inside. Not that
I want to go out either. The truth is, I don't know what
I want any more.

Paul seems to have been able to forget about that night,
but I can't. In my mind, I'm still in our bedroom, preparing
to bathe. I still see him in the corridor. I still relive the blade
hitting him again and again. I'm still there, digging his grave.

I'm awoken by a sound in the en suite bathroom. My
eyes open and I see Paul emerging from it, putting on a
shirt. 'Morning,' he says.

'Hi,' I say.

He shrugs his shoulders and purses his lips. 'I'm sorry,'
he tells me again.

'I know, you said so last night.'

'I did want to get back early. I wanted to spend time
with you.'

'You did what you had to do.'

'Are you sure you're all right?'

I sit up and puff a pillow. 'I'm not sure of anything, Paul,
I think you know that.'

He pulls on some jeans. 'I've had a message from Laurence.
He's asking if we'd like to have dinner with him and Amanda
tonight. What do you think?'

He can tell from the expression on my face that I'm
reluctant.

'They can come here and I'll cook if you prefer not to
go out.'

'No,' I say, quickly, 'I don't want them to think anything's
up. We always go out.' Laurence is one of Paul's oldest

and closest friends, and we used to see him and his wife, Amanda, frequently. Amanda is my best friend and we speak all the time, but we haven't gone out as a four since before Paul started the job, the longest gap there's ever been in our meet-ups. It wasn't just the job, of course; it was also me . . . I haven't felt like going out much.

He sits on the edge of the bed and strokes my hair. 'Look, Alice, the trial's over and the next one doesn't begin for a few weeks. That means I won't need to be in London so much. I can do a lot of my case prep here. I can be here for you.'

I smile but don't speak.

'Things will get better, you'll see.'

'I hope so.' I wish I had his confidence. Or naivety. I can't quite decide.

'They will, I promise.' He leans over and kisses my forehead.

I don't get up for some time and when I do finally emerge downstairs I find Paul sitting at the kitchen table, reading a newspaper and drinking a coffee. I put the kettle on to make a green tea.

I walk over to him. 'When does the next trial begin?' I ask.

He looks away from the article he's reading. 'Last week of March.'

'Does that mean I have my husband back?' I say playfully.

'Yes,' he says, standing up. 'Yes, it does.' And he places his hands on my hips and pulls me closer and kisses me on my lips.

P

'To you.'

'Yes, to you,' Amanda repeats.

We all hold up our glasses. 'Thank you.' I bring mine to Amanda's and then to Laurence's and, finally, to Alice's. My eyes hold Alice's eyes in a bid to encourage her to enjoy the moment.

We're dining in our favourite Thai restaurant in St Albans. We usually meet Laurence and Amanda in London – our favourite restaurant as a foursome is in Covent Garden – but Alice couldn't face the busyness of the capital. 'I'll feel like I'm trapped in a maze,' she told me, even though she knows London really well and used to spend a lot of time there. I wanted to say, 'Nonsense,' but I didn't want to risk upsetting her. After all, I half anticipated her turning down the meet-up.

'It's been too long,' Amanda says, smiling.

'Too long,' I repeat.

'Let's not leave it so long till next time,' Laurence adds. I turn to Alice. 'Yes,' she says shyly.

'So what's it like?' Amanda asks me. Peripherally, I catch

Laurence leaning back and turning his attention away. He's heard it all before.

'It's only been one trial so far, but it's quite . . . actually, it's exactly what I thought it would be, but it's been bloody difficult. There's been no greater highlight of my professional life. I couldn't have wished for more.'

'Well, we're thrilled for you,' she says, lifting her glass again. 'One more congratulations.'

I pick up my glass and we bring them together.

Amanda empties her glass in one. 'Order me another, honey,' she says to Laurence. 'Alice, shall we?' She gets up.

Alice isn't paying attention, doesn't seem to realise what Amanda is suggesting, despite it being a regular routine of theirs. *It has been a long time.*

'Alice?'

She shakes her head and comes out of her daze. 'Yes?'

'Toilet?'

'Oh, sure,' she says, getting up.

Amanda gives Laurence a kiss on the cheek and they make their way off. Both ladies are wearing long, sleek dresses. Both have appealing figures and the dresses hug them.

'Is she okay?' he asks me.

I shrug. 'I don't know. She's been . . . well, it's why I've not asked to meet up like this for a while. She's . . . just going through some things. I don't know. It's been . . . hard.'

'Anything I can help with?'

'Yeah, give me an excuse to come out more often.'

'That's a deal.'

'How's the office?'

'Oh, busy, you know, the usual. Busy means lots of money, so all good on that front.'

'Good,' I say. 'Good.'

He leans forwards, removing some folded papers from the inner pocket of his jacket. 'That reminds me, and before the ladies return, I've got these for you to sign.'

A

Amanda and I are standing in front of the large mirror in the ladies'. She's touching up her mascara. I'm holding my blusher, but instead of reapplying it I'm staring at myself in the mirror. My eyes are tired. My face is drawn. I don't look as young as I did only recently. I don't feel it, either.

'Is anything the matter?' she asks suddenly, rubbing the small of my back.

I exhale, too loudly, too obvious.

'What's up?'

I put down the blusher and lean against the sink. I want to tell her. I want somebody to speak to, somebody who knows absolutely nothing about what we've done, who can act as a receptacle so that I can release what's inside of me and then, I hope, feel better. But I know I can't. 'I don't know,' I lie.

'I'd hate to think you're struggling with anything.'

'Struggling?' I ask, more to myself. 'Struggling with . . . life at the moment.'

'But life's good, isn't it? Paul's job?'

'Paul's job is good, yes. Or at least it sounds it, doesn't it?'

She steps closer and speaks quietly and in a serious tone. 'Is it like before, Alice?'

'Is it . . . I hadn't really thought about it. I guess it is, yes. But then . . . I had reason. Such a clear reason.' I drift away, mumbling, 'The babies.'

'But, look, if the depression has returned . . . I mean, do you ever still see the doctor?'

'No, that stopped a long time ago now.'

'What about the pills? Have you thought about contacting him and asking him if he can give you more pills? They made you feel better once—'

'I don't want to stuff myself full of bloody pills again, Amanda.'

'I'm sorry, I just thought . . .'

'I know, I know you did. It's all right.' I place my arm around her. 'I'm sorry. I can't explain it. I can't, it's just how I feel.'

'Is everything okay between you and Paul?'

'Yes.' I pause. My face frowns on its own. 'I don't know. He's married to his work.'

'Laurence is, too.' She squeezes me. 'That's men for you. Or lawyers.'

Holding on tightly, I say, 'You know, if it weren't for that new job, I'd swear he's got himself a woman on the side. I never see him. I . . . I need him.'

'I know you do, honey. But it's Paul. Paul, remember. He wouldn't do anything like that.'

'No, I know he wouldn't. It's how it feels, that's all. I wish he were around more.'

'And I'm sure he will be. New job, getting settled, that sort of thing. Look, in the meantime, let me be around more. Any time day or night, call and I'll be there. Stay in, go out, it's up to you. Whatever you feel like.'

'Going out? The desire's escaped me, Amanda.'

In the mirror's reflection, I can see my words have hurt her.

'But I will. Thank you, I will.' Then I laugh. 'You probably won't be able to get rid of me soon.'

P

'Sure.' I pull out a pen and sign my name on the papers where Laurence points to. 'What am I signing away here?'

'Not your life.' I know the comment is a joke, but it hits home. I pause for a moment, my eyes on the page. 'Is everything all right?' he asks.

'Yeah,' I say. 'Funny. So what are these?'

'Some money transfers and something to finalise the latest purchase.'

'Excellent. And how have we done with it?'

'Doubled.'

'You are a talented man, Laurence.'

'Indeed I am, Paul.' He picks up his glass. 'Cheers.'

'Cheers.'

We finish our drinks and signal to the waiter that we'd like another round.

'How are you doing for money?' he asks.

'Not bad.' I look towards the toilets. The ladies haven't reappeared. 'What are you looking for?'

'One seventy-five.'

'A big one?'

'Give me six months, we'll treble it.'

'Treble?'

He nods his head firmly. 'Treble.'

'When do you need it by?'

'Can you manage two weeks?'

'Should be okay. Is there anything in the online account you can use?'

'Ten each.'

'Okay, so one sixty-five within two weeks.'

'Two weeks?' Amanda asks, sitting down. 'What's happening in two weeks?'

Alice is standing by the table. There's hesitation in her movement. 'Two weeks,' I say, looking at her and lying, 'before I've got to get working properly on the prep for the next trial. That means I've got a bit of breathing space.' I hold out a hand and Alice places hers in it. 'I've neglected my wife since starting this job, so it gives me some time to make up for everything.'

As Alice turns and sits down, I wink at Laurence, giving him a subtle nod.

Treble the money, six months. Sounds perfect.

A

When we were in the toilets, Amanda asked me if something was the matter. I can't conceal that I'm struggling. I'm finding it so hard to focus my mind on the here and now rather than on the that-night-when.

As we returned to the table, I could tell Paul was lying. He and Laurence weren't talking about two weeks till he has to start working on his next trial. He told me it isn't due to start till the end of March. He was probably gossiping with Laurence about me and how I've become. I wonder what he's said, how it would be possible to indicate that something's happened without actually saying what has happened. He couldn't risk saying too much, so I know our secrets are still ours, but I hate the idea that I'm now the subject of idle gossip.

I drift in and out of the conversation for the rest of the evening. We've always had such a good time together, the four of us, but tonight something is different. It's me, I know it is, but Laurence also seems slightly off. I desperately want to lift myself up, knock back a few glasses and laugh. I want to laugh and have fun. I haven't had fun since before

I killed that man. And I fear I will never have fun again.

Intermittently, I catch sight of Amanda staring at me. She's concerned about me and, at the end of the night, she gives me an extra-long hug. 'Any time you want to talk, just give me a call,' she whispers.

'Thanks,' I say, and kiss her on the cheek.

On our way home, Paul and I walk arm in arm. We live close enough to the city centre to make our way home on foot.

'I don't think you had much fun,' he says softly.

I decide to be honest. 'I didn't.'

'I'm sorry.'

'For what?'

We stop and he looks me in the eye. The street is quiet. 'I don't know.' He kisses me on the lips and holds me tightly.

When he releases me, I ask, 'What if this feeling never goes away, Paul? What then?'

He thinks for a long time. It's like I've asked him a rhetorical question. 'Everything will be—'

'But what if it's not?' I cut him off, not wanting to hear the same response as he's given me several times before.

He smiles wistfully and purses his lips. He runs his hands slowly up and down my arms, like he's trying to warm them. 'I don't know,' he says. 'I honestly don't know.'

13 March –
Four Weeks Later

P

'I don't want to be home alone,' Alice said to me when we woke up this morning.

I had to come to the Old Bailey today for a pre-trial meeting. Because I'd been thrown straight into my first trial within days of starting the job, and because Alice hadn't wanted to venture far from the house, she hasn't seen where I work. It took much convincing, but I've managed to bring her along with me today. Friday the thirteenth.

Each Circuit Judge is assigned their own private secretary. Mine is Belinda, who was my secretary at Blacksmith's for the past three years. She's young but good at the job. And she knows how I like things to be done, so when I was offered a court-appointed secretary I refused. I was pleased when Belinda agreed to come with me.

As soon as Alice said she'd like to come here, I called ahead and asked Belinda to free up some time to show Alice around much of the building. I said I'd show her the more interesting parts when I became free.

I'm based in the new building, where there are three courtrooms on each of three floors, so nine in total. The courtrooms are more spacious than in the old part of the building, where there are six, including the most famous, Court One. It's the place where some of the most notorious crimes in British history have been tried. Court Two is usually saved for cases trying high-security crimes, things like terrorist cases.

Despite the history in the old part of the building, most of the judges I've met prefer working in the new part because the workspace is more comfortable, each courtroom can house more people, and there's more room for the jurors. Any judge will tell you, you can't underestimate a jury's comfort.

Before my meeting, I take Alice into Court Twelve, which isn't being used today. I want to be the first to show her the inside of a courtroom. We're standing in the middle of what looks like a theatre auditorium, surrounded by green padding and varnished wood, carpets, tables, high walls. It's intimidating in here but awe-inspiring as well.

I take Alice by the hand. 'Here,' I say, and we step up and walk across the dais. I hold out a chair for Alice and, as she sits, I say, 'Ma'am'. Then I sit next to her. Satisfied and feeling I've truly arrived at the place where I was born to be, I point directly ahead. 'The dock,' I say. 'It's where the defendant sits. Several attendants will sit with him, and his or her future will be determined by twelve strangers sitting there.' I signal to our right.

On the wall above where I'm sitting is a coat of arms, below which is the Sword of Justice, pointing down towards us, or whoever sits in the judge's seat. 'The Sword of Justice points at the one who's supposed to deliver the verdict swiftly and fairly,' I tell Alice.

She looks genuinely interested and impressed, and I'm pleased she's here.

'You deserve this,' she says.

'I couldn't have done it without you.'

'You were made for this.'

I touch her hand tenderly.

I catch sight of the time. The last thing I want is to leave Alice and start hearing about the Cravens, but I can't delay any more.

'What's the case about?' Alice asks when I tell her we need to make our way to my chambers.

My throat dries up. I don't want to say. I don't even want to hear about it myself. 'That'll take too long. Best be one to save for another day.'

As we walk to Belinda's office, which is down the corridor from my chambers, I think about the Cravens and what they've done. As soon as I received the case and read the crib notes, I didn't want to be involved in the trial, but I've tried and failed to be switched with another judge. There's no valid, convincing reason I can give the decision makers and as a newcomer I don't carry any weight yet. I can't press too hard, and risk making my desperation to change obvious, so I'm stuck with the case. I don't know how I'm going to manage my way through it without the cracks starting to show.

'Morning, Belinda,' I say as cheerfully as I can. 'Alice, you remember Belinda?'

'Of course,' she says, smiling.

They shake hands.

'Take good care of her,' I say.

'Don't you worry,' Belinda says, 'I will.'

'I won't be long,' I tell Alice.

'They're waiting for you,' Belinda says. 'Everything you need's in there.'

I thank her, but I don't hear my words. I kiss Alice on the cheek and step out of the office, bracing myself.

A

'Do you still keep a bottle in your drawer?' I ask. 'For special occasions?'

'You remember that?' He looks impressed.

I nod.

'Of course I do.'

'Pour us one, then. Being here with you, this is a special occasion.'

'How was the tour?' he asks as he goes behind his desk and removes a bottle and two glasses from a drawer. 'Was Belinda friendly?'

'She's lovely, yes. Very pretty. I'd forgotten how much.' A pause. 'It was good, but I'd have preferred it to have been with you.'

Behind him, on the wall, are some framed newspaper cuttings. In one, he and I are standing side by side. It seems like yesterday when that photo was taken. Such a big day and him so full of nerves. He was awkward in front of all those people and the cameras; Paul, normally so confident, cocky even, yet when we were posing for that photograph, I could feel his arm, which he placed behind my back, shaking. In the picture, he's smiling, but the smile concealed so much fear.

He holds up his glass. 'Cheers,' he says.

We toast our glasses together.

'Cheers,' I say. I'm not used to drinking neat spirit, so I wince.

'Takes some getting used to,' he says.

'It's okay,' I say, wanting to please him.

He drinks with ease. 'So, after the drink, do you fancy the real tour?'

'The real tour?'

'You know, by somebody who really knows what he's talking about.'

'And who would that be?'

'Me, of course. Plus, with me nothing's off limits.'

'Oh, really?' I've missed the playful Paul. I place a hand on his chest. I love its shape. 'Well, in that case, how could I possibly resist?' I put the glass to my mouth and look deep into his eyes, but when I swallow the bourbon, I squeeze them shut; the burn is intense.

'Let me show you a couple of special things.'

Leaving his chambers, we walk through a series of corridors, which I don't recognise, even though I've only just finished touring the building, and we emerge through a set of large wooden doors.

'This,' says Paul through big eyes, 'is the Grand Hall. It's closed to the public. Very few people get to see it.'

'Well, I feel privileged.'

I step onto the black, white and beige patterned floor tiles. I gasp. The vast space is magnificent; everything looks so expensive and elaborate. The whole thing reminds me of the most ornate cathedral. At the top in the centre is a high dome that reminds me of St Paul's Cathedral, with glass windows around its peak. Smaller half-circle windows appear in other raised sections of ceiling. Murals cover most of the ceiling and there are patterns on the walls. In the murals, there look to be lots of noblemen, and St Paul's Cathedral features prominently. At ground level, there are statues along both lengths of the hall.

'I get to come to work here,' he says, filled with wonder. 'This place has such history. I pop in every day, just to remind myself how lucky I am.'

He leads me forwards, talking as we walk. 'That,' he says, pointing, 'is the entrance to Court One. The Krays were tried in there. The Yorkshire Ripper, too, and Ian Huntley. That picture above the door is of Lady Justice, the Goddess of Justice in Roman mythology. She's standing on the steps of St Paul's, and next to her is Moses as he receives the Ten Commandments. To Justice's left is Alfred the Great, who was a lawgiver and king in the ninth century. They're a reminder of how we're meant to behave and what happens when we stray.'

We're surrounded by people, lots of comings and goings. I can't help but wonder who they all are, whose role is what, what each of them will do or has done to be here. Who's done right? A judge, a prosecutor, a witness. And who's done wrong? A defendant.

'Much of the original artwork, which was by an artist called William Richmond, was damaged during World War Two when the Nazis' bombs struck in 1941,' Paul explains. 'They were recreated in the fifties, when they also added a lot of pictures commemorating the Blitz.

'That's Charles the first and there's Charles the second,' he says, indicating two of the statues near us. 'And this,' he says walking towards another, 'is Sir Thomas Gresham. He was a former Lord Mayor of London, which of course is the city that owns the building, so he's here to represent that everlasting connection.'

'Who's this?' I say, spotting one statue that's very different from the others. I turn to Paul. 'A woman?'

'That's right,' he says. 'Elizabeth Fry.'

'And that name's supposed to mean something to me?'

'She's given short shrift, is Elizabeth. She deserves to be better known than she is. Although they did stick her face on a fiver a few years ago, but still, every time I say the name to people all I get in return is a blank face.'

'So who was she?'

'She was a Victorian prison reformer who fought for prisoners to receive more humane treatment, and she succeeded in gaining Queen Victoria's support. Not an easy feat, I'd imagine. She has a nickname that's interesting.'

'Oh yes, and what's that?'

'They call her the Angel of Prisons.'

Perhaps I'll start praying to her, I think but don't vocalise. I don't want to put a damper on what's starting to feel like a date, even though my fears remain lurking within.

There are what seem to be quotations inscribed at various intervals. I pause at the last one.

The law of the wise is a fountain of life.

Paul sees me reading it and says, 'This and the others, they're axioms, which are statements we're supposed to believe that might provoke further reasoning or argument.

Obviously they're here to be believed,' and he adds with a heavy dose of sarcasm, 'and aren't they oh so true.'

Life, I think, *which I took, and the law, which waits to punish me.*

'Pretty inspiring stuff,' he says. He may be asking me a question, I'm not sure.

'Absolutely,' I answer, just in case.

'Do you want to see something even rarer? Something that almost no one has ever seen?'

'What's that?' I ask. 'I thought this was the special place.'

'Even more of a secret than this place. I have to warn you, it's not nice, but believe me, it's worth it.'

'Okay then,' I say tentatively.

He leads me back in the direction we came from and we end up in a fairly unkempt stairwell. We walk down a couple of levels. Paul opens a door to reveal the end of a long concrete walkway. There are dirtied off-white brick walls on both sides and every eight to ten feet there's an open archway made of the same bricks. The concrete floors are stained and every so often there's a large square manhole cover on the ground.

The corridor is completely empty. An eerie sensation spreads through my body. 'What is this place?' I ask, starting to feel uncomfortable.

'This,' he says proudly and impressively, 'is Dead Man's Walk.' He starts moving along it and I, now reluctantly, follow. 'There are all kinds of passages and spaces underneath the Old Bailey. You know, there's even a river. This has been here for almost three hundred and seventy years. In the past, when a criminal was sentenced to death, he or she would be brought down here and this would be his or her final route to execution. They would walk south along here, as we're doing now, to an outdoor space that was next to Newgate Prison. The prison and the court were at one time connected by this. In that open space, those convicted would be publicly hanged.

'These archways,' he says, tapping one as he walks beneath it, 'used to have doors in them.' There's moss on the bricks, an acrid green, and spiders' webs are everywhere. The place gives me the creeps.

We reach the end. 'Here you'd turn west,' he says, pointing before he moves, 'into this space, which was called The Birdcage. It used to have a net above it, up there, and it was the final place where the condemned would be able to look up and see the sky. It would be his or her final sight of natural daylight. Then they'd go through this exit and have a bag placed over their head and they'd be led, blindly, out and onto the scaffold where they'd hang and die for their sins and crimes.'

'Sins *and* crimes?'

'Same thing to religious people, and that's what they were back then.'

I retreat from Paul, moving back to the southern end of Dead Man's Walk, and stare down its length, which seems like an eternal darkened hollow tube. In my mind, I'm suddenly here under a different guise. Stepping out of an armoured van. Handcuffed and escorted by guards. Being marched along Dead Man's Walk, the angry public waiting to watch me face my fate. Guilty of my sins and crimes.

'Are you okay?' Paul asks, hastening towards me and taking hold of my arm, pulling me back to reality.

Without realising it, I've started shaking. *I can't be here any more.* 'Yes,' I lie, but my body says otherwise and he can tell.

'It's not a place for everyone,' he says. 'Look, I'm sorry, I didn't mean to . . . Come on, let's go, it's okay,' and he hooks our arms, leading me up and out of the building and into fresh air.

London's polluted air. I take a deep breath and cough.

Paul waits patiently, gently rubbing my back. 'It's okay,' he says. 'It's okay.'

I start crying. 'I couldn't, Paul. I'm sorry, I just couldn't.'

'Ssh, there's nothing to worry about.'

But the more I try to calm down, the more anxious I feel. 'I saw myself, Paul. I saw myself down there. It's what I deserve. For what I've done.'

'Oh Alice, not again. Don't start this now.'

'I can't, Paul. I can't go on pretending.'

'There's nothing to pretend about. It's done. Things are getting better. I swear, things are, and they'll keep getting better, if only you let them.'

'I'm scared, Paul.' I grab hold of him, as if for dear life; I don't ever want to let go. 'I'm scared I'm never going to be able forget about what happened.'

'You can.'

'What I've done.'

When I step back and look into Paul's eyes, I see he understands what I mean. There's pity on his face. His eyes and words give two very different messages.

'It's okay,' he says simply and ineffectively.

'I can't believe you, Paul. I just don't.'

4

A wheeled-in whiteboard had been placed at the side of the stale incident room. Stale in appearance and stale in smell. Peeling white paint clung onto each wall, and one notice-board, sparsely filled with yellowed and creased pieces of paper, was affixed centrally to the largest one. A table filled the majority of the room, and around it were close to a dozen chairs.

Detective Sergeant Katherine Wright and DC Ryan Hillier were looking down at the table, which was covered with folders that had been emptied of their contents: paper-work and pictures.

Key details were written on the whiteboard. Names of the three victims, dates, estimated times of death, addresses, details about them, information about the crime scenes.

Victim number one, 04/09: Richard Dollard, thirty-seven years old, solicitor.

Victim number two, 12/09: Ethan Fleming, thirty-seven years old, barrister.

Victim number three, 20/09: Simon Michael Ryman, thirty-five years old, solicitor.

'The obvious link is their jobs,' said Wright, 'so we need find out if there's any other connection between them. Did they know one another, for example. Speak to their families, their friends, employers and colleagues and find out if there's a deeper link, or whether this is merely a coincidence.'

Pulling a ball of piano wire from a carrier bag, Wright added, 'I picked this up on the way in today. Feel that.'

Hillier ran his fingers along it. 'Shit, that is fine.'

'It'll slice through skin without much effort at all. And imagine putting effort into it, what do you get?'

'A bloody mess.'

'Exactly.' She picked up the picture of victim number three, Simon Michael Ryman. 'A bloody mess indeed,' she agreed, surveying the carnage the shot presented.

'I'm meeting with Simon Michael Ryman's family at three o'clock this afternoon,' said Hillier.

'Let me take that one,' she said. 'Get back to everyone you've interviewed so far, distribute lists to the rest of the team, and get them onto Dollard's and Fleming's families. We've got to find a connection deeper than profession. It's got to be here somewhere.'

DC Theo Yardley knocked on the door. 'This has just arrived,' he said, entering and handing Hillier a brown A4 envelope.

Hillier thanked him and Yardley left. He opened the envelope. 'Report from Emerson,' he said.

'How many different sets of prints?' she asked impatiently.

'Thirty-three clear,' he said, 'and several other partials.'

'Okay, get back to Emerson and ask for comparison

prints between those found at all three scenes. Are there any that match?'

'He's already done that,' Hillier responded, reading further into the report. 'Here, it says . . .' He paused, reading. 'No, nothing at all.'

'Nothing?' she asked, incredulous. 'Not one single print that links any of the three scenes?'

'Not one, no.'

'Fuck.' She lowered her head and pinched her brow. 'What about other traces? Anything at all?'

'Just looking.' He was scanning the DNA readouts. Finally, he dropped the pieces of paper on the table. 'Lots of hairs and fibres, but nothing that matches. Useless.'

She closed her eyes. 'He's good,' she finally said. 'Too good.'

'That he is,' Hillier agreed.

Wright walked over to the whiteboard and stared at the names upon it. 'Surely he can't be that good.'

Hillier walked towards her. 'Killers always cock up, right?'

'Eventually,' she mused.

'So?'

'He's too clean. Not a trace of him at the scenes. Not a trace of how he got in or out. Piano wire – no one in this building has heard of anyone ever using piano wire as a weapon.'

'So a professional, like you predicted?'

'That's right. These are hits, Ryan, I'm certain of that. But there must be a connection. We must be missing something.'

'Like what?'

Frustrated, she said, 'I have absolutely no idea.'

P

A piercing scream wakes me. I touch my chest and realise I'm in a cold sweat – I have absolutely no idea what I was dreaming about. It must have been some kind of nightmare.

Sleep-muddied and breathing heavily, I assume I've woken to the sound of my own screaming, but the noise continues to reverberate in my ears, even though my eyes are open and I'm wide awake.

It's Alice. She's writhing on the bed next to me.

I reach for the bedside table lamp, but my hand connects with a glass and there's a thud as it lands on the carpet. 'Shit.'

When I manage to switch on the light, I turn and see Alice. She looks like she's in pain. Her high-pitched wailing drills into the centre of my skull, the agony she's experiencing contagious, and I reach out to her, running my hand across her ricocheting forehead. 'Alice,' I say, and then a soothing, 'Ssh.' But she screams even more shrilly, so I raise my voice and try to cradle her in my arms. 'Alice!'

Slowly, she quietens and settles, but she keeps sobbing. I hug her tightly. My heart's pounding and I desperately want to help her but don't know what else to do.

'The tunnel,' she wails.

'Alice, what—'

'Dead Man's Walk! The police! They were . . . here . . . and they took me . . . there.' Her whole body is shaking.

'Alice, nobody's here except you and me. No police. It's the middle of the night. Look. Just you and me. You're fine.' I don't believe what I'm saying, so I repeat it, as much for me as for her, 'You're fine.'

'They knew what I've done, Paul! They knew!'

'They don't know anything,' I say. Then hollowly: 'There's nothing to worry about.'

'I can't forget. You told me to, but I can't. I still remember. The first lie, it's led to this.'

She rolls away from me and curls into a ball. I'm left propped up on my knees, looking down at her. Seeing but not understanding. Helpless.

Her convulsions slowly subside. I touch her gently.

'Why did you take me there, Paul?' she mumbles. 'Why?'

'I didn't know, Alice. I didn't know you'd react like this. I'm sorry.' Words can't possibly express to her how regretful I am. I'm searching for anything, any way forward for her. I try, 'Listen, why don't you go back to the charity shop and offer to help them for two or three days a week again, anything to take your mind off things?'

'It was too difficult. It was too claustrophobic. I can't go back. I don't want to go out, Paul.' She sits up suddenly. 'I don't want to stay in either.'

'What then? What can I do for you if you can't help yourself?'

'You can turn back the clock.' She points at the alarm clock and, as she's speaking, she turns towards it. 'You can take time in your bare hands, squeeze it and turn—'

She screams again, her hand still pointing.

'What is it?'

I look at what she's pointing at. The alarm clock. I see it.

'It's 3 a.m, Paul. Three fucking a.m!'

03.00.

She stares at me, innocently, pleadingly, helplessly. I have no words. Am helpless to help.

Except—

I've got to get her out of here, away from this house and the memories of what we did. Away from that man's inescapable shadow.

5

Detective Constable Ryan Hillier arrived at 35 Denbigh Gardens a little after 11 a.m. The journey to Swindon had taken just over two hours. Yesterday, he met with Karen Dollard, Richard Dollard's sibling, who was his only surviving relative, and wanted to keep the momentum going, in the hope that they'd be able to establish some further connections between the victims.

Karen Dollard had painted a picture of a highly ambitious, hard-working young man, one who put his career before all else. He wasn't involved in a romantic relationship as far as she knew, instead choosing to pour his energies into his work at the law firm, determined to reach career heights as quickly as possible. She said when they last spoke he was excited about applying for a new position, something he described as a major step in what he termed *the right direction*.

Denbigh Gardens was in the middle of an affluent yet rural part of the town. The street, which was a close, contained only detached houses that looked grand in contrast to the average-sized home Hillier woke up in on a daily basis.

A large horse chestnut tree sat at the end of the path that led to Ethan Fleming's parents' front door. It shaded the front of the house, which comprised two large ground-floor windows and three upstairs.

Hillier knocked on the door and was quickly greeted by a man who looked to be in his early seventies and whose eyes, which conveyed remorse and self-reflection, appeared to have aged him significantly.

'Mr Fleming?' Hillier asked, and then introduced himself.

'Come in,' Alfred Fleming said softly. 'We've been expecting you.'

'Thank you,' Hillier said, wiping his feet on the outdoor mat. Despite this, he took off his shoes when he was inside.

'Would you like a cup of tea?' Alfred Fleming asked.

Hillier's head told him to say no, but he couldn't resist. The journey had been draining. 'That would be lovely, thank you.' He followed the old man into the kitchen and watched silently as the mugs of tea were prepared with great care.

As Alfred Fleming was finishing, Hillier asked, 'Is Mrs Fleming home today?'

'Oh, yes,' he answered. 'She's just preparing. She'll be down shortly.'

'She really mustn't go to any trouble,' Hillier said. 'Neither of you should.'

Fleming looked at him sceptically. 'It's a different kind of preparation, I'm afraid,' and Hillier instantly understood what he meant.

'I am truly sorry for your loss.'

Ethan Fleming's father paused and said, 'So am I.' Then he repeated quietly to himself, as if for reassurance, 'So am I.'

Footsteps approached and his wife entered the room, her hand extended. 'I'm Judith,' she said. Hillier took her hand in his. 'Thank you for coming.'

'Let me thank you,' he said in return.

'Speaking to you is the least we can do,' she said, and then closing her eyes, 'After all, you're trying to find out who killed our son.' She bowed her head and coughed into a limp fist. Then she looked up at Hillier and smiled pathetically. 'I'm sorry.'

He shook his head gently. 'There's nothing to be sorry about.'

'Tea,' Alfred Fleming said, passing a beige mug to Hillier. 'I made one for you, too,' he told his wife and handed it to her.

Alfred Fleming led the way out of the kitchen, along a corridor to the right, which was adorned with family photographs, mostly of Ethan at various stages of his life, a kind of journey through it, from childhood to university to his rise in the legal profession. Before it was cut short. Walking along this shrine, Hillier thought the photographs were probably both at once a source of comfort and pain to the parents who would never see their son again.

They entered the lounge and went to the dining table. Alfred indicated a chair to Hillier and he sat down, placing his mug carefully on the table before him. He began, 'Please let me repeat my condolences and know we are doing everything we can to find the person or persons responsible.'

'We appreciate that,' Alfred Fleming said.

'Could you just start by telling me a bit about Ethan?'

'What would you like to know?' Judith Fleming asked. 'I said everything I could think of to the constable who visited a few months ago.'

'I appreciate that. I'm conducting fresh enquiries to see if anything was missed. Please, just talk about him generally, tell me anything you'd like to tell, that's always a good starting point.'

'You've done many of these kinds of chat?' Alfred Fleming asked, Hillier couldn't tell whether indifferently or dismissively.

He looked the old man in the eye. 'Far too many times for my liking, yes, but I've found that listening about someone as told by their loved ones gives me a good starting point and sometimes even leads me to some information I might not have learnt if I'd just started by asking routine questions. So please, I'd appreciate it if you could just speak about him to a stranger who has never met him and doesn't know anything about him. Perhaps start off by telling me what you're especially proud of.'

'Oh well, that's easy,' Judith said, exhaling. 'He was wonderfully gifted academically.'

'Yes,' Alfred Fleming whispered.

'There really wasn't anything he couldn't do. He wrote beautifully, he understood everything he read, had a head for maths, a mind for science, cared about the world, was curious about the past, and it was early when he fell in love with the idea of being a lawyer, what, when he was fourteen or fifteen. He just knew, it was his calling. And when he began to look into the various options available to him after he started studying law and government politics at A Level, he discovered what a solicitor does and that appealed to him more than anything else. Once he knew what he wanted to be, there was simply no stopping him.'

'That's right,' Alfred Fleming added, 'once he set his mind on something, he didn't change it. That was our Ethan. He was so determined to achieve what he wanted. I always say, if he'd been as sporty as he was brainy, he'd have broken records.'

'Was he competitive?' Hillier asked.

'He wanted to be the best he could be,' Mrs Fleming answered, 'so if that meant competing, he had no qualms. He was confident in himself and achieved all that he set out to.'

'Well, almost,' her husband murmured.

Judith Fleming shot a look at him. Some kind of venom, Hillier thought, or disappointment.

Silence prevailed, so Hillier asked Alfred Fleming, 'Could you tell me what you meant by that?'

'By what?'

'Almost,' Hillier repeated. 'You said he almost achieved everything he set out to.'

Alfred Fleming drank slowly, then after placing the mug on the table, he cupped his hands. His wife sat forwards. 'He was ambitious, always with his eye on opportunities. He'd had more promotions than most people can count hot dinners. But what he really wanted to do was open his own practice one day. He wanted his name on the building, on the letterhead. He was a proud young man, was our Ethan. He had plans to do it last year, with a friend from his university days, but they had some kind of falling out, or things didn't work out for one reason or another, I don't know why, he didn't say. I think he was a bit embarrassed by it, so I didn't ask. But I know he took it hard.'

'This friend,' Hillier asked, 'do you know his name?'

'I'm afraid not, no.'

Hillier gave Judith Fleming an inquisitive glance. She shook her head.

'What university did he go to?'

It was Mrs Fleming who answered. 'He completed his law degree at Jesus College, Cambridge.'

Hillier's eyes sprang open. 'Sorry?'

'As we said, he was a smart young man. It was natural he went to Cambridge or Oxford. He liked the College the moment he stepped foot in it, so Cambridge it was.'

'*Jesus* College?'

'That's right,' she said, beaming with pride.

Jesus College.

A

I've struggled since October. Struggled to concentrate by day and struggled to sleep at night. Night after night, I've tried to cry myself to sleep. So often, because of his job, Paul hasn't been here. I know he's tried, and I know he's done his best, but it hasn't been enough. I've needed more. I've needed him.

I need more.

I'll support you, he told me that night. *I'm here for you.* I still need that. I still want that.

But Paul isn't here, again.

I think back to my conversation with Amanda when we recently went to dinner with her and Laurence. She mentioned the doctor. He helped me once, as far as I could be helped then, so maybe he is my best bet right now.

He's based in Harley Street. Paul spent a fortune on helping me four years ago. I didn't want to come to London, but Dr Barks is a patient, caring psychiatrist, the only one I know, and he'll remember me, so today I make an exception.

The receptionist who welcomes me in such a sensitive and friendly manner has a different face from when I was last here, but Dr Barks hasn't changed much. A good life. A relaxing life, spent listening to people's problems.

'It's good to see you,' he says softly, gently taking my hand in his. I'm expecting him to say more, something empty and vacuous like *How are you?* or *You're looking well.* Only the answer to the first can't be good – I'm here, after all – and the second statement would be a lie – I look like shit and I know it – so he says nothing else.

Instead, he leads me to the patient's chair, a sofa of sorts, and uses his other hand to indicate that I should take a seat on it. Or lie down, whatever is more comfortable.

I sit, perching awkwardly on its side, like I used to.

'What can I do for you?' he asks, his calming, neutral face greeting me.

'It's like before,' I say.

When I don't elaborate, he asks, 'How are you feeling?'

'Down. Without energy.' I think carefully. 'Without hope. Afraid.'

'Do you have any idea what the cause may be?'

Yes! I want to shout the word at him. I don't know what to say in its place that will satisfy me.

'Do you know what you're afraid of?'

Yes, yes, yes.

'Is it linked to what happened before?' he asks.

'It's the same kind of feelings.'

'Are you and your husband, if you don't mind me asking, still hopeful of having children one day?'

'No,' I say, suddenly entranced, taken back to the time when that was exactly what we wanted. *I can see our children.*

'But the feelings mirror those you experienced back then?'

'Absolutely.'

'You used to say the pills I prescribed helped you to relax.'

'That, they did,' I say, still half in, half out of the room.

'Shall we try those again?'

'Whatever you think, doctor.'

I can see them.

When I return home, I head straight for the kitchen. I pour some red wine, washing up the glass and putting the bottle back into the cupboard, before I flick the switch on the kettle. As it heats up, I stare out of the window. The back garden is overgrown, but I can't see anything other than a blur of dark green.

We did want children.

The front door opening snaps me back to attention. Paul walks in, a wide grin on his face. He puts a newspaper on the side unit and kisses me on the cheek. 'I'm going to take you away,' he says unexpectedly, as the kettle starts to boil.

This isn't like Paul. 'How?' I ask. 'You've just started a new job.'

'I have a couple of weeks till the next trial begins. I can shuffle things and make it work. You need to be out of here, away from all the reminders.' He takes me by the shoulders and runs his hands caressingly up and down my arms. 'I want you to forget all this. Let's go away to somewhere you can remember what it feels like to be you again. Let's get you better.'

P

So close, yet so far. There's no other way to describe what being married to Alice is like now. Things have to change. I have to try harder to help her. I have to find a way to break through.

This is the start. The chance to be refreshed. I'm hoping a change of scene might be the solution.

Three nights in the Big Apple, time for her to regenerate and become anew. A chance for us to return to who we were before last October. And perhaps, selfishly, a chance for me to temporarily forget about what's to come at work. *The Craven trial.*

The following morning after I booked the trip, when I told Alice what we'd be doing, I said to her, 'Bring the red dress.'

She smiled, I'm sure transported back to the days when she first put it on. It was the first gift I bought her after I completed my placement years and got a job as a fully fledged barrister.

We arrived early for the flight at London Heathrow Terminal Five. I had it all planned out. Time for food and time to have a couple of drinks. Time to relax.

The flight from London Heathrow to New York's JFK takes a little under seven hours. I secured business-class tickets – an absolute fortune thanks to the last-minute nature of my booking, not that they're ever cheap, but I was sure it would be worth it. Besides, little matches British Airways' Club World service, which would make Alice feel special and hopefully encourage her to forget all her ills.

She was initially reluctant to drink much alcohol in the airport, but the lure of champagne as we settle into our seats quickly encourages her. In fact, by the time the plane starts taxiing to the runway, we're both on our third glasses.

As the plane takes off, I'm convinced this will be a special trip, that this will help things change. *This is the start. She can get better.* I hold her hand as we sit facing rearwards on two centre seats, lift it towards my lips and kiss it. She places her head on my shoulder and the weight of the world seems lifted, transporting me back many years to the first time we shared a flight abroad, a trip to Mauritius. Back then, we were in economy, young, broke, ambitious. How times have changed.

We're staying at the Roxy. It's on Broadway and 36th Street, nice and central, just a few blocks south of Times Square.

In Manhattan, patches of snow lie on parts of the pavements and cover some of the little greenery that's in view, and I'm relieved the forecast I checked this morning predicted it wouldn't snow again until after we leave. But it's bitingly cold, so much so it hurts.

The word Roxy is surprisingly discreet in dark red italics above a rotating glass door. As we step through, we enter into a wall of booming music with a dance beat and a young clientele. I want to take Alice back into the past.

The foyer comprises cream marble walls and floor, a high ceiling and eight dark wooden desks, equally separated into two rows at both sides, resembling stand-up pianos. Behind each is an attractive young woman. One of them checks us in. The elevators, she says, are further along, through a gap between an office, which reminds me of a DJ's booth, and a luggage hold room.

Our room is on the seventh floor. The hotel's top floor, where the rooftop bar is, is the thirteenth. When we emerge, we teeter along the corridor, happy, full, drunk and, above all, content.

Our room is fairly small, typical for New York, but the bed is spacious and comfortable and there's a great view from the window. The bathroom is luxuriously decorated with a quirky-looking sink and a walk-in shower whose base is part of the tiled floor.

'It's interesting-looking,' Alice says. 'Unusual.'

'I thought you'd like it.'

'I do.' She comes to me and kisses me. 'It's the kind of thing the teenage me would have got excited about in holiday brochures. I feel alive, Paul. Even the air is different. Thank you.'

A

I'm woken by the sound of the door shutting with a heavy thud. The room is still dark and I use my hand to feel if Paul is by my side. He isn't. My heart suddenly beating fast, I sit up and crawl over to the window, which is by the foot of the bed. Feeling around, I work out how to open the blinds. Daylight pours through.

Once my eyes have adjusted to the light, I lean against the window and peer down. The road is busy, people streaming in all directions. I see Paul coming out of the hotel and heading down the street. I want him to look up and see me, but he doesn't. I hope he's going to return. I know I'm being unreasonable, but I'm afraid that he might leave me here all alone.

To distract myself, I decide to wash and get dressed, but first I switch on the television to plug the room's silence. The warm water goes some way to helping me feel better.

'Thought I'd get us some breakfast,' Paul says, re-entering the room as I exit the shower.

Relieved, I leap over to him and hug him tight.

'What's the matter?' he asks.

'I was afraid . . . I know it's stupid, but I was.'

'You thought I'd leave you here?'

I look away shyly. 'I don't know. I'm sorry.'

He touches the side of my face. 'You have absolutely nothing to be sorry for. I'm so pleased to be here with you. And for you.'

After breakfasting on croissants and coffee, we walk up to Central Park, spending some time by the main lake and wandering amid the cyclists, joggers and tourists. It's cold, but there's a brilliant blue sky and a freshness in the air. We buy some roasted nuts from a vendor and feed the squirrels. I'm amazed by how close they get to us. We walk arm in arm, slowly and without any care in the world.

We spend a couple of hours in the Met, experiencing the exhibits and the vast open spaces. It's so calm and peaceful inside, just like in Central Park, both in stark contrast to the rest of the chaotic, busy city.

After, we spend a few hours shopping, heading south down Fifth Avenue. It's one of the fashion capitals of the world, and Paul knows how much I love fashion. By the time we're finished, I feel spoilt and happy.

A meal at a French restaurant follows, including a nice bottle of wine, which makes me feel more relaxed and centred than I have in many months. As we leave, I thank Paul with a deep kiss.

'One more surprise,' he says.

He hails a cab and we arrive at the Rockerfeller Center at about 8 p.m. 'Ha!' Paul laughs as we walk into the entrance and find it empty of people.

'Is it shut?' I ask him.

'No, the trick is to arrive an hour before closing time and you can breeze straight through.'

Which is precisely what we do.

The view of New York City's lights from so high up is breathtaking. I feel like I'm floating on air; I haven't been this happy in I don't know how many years. I hug Paul.

We look across, down and around, his arm around me the whole time. I nestle against him. He is my husband and I love him more than words can say.

'Thank you,' I say.

'What for?'

'For this. For every minute we've spent here.' I don't look at him. 'For everything you've ever done for me.' I know he knows what I mean.

'You have nothing to thank me for. Your pleasure is mine.'

'I love it up here. We're so close to each other while so far away from everyone else. They all look so small down there. We can just about see them, but they can't touch us. Only you can touch me.'

He squeezes tighter.

I face him. 'I want to go back to the hotel room and I want to make love to you.'

He lowers his arm and runs his hand over my hip. My legs become weak and I sink into him.

'Take me there,' I whisper.

He cups my chin and leans down, planting his lips against mine. Our kiss is deep, sensuous. I place my hand on the side of his face.

My Paul.

A

The following morning, we wake up naked in each other's arms. We take our time getting ready, then breakfast in a nearby Starbucks. Afterwards, we take a cab south to Church Street for our final day here. It's drizzling lightly. We walk to Vesey Street and find ourselves facing the former site of the World Trade Center, now One World Trade Center. I'd specifically asked that we come here; it's something I must experience.

As we pass Greenwich Street, the whole of New York City seems to change; the loud noises of every other street and avenue are dulled and it's suddenly immensely quiet.

We stand in front of One World Trade Center and tilt our heads up. One hundred and four storeys – or 1,776 feet – high, it's the tallest building in America and the fourth tallest in the world. The sheer scale of the building takes my breath away. 'I read that its height in feet – seventeen seventy-six – is actually a reference to when the Declaration of Independence was signed,' Paul says.

From West Street, we enter Memorial Plaza, the official memorial to the victims of 9/11. Located where the foundations of the original Twin Towers were are two large black square basins that are cut deep into the ground. One acre each, water flows down their sides, like a waterfall.

We walk slowly around the nearest pool, originally the site of the North Tower, passing the names of the 2,983 victims, which have been inscribed on the parapets of the pool's walls. We finish circling the first, then walk over to the second, where the South Tower once was, and begin walking around it. The victims' names are not inscribed text but carved into the memorial, and gaps are left in the lettering, where every so often a single red or white rose rests. I cling hold of Paul, melancholia overflowing me.

I forget myself and stare at the water for a long time. Specific thoughts evade me. Eventually, Paul asks, 'Shall we go in?'

The 9/11 Memorial Museum's façade reminds me of the Louvre. Glass and triangular above ground, most of the museum itself is housed underground, in and around the foundations of the original Twin Towers.

An escalator takes us down and we enter a large open but dark space. The quiet outside has followed us; there are plenty of people in here, but they can barely be heard. We follow the stream of visitors, through the exhibitions, reading about and watching and listening to the sights and sounds of that terrible day. By the time we reach the lower ground level, which is where the main exhibition is, I feel so submerged I don't know if I'll ever be able to get back up. 'Those poor people,' I say, teary. It's the most intensely moving experience of my life.

Tracing our way into the pits of the museum, we scan the exhibits, from the birth of Al Qaeda and the day of the attacks to the aftermath and the consequences that linger today. It's taken us almost four hours to get this far.

We're sitting on benches inside a darkened room, which has entrances and exits off two sides, with the other two walls used as projection spaces. On them, images of victims appear as their loved ones, who can be heard but not seen, recount memories of them.

The sadness becomes overwhelming and when I hear the story of a man whose wife was due to give birth to their child within days of the attack happening and she recalls her final conversation with him, 'Look after our baby, make sure she knows I love her every day I'm not here,' I can't take it any more and escape, gasping for air.

Paul follows me out. He stands next to me. I can tell he wants to speak, but he remains quiet.

'I need fresh air,' I say and I move quickly towards the escalator. As I reach the top, I push an emergency exit door open and emerge into Memorial Plaza. I suck in as much fresh air as I can. I can't hold back the tears.

I thought this was working, I thought New York was helping, but this place reeks of death; it's overwhelming.

'Aren't you having a good time?' he says eventually, trying to hide the irritation in his voice. At least, I think it's irritation.

'The loss,' I say, choking back the tears. 'They've all lost so much.' I hold him. 'We've lost so much.'

'We haven't lost each other, Alice.'

'How can we have each other, Paul, when I don't even have myself any more?'

That silences him. I turn and look at him, but he glances away. There's something strange in his eyes. He's started to have enough of me, I can tell. But I can't help it. This is me right now. This is who I am and how I feel. I can't help it.

I'm worried I'm losing him.

We drift over to a bench, sit on it, and time passes. First, we remain in silence and apart, then we move closer together, and then Paul finally speaks to me. 'Come on,' he says, 'things will get better.'

I shake my head. 'They won't.'

He takes me by the hand. 'Dinner.' He pulls me up, not letting me continue. 'And drinks. Lots of drinks. You've got to keep moving forward, remember. So let's keep moving forward.'

We settle in an Italian restaurant that Paul says is family-owned and known for a great wine list. After we're seated and have ordered, Paul says, 'Do you remember the first meal we shared on our first trip abroad?'

'Oh, you mean that godforsaken Spanish menu,' I laugh, but all it does is mask my unhappiness. 'Squid isn't your thing, I think we learnt.'

'Hey, I didn't know it was squid. They said it was their speciality.'

'Well, it was special all right. Can we have some wine now, please?'

I hope the wine, a full-bodied white, will help pick me up.

When we're on our second glass, I look at Paul and think, *We've lost too much. How can we ever go back to where we were?*

'I'm sorry,' I say, attempting to reconcile what I've done to our trip. 'I don't know what came over me. I was being silly.'

'Not silly at all,' Paul says. 'I felt it, too. But I'm thinking about it in the most positive way I can. That place, and what happened there, makes me realise we're lucky to have what we have.'

I smile at him, but I'm not sure I hide my true feelings successfully.

'Life can be taken away so quickly,' he says. 'So we've got to enjoy every day we have. We have to make the most of our time together, Alice, every moment.'

'You're right,' I say, even though I'm not convinced. 'I'm glad we're here.' At least that's how I felt until today.

Paul picks up his wine glass. 'To us.'

I bring mine to his. 'To us,' I repeat. But I fear my voice is hollow.

My head doesn't hurt when I wake up in the morning, despite the amount of alcohol I drank, and I open my eyes, uplifted. 'Last day,' I say, even though I know Paul is still asleep and can't hear me. We fly this evening. 'Last day.' Thoughts of returning home, and memories of the museum, overshadow the happiness I experienced the day before yesterday. I can't blank them.

I look at the man I am forever entwined with. He's the man I love, but I feel so little, at least compared with how much I felt forty-eight hours ago.

He is the man who figured out how to save me; he knew what to do with the dead body. I owe him everything, yet I fear I'm able to give nothing.

The strain on his face after each spadeful of earth was thrown over his shoulder was ugly and painful. He pushed himself further than he'd ever gone and he did that for me, despite the danger it put him in. He risked his career. He's waited for so long to achieve his goal, he's fought so hard for it, and now he's got it and he's achieved the success he's striven for, it could be gone in an instant.

That's what he did for me.

I look over to him and know I should feel deep love. I know him intimately and no one will ever know me better than he does. But I'm still feeling hollow. I can't get away from the loss.

Regardless, we have no choice: together, we are co-conspirators, so we must remain united, forever. We must always be there for each other, no matter what.

6

When Hillier's meeting with Alfred and Judith Fleming had been concluded, without resulting in any further revelations, he was on the phone with Detective Sergeant Katherine Wright.

'He went where?' she asked, a shudder of expectation in her heart.

'Jesus College,' Hillier repeated. 'The same as Richard Dollard. He was on the same course at the same time, too.'

'Get there,' she said.

'I'm already on my way.'

Which was where he was now.

Founded in the late fifteenth century, Jesus College is one of the University of Cambridge's largest sites. The office of the registrar, Gethin Hughes, was situated off Library Court, next to Quincentenary Library, which was built in 1996 to commemorate the five-hundred-year anniversary of the foundation of Jesus College.

Gethin Hughes was a friendly man with intensely dark short hair. 'What year?' he asked.

Detective Constable Ryan Hillier smiled. 'Two thousand and one. That would be great.'

Gethin Hughes winked at him. A camp man, whose hands moved too much while he spoke, he added, 'I wonder if I could ask why these names are of interest to you?' His voice rose substantially at the end of the question, the pitch awkwardly high.

Hillier leant against the counter desk behind which Hughes worked. He wanted to convey an impression of casual interest. You never know who you might need to call on.

'You could ask, but I'm afraid I can't tell,' Hillier responded with a hint of flirtation in his voice, which he kept soft, seeing that it had helped him to bypass formalities to get this far. 'But you will be helping me with something very important, that much I can assure you.'

Hughes retired to the back of the room, where he sat at a computer desk and busied himself. It wasn't long before he returned. 'Here you go,' he said, presenting some sheets of paper.

'That was quick,' Hillier said. 'I'm impressed.'

'Any time,' he said, a flick of the wrist suggesting it had all been too easy.

'Do you mind if I take this?' he asked.

'No problem,' Hughes said. 'And,' he added, pulling something from his pocket, 'my card. In case you need me.'

Resisting the urge to laugh, Hillier took it and thanked him. Outside, he found a bench, one of many surrounding an attractive square of green grass, itself surrounded by several ancient buildings. Students walked and milled around, some sitting at the benches eating lunch.

Hillier started searching through the names, his finger running over the list. Name after name. And then there it was: Richard Dollard. And then: Ethan Fleming.

He continued scanning, name after name, his finger moving slowly down the page. But nothing else. He went back to the start and repeated. His eyes passed the words Ethan Fleming and Richard Dollard again. His eyes glazed over. A lapse in concentration. The names merging into one. Then a pause.

'Wait a minute.' He looked up at the sky. 'I should have known.'

Removing his phone, he dialled. 'Katherine,' he said, when DS Wright answered, 'remind me, how old was Simon Michael Ryman?'

She didn't need to check. 'Thirty-five,' she said without hesitation.

'Tch, idiot.' Feeling as if he needed to explain: 'Me, not you.'

'What? What's the matter?'

'I'll call you back.' He rang off and went back into the administrator's office. 'Gethin,' he said, his smile beaming. 'Listen, sorry, I was confused. Can I have the names of those who would have graduated two and three years later, so 2003 and 2004?'

'Won't be a problem. Just give me a moment.'

Hillier had the pages in a few minutes and went back outside. This time he didn't sit; he started finger-trawling through the names as soon as he was away from Gethin Hughes' sightline, mouthing them one by one. He saw and said them all.

'And here you are,' Hillier said. On the page: Simon Michael Ryman.

He redialled. Before Wright said anything, he said, 'Simon Michael Ryman was two years younger than Ethan Fleming and Richard Dollard. He graduated from here two years later.'

'Where are you? Are you in Cambridge yet?'

'Yes. They all studied here, Jesus College, all three of them, only Simon Michael Ryman graduated two years later than Dollard and Fleming. This is our link. This must have something to do with it all.'

'Seems likely.'

'Some kind of revenge story, some kind of rivalry perhaps.'

'It's too early to tell. Look, get back here with those lists.' She paused. 'In fact, do you think you could get the names of everyone who's studied on the course since, let's say, 1996?'

Hillier looked through the door and saw Gethin Hughes, who was watching him and gave a quick wave. 'Something tells me that won't be difficult.'

29 March

P

We flew back to London. We resumed our lives, content.

At least, that's what I thought.

New York was exactly what Alice needed, at least until we reached the 9/11 Museum. I should have known it would be a mistake, but she'd insisted on going. Still, everything else about the trip was a success. That should count for something.

We arrived home, somehow changed and yet somehow exactly the same as before. Both anew, both unchanged.

We felt better together, like we fit more comfortably, like we were more connected. But the one thing we could not change, nor could we deny, was what we had done and what we had gone away to forget. When we returned home, it was waiting for us.

Now the Craven trial has reared its ugly head and it's something I can no longer ignore; the time has come to dive into it, regardless of my hesitation, which means Alice will have to deal with being alone a lot more.

'I have to go back full-time from tomorrow,' I tell her, as I approach her in the kitchen. She's standing in front of the sink and staring out of the window into the back garden.

'Tomorrow?' she asks, her voice managing to cover what she's thinking about it.

'I've stayed away as long as I can.'

'I know you have.'

She still hasn't looked round at me.

'Will the days be long?'

'Like last time, I suspect,' I say, stepping towards her. I place my hands on her hips.

'I felt so alone,' she says.

I lift my hands to her shoulders and massage gently. 'I'll be back as quickly as I can every day, but I have to go. You know I do.'

'I know,' she says, nodding.

'Alice, I'm doing this for us.'

She sniggers but still keeps her face away from me.

'What are you laughing for?'

She turns around. There are tears in her eyes. 'This is all about you, Paul. It's all you've wanted. I just want a husband.'

I'm confused by the sight of her tears. 'Someone needs to pay for all this, Alice?' I swipe my hands around, indicating our home. *I can't believe how selfish she's being.*

She sniffs. 'I want to move.'

'I know, I've thought about it too.'

'I can't live here, Paul. When I'm with you, okay, I can manage, but alone every day, no, I can't do that. Not here. Not where he was. I want to leave this house.'

'This was supposed to be our dream home.'

'It was, until he turned it into a nightmare. No, I can't, Paul, I want to leave. If you're going to be gone for hours on end every day, I want you to sell it. I don't want to be here alone.'

I try to sound convincing. 'Let me look into it. I'll see what I can do.'

'Please, Paul, I mean what I say.'

'I understand, Alice. I understand. And I mean what I'm saying. I will try my best. Trust me.'

I hope I sound sincere. The truth is I don't know whether selling this property, without substantial downsizing, is a realistic possibility. I have several investments banked against the equity I have on this house. She doesn't know about them.

'I trust you,' she says, and she brings her lips to mine.

'I love you,' I say.

She smiles but doesn't return the words. Something niggling at the back of my mind tells me I may not hear them again for a long time.

'I'll do everything I can to be back by seven.'

P

'Coffee?' Belinda asks, leaning into my chambers.

Something stronger, I think but don't vocalise. I knew this prep would be hard, but I didn't predict just how hard I'd be hit by what I have to read.

'I'd love one,' I say with a forced smile, 'and bring one for yourself.' She looks surprised. Anything to get me away from these documents.

I read the Cravens' story and I see Alice and me. *Us*. I don't want to do it. I lean back in my chair and lift up my arms to encourage the sweat to cool.

I need a distraction, I think, or just something else to do.

Belinda brings in my coffee and I thank her. 'Where's yours?' I say, seeing she has empty hands.

She smiles shyly and says, 'Give me a sec.'

'Please,' I say, indicating the chair opposite when she returns.

Even though she's worked with me for three years, she doesn't know me particularly well. Everything has always been strictly professional and it's clear she feels awkward or uncomfortable around me. That's how she looks once again right now.

'It's okay,' I say. 'Just relax. I could do with the company. This stuff is driving me mad.'

'The new trial?' she asks, leaning forwards slightly.

'Yup. Starts in an hour.'

Her top is low-cut and she unintentionally reveals more than I'm sure she hopes to. I look. She has lovely skin. She's young, after all, only twenty-five. There's something about her smile that relaxes me. 'And how have you found things, I mean, since we came here?'

'I like it.' She smiles. It's a pretty smile. 'But I do miss all my friends. It's very . . . separate here.'

'How so?'

'I assume it's because no one's based here all year round. Either that or they're just stuck-up, arrogant pricks.'

'Probably the latter,' I laugh. She laughs, too. Her smile is beautiful, her teeth a gleaming white and perfectly aligned. 'I'm glad you came with me,' I tell her. 'I don't think I could have managed without you.'

She leans forwards. 'I'm glad, too.'

A

'I want to move house.'

That's what I told Paul over two weeks ago and he's not mentioned it since. He's been working all the time and I've hardly seen him.

Seven o'clock? If he's home by nine, I'm lucky.

I feel so lonely. For a couple of weeks, I got used to Paul being with me much more than usual, just at the time when I needed it most, and now he's back to his normal routines, first as lawyer, now as judge, and I can't accept things being the way they once were.

I loved being with him in New York, until that last day when it all came tumbling down around me – the loss, I couldn't take it; it resonated and made me think about us. I regret how I behaved, that I couldn't suppress how I was feeling and broke down, that I fled from the museum and concerned Paul, but it was too much to handle. I feel like an ungrateful bitch – he took me to New York and look at how I behaved. But I couldn't help it.

I haven't been able to forget that wave of emotion that swept me away, and now I'm alone again. Only Paul can bring me the comfort I need, but there he is, so near and yet so far, every day at the Old Bailey and returning home so late and too exhausted to even talk.

It's Wednesday and I spend much of the day staring out of the rear kitchen window, sipping on gin and tonics. Our garden has been a visual haven of sorts for me. I can't explain why. Perhaps because it's outside of the house, away from where he was.

At some point, I get tired and head upstairs. The bed isn't made from when I woke up earlier, so I climb atop it. My eyes close instinctively – this happens frequently – and pretty soon fall asleep.

I don't know how much later it is, but I awake in darkness with a heavy head and even heavier heart. I feel hungover and sad. My senses have been dulled, perhaps by the room's darkness, its blinds so tightly placed together that not a centimetre of light makes it past them, or perhaps by the excess of alcohol I've consumed. I have a strong thirst and regret having drunk so much gin and tonic this morning. Even though alcohol is the only way I feel I can stay in this godforsaken place without Paul.

And then a noise, the very noise in fact that woke me up. It comes from downstairs and sounds like a chain rattling. Now there's a metallic sound being pounded and then glass shattering. I sit up and pivot to Paul. But he isn't here. He's at work.

Shivering, I get up and edge towards the bedroom door. From the doorway, I can see along the hallway. I step into it, spot-lit, and then I stop, frozen by the footsteps I hear coming up the stairs. I wait for Paul to appear at the top of the staircase. It must be him.

The footsteps get closer, louder, and then not Paul but a shadowy figure appears, much larger than Paul, with less hair, and soon he's in the corridor and coming towards me. Nearer and nearer, still in darkness, but when there are only two or three metres between us I snatch at the light switch and the hallway lights up like Broadway.

It's him, the man I killed, and his neck and white T-shirt are plastered in dried blood. I stare into his eyes and he offers me a twisted smile. He brings out his hands towards me and I scream, startled by some kind of wire that he's holding between both hands.

I scream and scream and then my eyes open. Daylight is seeping through the curtains, Paul isn't by my side and I'm alone, but that also means the man isn't here. I'm covered in sweat and so is my side of the bed. A glance at the alarm clock tells me it's only 1 p.m.

Trembling, I grab my mobile. I want to call Paul. I need him. I can't take this any longer. What we've done – what I've done – will plague me forever and I need his comfort. I need his arms around me now.

It was all my fault, Paul, all my fault, and I'm sorrier than you can possibly imagine. I killed him. I did it.

A romantic meal. I have to try to reconnect us. Paul tried to in New York and he succeeded until I let myself get carried away. Now it's my turn to take charge, have a purpose and make myself better.

I decide to cook Paul a three-course meal by candlelight. I'll buy a bottle of the best champagne – he's loves it, particularly on special occasions, and tonight can be a special occasion. The night when I change back to normal for good.

I spend the whole afternoon preparing, the anticipation building in my stomach. I'm going to make things right, I'm determined, and I tell myself repeatedly throughout the day that I'm going to make myself better by focusing on us.

A little after eight, I hear a car pulling into the driveway. I look through the blinds and see Paul approaching. I'm relieved he's here because there was always the possibility that he wouldn't turn up till much later.

I hear a key in the front door. It opens. But then silence, so I go into the hallway, champagne glasses in hand.

'I've made you a meal,' I say.

He looks back at me, blank.

'Surprise.'

He runs a hand over his face. 'I need a wash, Alice.'

'A wash?' He's ignored the glass of champagne I'm holding out to him. 'Why?'

'Because I feel dirty.'

Without another word, or even a glance at me, he makes his way upstairs.

By the time Paul comes down, well over half an hour later, the food is almost ruined. I'm sitting at the dining table, all the food laid out, our champagne glasses standing unattended. Just like I feel.

I pause as he comes into the room. Then: 'I said this was a surprise, so . . . surprise.'

'I'm sorry, I didn't realise.'

'But I said, "Surprise".'

He holds up his hand, a newspaper clutched between his fingers. 'I wasn't really listening. I've had a hell of a day. The things I've had to listen to . . .'

I get up and take him by the arms, but he keeps hold of the paper. 'What's the matter?'

He shakes his head. 'It's just this trial . . . I can't talk about it. I don't want to . . . Look, I'm sorry.'

He won't make eye contact with me, so I take him by the chin. 'Darling, I'm here and I've prepared a meal for you. Forget all of that.'

He shakes his head again. 'I can't. I'm too involved.'

'Then tell me.'

Now he looks me in the eye, properly and for the first time. I don't know what he sees, but he says, 'Please don't.' He doesn't say any more, just turns away from me and takes a seat opposite where I planned to sit.

'I bought champagne,' I say, without turning to him.

'A toast to *us*,' he says, and I hear him swallowing as I stand, alone and without a glass. When I turn around, his is empty.

'I made this meal to say I'm sorry for how I've been since New York.'

He looks sad. 'So am I,' he says.

'How am I to cope then?' I blurt out, suddenly unable to prevent the building emotion from escaping me. 'I need you, Paul.'

'And I need you.'

'Then tell me.' I grab him and hold his gaze. 'What's happened?'

He tries to brush me off. 'The trial . . . it's making me wonder whether I'm cut out for this job.'

'But it's you, Paul. It's meant everything to you for so many years. We put our whole lives on hold for it. Kids, I mean—'

'I know what you mean,' he snaps. 'Don't you dare blame me.' He pauses and fixes his eyes on mine, shaking his head definitively. 'No, Alice, not now. I don't want to talk about this.'

I lean in and kiss him on the cheek, but he pulls away and walks out of the dining room, leaving me with my overcooked meal.

It was supposed to make everything better.

'Surprise,' I say to myself. 'I've made you a meal to say I'm sorry.' And I cry.

7

Detective Sergeant Katherine Wright and Detective Constable Ryan Hillier got out of the car. After discovering the three murder victims had completed law degrees at the same university – two in the same year and one two years later – but with no other leads gained by interviewing the victims' closest families and friends, Wright felt they had no choice but to work their way through Hillier's list of all the students who had completed the same course, visiting each individual. It was a long, arduous task: seventy-three people in total. The entire team was making similar visits as part of the exhaustive investigation.

They entered the building and Hillier enquired the way of a security guard. He and Wright walked down a long corridor and came to an office door. He knocked. 'I'm looking for Judge Paul Reeve?' he said.

Belinda Adams looked up from her work. 'His Lordship's chambers are down the corridor. Who's asking for him?'

Hillier explained.

'Just one moment.' She picked up the phone and dialled. 'Paul, two police officers are here to speak to you about an investigation.' There was a long pause and Wright and Hillier waited patiently. Belinda nodded a few times. After putting down the phone, she said, 'This way, please,' and led them back along the corridor through which they'd come, knocking on a door. 'One moment, please,' she said and went in, closing the door behind her.

It was a few minutes before she reappeared. Next to her was a man.

'Mr Reeve?' Wright asked. 'Or is that "Judge"?'

'Paul, please.' He held out a hand, which she shook. 'Do come in.' He shook Hillier's hand as well. 'Please, take a seat.'

They sat down and he returned to his deep leather swivel chair on the other side of the desk. 'A drink?' he asked.

Both gave thanks, but no.

'Thank you then, Belinda.' She left the room.

Paul leant back on his chair, effecting composure and calm. 'How can I help?'

'We're investigating three murders.'

Paul leant forwards. 'Oh, goodness.'

Wright nodded. 'Two of the victims were on the same university course as you at Jesus College. The other one was on the same course but two years later. Do the names Ethan Fleming and Richard Dollard ring a bell to you?'

'Of course.'

'Did you know them well?'

'Yes.'

'Is there anything important you can tell me about them?'

Paul sank back into his chair. 'Richard, Ethan and I were friendly. Good friends.'

'What about Simon Michael Ryman?'

'I didn't know anyone called Simon.'

'Is there anything about the whole group dynamic – everyone you studied with – that you remember?' Wright asked. 'Or any individuals – does anyone stick in your mind? Anyone odd, anyone who behaved strangely, anyone who showed a dislike towards them?'

He shook his head again. 'No, nothing that I can recall.'

'Can you tell me the names of the people you were closest to?'

'Sure. Aside from Richard and Ethan, you mean?'

'Exactly.'

Paul said the names and Hillier wrote them down. 'Of those, the only one I'm still in touch with, with any degree of closeness, is Laurence Sanders. One or two of the others I see here and there, but we're not close in any way.'

'How would you define your relationship with Laurence Sanders?'

Paul's mobile phone buzzed on his desk and he glanced at it. 'He's my . . . best friend.'

'Do you know if he was on friendly terms with Dollard, Fleming or Ryman?'

Paul shrugged. His phone buzzed again, then again. He cleared his throat, picking it up. 'You'd have to ask him that, I'm afraid.'

Noticing that Paul's face turned marginally pale, Wright asked, 'Is something the matter?'

He shook his head too forcefully. 'It's just my wife. She's not very well at the moment.'

'Oh dear, I hope it's nothing serious.'

'Not at all, it's just—' He checked himself. 'Is there anything else I can help you with? You'll have to forgive me, I'm very busy with a trial.'

'Well, I don't want to alarm you, but we're paying visits to everyone who was on the same course as Dollard, Fleming and Ryman. We think you should be vigilant, wary, just in case. Have you noticed anything unusual in your life, anything suspicious, that's stood out as different in the past few weeks, anything that's made you feel uncomfortable?'

'No, nothing comes to mind.'

'Only your wife being unwell.'

'Only my wife.'

'Be sure to remain vigilant and if anything comes to mind or comes up, please let us know straightaway.' Hillier handed Paul a card.

'I'll do that, but honestly, everything's fine.'

'Good, I'm glad to hear that.' Wright stood up. 'And I hope it stays that way. Stay safe.'

'I intend to.'

As she made her way to the door, Wright turned around and said, 'Oh, by the way, many congratulations on the recent promotion. I read about it in the newspaper. How exciting for you.'

Paul twisted his head awkwardly. 'Thank you. It's been . . . interesting.' He indicated the piles of papers on his desk. 'Preparing these can be difficult. And these things can be quite disturbing. I've got a particularly hard one at the moment.'

'Not living up to your expectations?'

'In a way.' He shrugged his shoulders. Then he shook it off. 'No, that's not true. It's all I've ever wanted. It's just this trial, it's making me weary. I didn't expect to get such a challenging and disturbing one so early on.' He laughed to himself.

'What is it?'

'I just thought about my wife. She always reminds me of many years ago what I said to her about my ambitions. Apparently, I told her I'd kill for this job if ever the opportunity arose. Now that sounds funny: kill for something that's so mentally exhausting. I had no idea what would be in store for me.'

'Well, regardless, I've read that you've made history, so congratulations again.'

He exhaled audibly. 'Yes, history. That's right.' Then after an awkward silence: 'Thank you, Detective.'

Paul walked Wright and Hillier to the door. He handed her a card before he closed the door and leant against it, sighing deeply, relieved.

P

I drank heavily last night after work. So heavily I didn't make it back home till after midnight. I sent Alice a message, making up an excuse because I didn't want her to know how I'd caved in after meeting the police officers. I was expecting Alice to be awake when I returned home, even at such a late hour, to read me the riot act when she saw how drunk I was. But she was asleep, so I counted my lucky stars.

The alcohol was a must; I needed to recover from the time I'd spent with the police officers. I was startled when Belinda said they were there to see me. After we settled in my chambers, I kept expecting them to mention a missing man, my mind whirling around to come up with what I could to say to deflect them from the fact that Alice had killed someone and I helped hide the body.

I was relieved when they didn't mention him, but the sudden questions about the guys' deaths threw me and I'm worried how my reaction came across to her. Of course, I knew about their deaths, it was national news, but I think Detective Wright was testing me to see if I knew more.

And now they've visited me once, I fear they'll return. I fear I haven't said enough of the right things to appease them. In fact, I fear I may have said things that will encourage them to come back.

Alice's text messages didn't help. They arrived at precisely the wrong time and added further distraction. I'm certain I wasn't able to cover up the concern they made me feel. They've been happening so often recently, and they've been getting increasingly urgent, that I'm worried there'll soon come a day when I'm not going to be able to help her at all. Every time I'm not home with her – which is every day at the moment – I receive messages of fear and paranoia from her, mentioning things she's seeing, noises she's hearing, what's on her mind. And there's a lot on her mind. Nothing I say seems to reassure her.

Unsteadily, I get out of bed. Alice is still asleep. Something, perhaps the dull thud in my head, keeps me from waking her, even though I know I can't keep the police officers' visit a secret from her.

Miserable and suffering, I go downstairs, make a coffee and take two Ibuprofen. I know I deserve this; my stupidity last night caused it. I lean against the counter top and sigh, unable to see the wood for the trees.

Two police officers investigating murders snooping around. A wife who's losing control of herself. A dead man in my house and a secret I have to keep hidden at all costs. I'm worried about how many lies will be necessary to cover this up if I can't reel Alice in.

Everything's converging and I fear I'm starting to lose control.

'You're still here?'

Alice's voice surprises me. I spin around uncomfortably. 'Jesus, you scared me.'

'Scared?' she says teasingly.

I exhale. 'I wasn't expecting you to appear so suddenly. You were asleep a moment ago.'

'No, I wasn't.' She looks sad. 'Nor was I when you stumbled in last night. Drink rather too much?'

'You saw?'

She nods. 'I saw.'

'Sorry, it was—'

'Don't bother,' she says and starts preparing a coffee for herself. 'Don't feel you have to lie to me.'

'Alice—'

'Or explain. Believe me, if I had a good reason, *I* would.'

'Alice, you can.'

She spins towards me. 'No, Paul, I can't. Not any more. I just . . . can't.' She ignores the mug in front of her and stares out of the window.

I wait for her to say more, but she doesn't. 'Speaking of unexpected visitors,' I say, sipping my coffee, trying to be calm about it, 'two police officers came to see me yesterday.'

'Why?' she asks dreamily, her stare remaining fixed.

'For a horrendous moment, I thought they were going to ask about him,' I laugh, 'but they weren't. Three guys I studied with at university have been murdered.'

That gets her attention, and she turns to face me. 'Murdered?'

'Yes, but I knew about that. That's not what matters.'

'How can that not matter? They came to see you.'

163

'That's not what I mean. I mean, I don't want them to have a reason to come back. I don't want them snooping around my life. God knows what they might find.'

'Why did they come and see you then?'

'They were asking about Richard and Ethan.'

'Richard and Ethan?'

'The ones who were killed.'

'You said three.'

'And Simon . . . Mike.'

'And what do you know about them? *Do* you know anything?'

'No, of course not. Don't be ridiculous. But that's not what matters anyway. They also suggested I might be in danger.'

'Jesus, Paul—'

'I'm fine, don't worry about me.'

'But don't you see, Paul?'

'Don't I see what, Alice?' The pounding in my head is reducing my patience today.

'Him. The man in our house. The man I killed. What if he were there to kill you, too?'

I laugh. 'Me?' *The idea's ridiculous.*

And then I think about it for a moment.

'Me.' And I know I've made a big mistake.

A

Each day, I'm able to rest less and less. I can't stop thinking about the man I killed.

But now I also can't stop thinking about Paul. If that man came to our house to kill him, and if he killed Paul's old uni friends, there must have been a reason. What if Paul's life is still in danger?

While Paul is at work, I worry about him continuously, like a fearful child in the dark. I picture his journey there, his time at the Old Bailey, the corridors he has to walk down all alone, and his journey home. So many opportunities, so many moments when he could be hurt, when someone could attack. And they'd get him, I know they would.

What if he's taken from me? I'm already struggling to cope. How could I survive without him?

Then another thought comes: what if the police come to our home to see Paul when I'm here alone? How can I possible deal with them? Pretend I don't know anything they're talking about or reveal what Paul has said to me about it? Worse, what if they challenge me, telling me they know there's more to Paul's story, what would I say then?

I have to speak to Paul, but he's at work. I need to make sure he's safe and we must figure out exactly what to say if the police come back. We need a plan. *I* need one, certainly. Before it all goes horribly wrong.

I call him, but I'm not convinced I'll reach him. He's probably in court.

I was right. There's no answer on his mobile, so I check with his secretary. Yes, court is in session, she tells me.

I can't wait, so I get up and dress. I feel like I'm left with little choice but to head into London.

8

Wright and Hillier, separately and together, worked their way through most of the list of alumni. They'd learned much about Ethan Fleming, Richard Dollard and Simon Michael Ryman, much about their relationships with their course and work-placement colleagues, but little that helped to advance the investigation.

Of the three, Richard Dollard had been the most social, the most experimental and daring. He'd used drugs recreationally and, at times, habitually, had enjoyed a lot of girlfriends and one-night stands, and had partied hard. At the same time, however, he'd studied hard and been a highly successful student.

Ethan Fleming had had a steady girlfriend for most of his time at Jesus College. She was a student at Trinity College, studying Humanities. He was a hard worker, a solid student, but to some extent had a rather unremarkable personality, despite what his parents had suggested to Hillier.

Simon Michael Ryman, the youngest of the three, seemed to have been the most exceptional academically. His tutors, placement mentors and fellow students had sung his praises.

He was so popular that the law firm at which he completed his placement offered him a full-time position, which he accepted and at which he worked until his death.

All good at their jobs. All successful and fairly wealthy. All clever young men. All with bright futures ahead. But with few other similarities, which frustrated the case and meant that Wright and Hillier had not progressed very far.

Tim Yardley had been abroad when Hillier had first paid him a visit. He'd taken a sabbatical year from his work and was due back in several weeks' time. Now that he was home, Wright and Hillier arranged to visit him, to run through the same questions they'd asked everybody else, in the hope they might learn something new.

A woman, wearing a partly open blue shirt – men's – partly covering white panties, opened the door.

'Oh,' Hillier said.

'Oh,' she repeated. 'Detective?'

'Ryan Hillier. And you are, Miss . . .'

'Sayles. Lucy Sayles.' She looked at Wright. 'Nice to see you again, Detective.'

'Nice to see you, too.' Wright cleared her throat, then turned to Hillier. 'We met a few weeks ago. Miss Sayles was in Richard Dollard and Ethan Fleming's class.' Then back to Lucy Sayles: 'Is there a reason you're here?' Wright hadn't intended to come across rudely, but she also didn't care if she offended.

'Tim's my boyfriend.'

Wright looked surprised.

'On and off,' she clarified as Tim Yardley appeared behind her and patted her backside.

'Let the good people in, darling,' he said cheerfully.

Lucy Sayles stepped aside and Wright and Hillier entered. They were at Tim Yardley's house in East Finchley. 'My parents' house,' he admitted as they entered a large open-plan lounge-diner. 'They spend six months a year in Spain. Are there basking in the sun right now, so I'm staying here till they return in the summer.'

'And what'll you do then?' Wright asked.

'Have to rent something, I guess. Or move into Lucy's,' he said, giving her a cheeky wink.

Tim and Lucy sat on the sofa and he indicated the armchairs to Wright and Hillier.

'You didn't mention being in a relationship together,' Wright said to Lucy.

She smirked. 'You didn't ask.' She rubbed her hand on Tim's knee and giggled. 'It's a sort-of relationship.'

'We're on again, off again,' Tim added. 'It's not important.'

'Besides,' Lucy said, 'you were asking about Ethan, Richard and Simon if I remember correctly, not Tim.'

'Do you remember them?' Wright asked Tim, jumping right to the business at hand.

'Of course I do,' he said. 'And since I heard about their deaths on the news, I haven't been able to forget them. Sounds horrific.'

'Where have you been travelling?' Wright asked, even though she already knew.

'Thailand. All over. Amazing country. I might even go back. Maybe take you.' He nudged Lucy. 'I saw those small islands they used in that Bond movie. You know, *The Man with the Golden Gun*. Stunning place.'

'These murders were on the news over there?' Hillier asked.

'Ever heard of social media, Detective?' Tim shrugged. Wright didn't like him; arrogant, smug, cocky. Born into privilege and not for one moment thankful for it.

'How close were you to them?' she asked.

Tim thought for a moment. 'Hmm, how much to say,' he said, seeming to vocalise what sounded like a thought.

Wright and Hillier sat patiently, but Wright had had enough of him and was close to losing her temper.

'Ethan Fleming was a good guy. A bit too good, if you know what I mean. Um, boring is the best word to describe him, if I'm being honest. A goody two-shoes, really. He was dedicated . . . to his studies and to his ugly-as-fuck girlfriend. He wouldn't have been into the things I was into. I was . . . how can I put it?' He laughed and then said with too much volume and suddenness, 'A stoner, you know what I mean.'

Wright remained unfazed. 'And what about Richard Dollard?'

Tim let go of Lucy. 'Ooh, Richard Dollard.' He inhaled deeply and rubbed his hands together. 'Now, Rich and I were pretty tight. We were, erm, you know, we were into the same things. Girls and drugs mostly, again if I'm being honest with you.'

'When was the last time you saw him?'

'Oh, a good few years ago now. We kept in touch after we started practising, but then occasional weekend meet-ups became a few times a year and eventually we lost touch. I can't even remember the last time we spoke.'

'Can you tell me about any girls he met during his university years whom he may have kept in touch with?'

'He met a lot, far too many to keep track of. He was a, erm, a free spirit. Too much of one, I'd say, to keep in touch with a girl much beyond the night he spent with her. His favourite thing to do – mine as well, I confess – was to leave before the girl woke up. Less messy that way.'

Wright looked at Lucy, a seemingly intelligent woman, and wondered what the hell she was doing with this creep.

He has money, she concluded.

'Do you know if he ever upset anyone? Any grudges or conflicts? Any of them – did any of them have any problems with others?'

'Nah,' Tim said, sniffing exaggeratedly, 'Rich was so relaxed, he never had a problem with anyone. Drugs'll do that to you, you know what I mean.'

'I know exactly what you mean,' Wright said coldly. 'What about Simon Michael Ryman? Did you know him?'

'No, not really. I saw him but didn't spend much time with him. He was younger and I was a snob. A bit of a prick, if I'm honest.' He laughed at himself.

Wright stood up. Hillier followed her lead. 'Thank you for your time, Mr Yardley.' Then Wright saw a collection of pictures upon a shelf above the fireplace. A group shot caught her attention. Everyone in it was in graduation garb, black cloaks and hats. She walked over to it and picked it up.

Tim approached and peered over her shoulder. He stood close to her. Too close. 'Time goes so quickly,' he whispered into her ear. Hillier found him as creepy as he was obnoxious.

In the picture, there were several rows of young men and women, smiles across their faces, beers in some hands, cigarettes, or something akin to them, in others. She scanned the image and found Tim Yardley. Behind him was Ethan Fleming. Then she saw that Yardley was standing next to Richard Dollard. They had their arms around each other.

Then another photo, in this one the three of them, arms again around each other. Only in the background, two others . . . 'Him,' Wright said, pointing.

Tim Yardley moved even closer. Wright could smell his scalp and felt sick. 'Paul?' he said.

Wright put distance between them. 'You remember Paul Reeve?' she asked.

'Remember him? Sure, we were tight.'

'And he's there with Simon Michael Ryman?'

'Yeah, they shared a flat. Two years, I think it was. Still, I didn't see Mike much. He was usually locked away studying.'

'Mike?'

'Yeah, that's what we all called him.'

A

A train journey and then a walk and I'm at the Old Bailey within an hour and a half. I stupidly haven't brought an umbrella and it's been drizzling since I emerged from Euston. Even though I've dashed along the open roads, I'm drenched.

'Shit,' I say, stepping into the Old Bailey. After showing my ID, I sign in at the visitors' entrance and ask to be shown the toilets. I want to make myself presentable before I see Paul. I want him to be pleasantly surprised, not shocked by my sodden appearance.

Once I'm dry, I make my way to his chambers and knock, but there isn't an answer. So I head down the corridor and enter his secretary's office. 'When will Paul be out of court?' I ask her.

'He hasn't been in. There wasn't a session booked in for today.'

'What do you mean?' I ask, stunned.

'Court wasn't in session today.'

'But he said . . .' *If not here, he should be home with me then. I need him.*

'He was here,' she says, anticipating what I want to know. 'But he's gone out to lunch and he said he won't be back this afternoon.'

'With whom?'

'I don't know.' She's playing dumb, I can tell.

'Where?' I say, numb. *Why would he have lied? He said he was in court every day.*

'The Hamilton,' she says, smiling.

Now I picture him sitting at the table with another woman across from him. Not his wife, no. Smiling at her. Plying her with alcohol. In bed. On top of her.

The bastard.

It's not paranoia – no – no, it's not.

She peers down at her desk, or at her hands. 'I'm afraid I just don't know. He left suddenly, saying he was going to lunch and that he won't be back afterwards.'

I don't thank her, just head out, moving with purpose and an urgency I haven't possessed for a long time. I hail a taxi, telling the driver where I want to go. And I urge him to be quick.

As soon as we arrive, I pay by card and jump out. It's a French restaurant, fine dining, expensive. An artificial waterfall with lights on the background wall is the façade that welcomes visitors. The way in is half a dozen steps up. I take them two at a time. My heart is pounding and I dread what I'm going to find.

There's a young woman standing behind a small desk near the door. I don't pay any attention to what she says as I enter; I walk right past her. 'Miss?' she calls, and I hear her trying to catch up with me. I pick up my pace, even though I haven't a clue where I'm going.

I push through some wide, heavy double doors. In front of me is the largest bar I've ever seen, with rows of alcohol bottles lined before a high mirror. I catch sight of myself, the anger spelled out on my face.

I have two route options – left or right – so I head to the right. The restaurant opens up into a large seating area and I scan the tables. I don't see him, so I turn around, colliding with the woman who was on the door.

'Miss,' she says, more aggressively this time.

I walk on without a word, already looking towards the other side of the restaurant, which I can't see properly yet. It's round a corner and then there's a large pillar blocking my sightline. From behind it, I see a woman dressed in black walking in the opposite direction. I step forwards and, behind the pillar, I find Paul sitting at a table for two. He's staring at his phone. It's only when the woman from the door bumps into me because I've come to a standstill in front of her that he notices a commotion. The smile on his face vanishes and he drops his phone onto the table.

'Oh,' he stutters, 'Alice.' He looks from the woman to me and back again. Then back to me. 'Alice.' And he stands.

'Who the fuck is she?' I blurt out.

'Wh—'

I slap him, hard. He's not going to talk his way out of this one. 'Who? I said. Who, you fuck?' and I'm shouting, so loudly that the whole restaurant has become silent and everyone's eyes are on me and people are staring and they're whispering to each other and I feel the woman's arms on me, pulling, and I shrug her off. And I shout again, unable to control myself, 'How could you?' and I'm crying, hysterical, with tears and snot and spit all flowing uncontrollably.

Paul steps forwards and takes me by the arms. I shake in protest, attempting to resist him, and try to strike him again, but he manages to keep hold of me. 'Alice, stop. Don't.'

'How dare you!' I'm wailing like a crazy person.

'Paul?' The inquisitive, confused voice is male and doesn't belong to Paul. It's familiar, though, quietly spoken and full of surprise.

I stop wriggling. Paul releases me. 'Laurence.' Paul's voice is shaky as he says the name.

'Alice,' Laurence says, quietly again, kissing me on both cheeks.

I look all around, at Paul, at Laurence, at the hostess, at the people sitting at tables. My eyes land on a woman in a black dress. It's the woman who was walking away from Paul as I entered. She's holding a menu and an iPad. She's a waitress.

I shrink. *Oh God.*

'Is everything all right?' Laurence asks.

What have I done? 'I'm so sorry,' I say as much to him as to Paul. I drop into a chair.

I can't hear the words coming out of Paul's mouth – there's a fuzzy noise in my ears – but I think he's apologising, both to the staff all around us and the diners nearby. 'She's been unwell recently,' is the only sentence I catch.

There are some reassuring sounds from other voices and then Paul is back next to me, crouching down. He says, 'Alice . . .'

'Your secretary said you weren't in court today. I didn't know. I needed to see you.'

'The primary witness for today was ill. We had to cancel.'

'I didn't know,' I mumble.

Paul caresses my back. 'It's okay,' he says, and I look up and see him nodding at Laurence. There's concern on his face, but he's trying to cover it.

'Oh God.'

'Don't worry.'

'I'm sorry,' I cry. 'I'm so, so sorry.'

He shushes me and brings his mouth close to my ear. 'Nothing to be sorry about,' he whispers. And he delicately kisses the top of my head. I feel like an idiot child.

'I'm so, so sorry.'

P

'Are you okay?'

I'm not. I managed to get Alice home yesterday afternoon, but she cried the whole way and then she cried for the whole evening. Nothing I did could console her. It reached the point when I'd told her that so often, I genuinely believed what had happened didn't matter at all; I was no longer in any way mad at her for what she'd done. But nothing worked. In the end, I'm ashamed to say I left her in the bedroom and slept on the sofa, after a good helping of Woodford Reserve to calm the nerves she'd brought out in me.

Now I'm here, back at work, hungover and worried like I've never been before.

'I'll manage,' I murmur to Belinda.

I force myself through the morning session and then go into her office to tell her I'm going to be out for lunch. The whole of lunch. But the sight of Belinda crying surprises me and forces my attention away from my own troubles and onto her.

'Are you all right?'

She tries to answer me but words don't come out.

'Come here,' I say instinctively and walk round her desk. She struggles out of her chair and falls into my arms. I shush her, almost parentally. 'It's okay,' I say, even though I'm clueless about the cause of her upset.

I seem to be telling that to women rather a lot at the moment.

I feel my mobile phone vibrate in my inner jacket pocket. Concerned that Alice is contacting me, but in a tricky position right now, by the time I try to answer the ringing stops.

I brush the hair from Belinda's forehead.

She slowly pulls back from me.

'Do you want to talk about it?'

'My boyfriend has left me.'

'Boyfriend?'

'We were going to get married this summer,' she says and then she falls back into me, the tears refreshed.

'Oh God,' I groan. My phone vibrates again. 'Jesus,' I mumble.

Belinda reaches round and grabs hold of me tightly. I can feel her breasts pressing against my stomach, any parental instinct I may have had vanishing. Sexual sensations mix with those that are wary. I seem to be a magnet for unstable women at the moment, first at home and now here at work.

I just want to be away from it all.

I glance at my watch. It's lunchtime. I reach round to Belinda's face and steer her away from me. 'Okay, here's the deal. How about lunch, and no relationship discussions? Nothing work-related, either. Just a nice meal and casual conversation, something to take both our minds off our troubles. How does that sound?' I reach for my phone, but the ringing has stopped again.

She sniffs and wipes away some tears. 'Sounds perfect,' she says through a forced smile.

'And a drink.'

'Hell, yes please.'

I pull out my phone. I'll give Alice a quick call back.

Two missed calls, but they're actually not both from my wife. Only one is from Alice, the second from Detective Sergeant Wright.

Shit, I think.

A

I wanted to surprise Paul, properly this time, but as I approached the Old Bailey I got cold feet. I became worried that he'd view me as this deranged and unstable woman he's married to, not as a companion who longs to be with him. Who needs him.

I tried to be spontaneous yesterday and look where that got me. The scene I made. Now I'm full of doubt, even though I want to do it the right way today.

Sod it, I think, and pay the taxi driver. Too much thinking is ruining me. *Just do.*

As I step out of the cab, Paul emerges from Warwick Passage. I'm about to call out to him, but he looks behind him, holds out his hand and then a young woman wearing a hood takes it. They quickly head off down the road.

I recognise it's his secretary, Belinda's, but why the hell is he taking her by the hand? I follow, ready to catch up with them, pulling at his arm and asking what he's doing. But I don't, because I did that yesterday and I'd misread everything. Perhaps the same thing is happening again right now.

But there's something about the way he's holding her, something about the way she's leaning towards him, that doesn't feel right.

It starts raining after they make several turns and they pause when they reach a French restaurant. *French,* I think, just like yesterday. And just like in New York, when it was only him and me.

Paul leads the way in. I wait outside. I want to go in, but I can't repeat what I did yesterday. Maybe it's just a business lunch. I'll wait and when they come out I'll know. I'll be able to tell. Then I'll know what to do.

9

Laurence Sanders worked for a firm whose offices were in Liverpool Street. His office was on the twenty-third floor and boasted spectacular views of the London skyline.

Detective Sergeant Katherine Wright was told by the friendly receptionist that Sanders wouldn't be long. Twenty minutes later, she approached Wright in the waiting area as she glanced over some glossies and asked her to follow. She led Wright to Sanders' office, a spacious and lavish set piece that was worthy of a big-budget Hollywood legal thriller. A huge mahogany desk faced off against the door, screaming importance to all who entered. In front of it were two deep leather chairs that Wright estimated cost more than the bed she slept in.

Behind the desk, Sanders sat in a tall leather swivel chair that encased his body with a degree of importance Wright had never come across before. To her right, a corner leather sofa sat in the middle of the room, a glass coffee table in front of it, facing a wall-mounted widescreen television. Bookcases lined either side of it, heavy leather-bound books filling them. They looked untouched but gave off an air of knowledge and intellect. An attractive square rug covered the parquet floor beneath the sofa and table.

'Good afternoon, Detective,' Sanders said without rising. 'Please,' he added, indicating the chairs opposite him.

Wright walked forwards, eyeing all four corners. 'This is quite an office.'

Sanders beamed. 'Thank you. I'm in litigation,' he said, as if that explained the extravagance.

'I won't keep you long,' Wright began, sitting down and pulling out her notepad. 'I'm investigating the murders of three individuals. Your friend, Paul Reeve, said you knew them.'

'Yes, he told me about that,' Sanders said. 'Dreadful business.'

'How did you know one another?'

'We were at university at the same time. Not the same campus, mind you, but I was at King's at Cambridge and everybody in Law mingles.'

'What can you tell me about Richard Dollard and Ethan Fleming?'

'They were superstars.' Sanders sniggered. 'Richard, not in the academic sense but in the social sense. Wherever there was a party, Richard was at the centre of it. He was a lot of fun and had a lot of fun. Too much, one could say. But he eventually turned into a good lawyer, that I can assure you. Ethan was simply a natural. I don't think he had to try too hard.'

'Did you also know Simon Michael Ryman, a couple of years younger? He was known as Mike, I believe.'

'Mike, sure,' Sanders said. 'He bunked with Paul for a while. Hardly ever saw the guy, mind you. Head always buried in a book. Boring turd, if you ask me. But Paul and me and Rich as well as Ethan to an extent, we were close. It's a small world, the law division of Cambridge. There's a lot of camaraderie. The studying's intense, the training is difficult and the hours long, and the parties are . . . necessary, shall we say. *Everyone* parties.' He grinned with self-satisfaction.

'Can you tell me anything about Simon Michael Ryman?'

'Nothing that anyone who knows him wouldn't be able to tell you. Mike was introverted.'

'Why Mike and not Simon?'

'That's what the inner circle knew him as. Just a small group of us. Again, I didn't know him that well, but that's what they all called him, so I called him it as well. If memory serves, I think it was a gag at first, but it stuck. With the group, at least. Simon Michael Ryman was Mike, plain and simple. It was funny because I heard he actually wouldn't even respond to the name Simon after he got his first job.'

'How close were Paul Reeve and Simon Michael Ryman?'

'Close, I assume. They shared, like I said. I just didn't see much of Mike, but Paul must have. They aren't in touch now, though.' He checked himself. 'Weren't, I meant. Sorry. You know, before Mike . . . Anyway, something happened between them.'

'Do you know what exactly?' Wright said.

'Haven't the foggiest.'

P

There's nothing like the sound of a young woman's laugh and the look in her eyes that goes with it, one that says she's grateful and happy and enjoying herself.

I've forgotten what it's like. To be youthful. To enjoy the laughter. Life with Alice is . . . well, different from how it was before.

Now I've seen a different side to Belinda, and I'm enjoying her company. And she's enjoying mine, she's making that much clear.

She's only had one glass of wine, but that, coupled with some jokes and amusing stories from me, has cleared up her eyes and sent her tears packing.

'Thank you,' she says.

'Hey,' I try to joke, 'I didn't realise how much I needed this,' but then I realise I'm actually being serious: I realise that being here with Belinda makes me feel better. No matter what it's doing for her, I think it's doing me a lot of good, too. I need this. I need to get away from everything. I need a distraction.

Alice has become too much.

'No relationships, no work,' she says. 'We should have done this years ago. Tell me, informally, how does it feel to sit up there and be a judge?'

'Informally?'

'Yes, not one of those stock answers about respecting the position and always wanting to do it to serve your country. What does it really feel like to know you're going to determine people's futures? I mean, you hold a person's future in your hands?'

I think about it for a moment and then smile. 'It feels . . . fucking fantastic.' I let myself go. 'There's power in sitting up there. Everyone's watching you and there's this sense of awe. Everything you say goes. Anything you say, they're all listening. And what you determine, well, people feel the repercussions for years. There's nothing quite like it.'

Her grin is huge. She's beaming.

Adopting a serious stance, straight-backed, I add, 'And of course it's an honour to serve my country and a privilege to hold such a position of responsibility.'

She laughs and I do as well.

Speaking about it, I realise Alice has never asked me what my new job is like. Her days are spent thinking of herself and remembering what happened. I miss Alice's attention. I miss her wanting to know.

'I like this side of you,' she says.

So do I, I think.

She's nice to talk to. She's attractive to look at. She's good company to be with.

She has shoulder-length dark hair, lightly curled towards the bottom, tanned skin and deep, dark eyes. Her cheekbones are high and her lips are a dark pink. She's wearing a white suit jacket and skirt. She holds a wine glass in hand and sips from it, her lips toying with the rim, a smile creasing her face behind it.

She's thinking of something.

'What's the matter?' I ask.

'Nothing,' she says, lowering her glass and then fingering the rim as she holds it atop the table. 'It's just you. I always knew you were a nice guy, but you're always so business-like, so . . . distant. And now look at you, taking care of me.' She leans forwards. 'Thank you for being so kind.'

I smile. 'A pleasure.'

'Is it as good as you'd hoped?'

'What's that?'

'Being a judge.'

She's being playful. Maybe I blush.

'I don't know yet.'

'I do.' She leans forwards and unexpectedly I feel her hand on my knee, running slowly up my thigh. 'I do want to thank you,' she whispers.

My phone vibrates in my pocket. A text message. Swallowing, I pull it out.

It's from Alice. *Where are you? What are you doing? Why haven't you called me back?*

I sigh.

Belinda's hand squeezes. I put the phone back in my pocket.

'You've already said thank you, there's nothing else to say,' I tell her.

'Okay, so I want to *show* you how grateful I am then.' She pulls puppy eyes on me. 'You've helped me a lot.'

'Belinda, it's fine, I underst—'

'You've made me feel so much better already. There's only one more thing that can make me feel completely better.'

'Belinda, I—' *Oh God, I'm tempted.*

'I know what I want and I know what I'm asking for. You wouldn't be taking advantage of me, Paul.'

I start to protest. 'It's time we got back.'

She walks around the table and rubs her hands on my shoulders. Then she leans down to my ear. 'No one needs to know,' she whispers. 'No one.'

A

He hasn't answered my text message.

They emerge. *Shall I approach or shall I follow?* I could be overreacting again. I probably am. I just need to relax.

They turn in the direction from which they came. Relieved, I'm about to turn away, but they take an unexpected left into a road that curves right around to the left and therefore takes them away from the Old Bailey.

The rain is falling hard, she's sheltering beneath his arm. I'm soaked and alone.

I follow, at some distance. They eventually pass Bush House and walk on the right-hand side of the Strand.

The Waldorf Astoria. *No.*

They enter it. I go in as well and loiter in an alcove on the far side. They head to the check-in desk. I pretend to use a public pay phone. The clerk hands Paul a key card. I fiddle with the phone. They turn and start walking towards the lifts. When they get in a lift, I drop the phone and dash towards it. Above the doors is a clock hand that indicates which floor the lift reaches.

It stops on the fifth floor. *My God, what is he doing?*

What is he doing to me?

They're up there, on the fifth floor, Paul and his secretary. And I don't know what to do. I'm static and can't get my feet to move. I feel empty but curiously sick. I feel nauseous but curiously hungry. I feel cold but curiously hot.

I came here for you, Paul, because I wanted to say sorry. Because I wanted to make things right to you. Because I behaved badly yesterday.

But now, today—

Now, a hotel room can mean only one thing, I'm not stupid. How can we find a way out of our mess when he's here . . . fucking her? What's he doing . . . to me, to our marriage, to our future?

Soaked yet sweating, I can only leave. I can't wait here and confront him when he comes back down. I can't humiliate myself again.

It's still pouring outside. I forsake the hood on my coat. I don't bother with a cab. I'm already wet and why should I worry about what might become of me? I have nothing left. There's no one left to worry about me.

Instead, I drift along the Strand, slowly, aimlessly, getting even more drenched.

As I trudge along, I realise that the last time I was as wet as this was October last year. That night, when Paul and I became inseparable. Yet here he is as separate from me as he can possibly be.

And although I didn't see it at the time, we became irreconcilable.

I will walk all the way to Euston, I don't care how wet I get. I can't be more drenched than I was that night.

That night, which ruined everything.
I don't care any more.

P

Belinda and I lie side by side. Despite the no smoking sticker on the door, she takes a drag and I drink from the mini bar. The Johnnie Walker is smooth, so relaxing that I feel part of the bed and don't want to get up. I'm no longer a smoker, but she occasionally holds her cigarette in front of my lips and I puff on it. It's been a long time since I smoked regularly, but it's as refreshing as the booze.

She puts out the cigarette and moves closer to me. She starts playing with my chest hairs, running her hand back and forth over my stomach. 'That was exactly what I needed,' she murmurs.

'God, if this could be my life, things would be so much easier,' I vocalise without meaning to.

'Any time,' she says.

She leaves me lying there and jumps into the shower. She's in there a long time and eventually comes out, dressed. 'Back to work, I suppose.' She kisses me deeply.

I glance at my watch. 'I suppose.'

She smiles at me and says, 'Like I said, any time.' And then she leaves.

My phone rings. I peer at the screen, expecting to see Alice's name.

Detective Sergeant Katherine Wright.

I know I need to talk to her, but I can't, not right now.

The thought of Detective Wright and what Alice and I have landed ourselves in catapults me back to reality; as much as being with Belinda has been thrilling and an escape, and much needed, I can't be without Alice, she and I are tied inexorably together because of that night.

I am trapped.

And that leads to the first pang of guilt I experience. Lying here alone, I think of Alice. Perhaps she's at home, alone in our marital bed, still suffering with the guilt she feels. I should be there with her.

Again, Belinda said. I can't. I mustn't. 'It can't happen,' I tell myself. And I mean it.

We have a secret, one that has to be kept, and being foolish with Belinda, although fun, can only jeopardise that.

I can't risk it.

A

I am without energy. Numb. It's been three days. I can't leave this bed.

I thought I'd wait till Paul came home before I confronted him. I thought I'd shout in his face and tell him to get the fuck out.

But I couldn't. He's fucking his secretary and I've killed a man. I need him, although I don't want him. I need him, although I think I might hate him.

He deserves that, surely.

I've barely eaten since I saw them going into the hotel. I don't feel hungry; I just feel empty. I don't know what to do.

So I just lie here, thinking. Which makes me feel worse. Three days ago.

Following them to the hotel. The room. The bed. And October last year.

It had been a long day. I was expecting Paul to come home for dinner. He was late and I was hungry, so I ate alone and left his food in the oven. I was preparing a bath. The steam in the room opened my lungs. I lingered, breathing in deeply. It relaxed me. That mix of hot from within and cool air outside was what I longed for. As the bath was filling up, I started undressing and made my way into the bedroom to prepare my night clothes. I removed my trousers and socks, was in a pair of knickers and a shirt, when I thought I heard someone coming up the stairs. *Paul,* I assumed. The sound from the running taps in the bathroom made it difficult to be certain. Floorboards, I definitely heard floorboards. Momentarily, I was happy because Paul was back. But instead of Paul, I saw a strange man entering the bathroom. I knew he posed a danger to me. The letter opener – it's so sharp – was just a few feet from me. I grabbed it and instinct took over.

As if I'm God in the clouds, I watch myself rushing on tiptoes towards the bathroom, desperate to not be heard. I press against the door and lunge towards him. He looks over his shoulder when I'm right behind him. He might be about to say something, I don't know. I lift the dagger as high as I can and bring it down and up and down repeatedly. I'm striking him with all the force I have. He's shouting as he's being struck, a shrill sound, an angry voice, full of hate and intent, but I can't make out any words. He falls as he keeps shouting and then the sound is muffled once his head hits water, blood spreading, and the water's turning red and I'm screaming and crying and I feel nothing but pain, even though I'm not physically hurt, I'm just in agony inside. The hurt stems from a recognition, before I truly understand what it is, that I've ruined everything, that I've destroyed my life, that I've changed everything for Paul and me forever and done something he won't be able to ignore and it's also something he won't be able to forget. He'll never forgive me, like right now I can't forgive myself, and like I can't forgive him for what he's done to me since.

I killed a man. The fact keeps me up most nights and if I do drift off, my subconscious attacks my dreams. I thought I'd always be able to turn to Paul in moments of despair. Now I doubt I'll ever be able to turn to him again.

As I lie here, I can't help wondering whether it would have been better if I'd been killed by that man. If he'd succeeded, perhaps there wouldn't be any of this suffering.

I imagine a blade striking me, pushing through the soft skin of my chest.

My eyes spring open. Gasping, I stir, the sunlight dazzling me. There's a figure standing at the end of the bed. I scramble back, against the headboard, and start to scream, but then I hear his voice.

'Still in bed?' he asks softly. It's an almost soothing sound, but now I know who he is and what he is, I can't let it be.

I peer at the alarm clock. It's gone 2 p.m. I'm silenced by thoughts of where the day has disappeared.

'Are you okay, Alice?' Paul asks. 'Are you still not feeling well?'

I lied to him two days ago the first time I didn't get out of bed. And I lied to him again yesterday when the same thing happened. 'I feel so weak,' I say, telling the truth but also lying, adding, 'my stomach.'

'I came back early because I thought, if you were up to it, I could make us a meal.' He waits expectantly, but I say nothing. 'Maybe just a salad, something light?' When I don't answer, he shifts uncomfortably and says, 'Alice, you have to eat to keep your strength up. Christ, you have to be strong.'

I turn my face towards the window. I want to shout at him, *I know!* I want to tell him everything I saw and watch him squirm. He'd try to lie his way out of it. He's a good liar. I know his dirty little secret. I want him to feel pain, like I am.

But I don't say anything. Instead, I mumble, 'Salad might work.' I don't look at him, though; I don't want him to think I'm grateful.

'Why don't you try getting up?' He walks round and attempts to encourage me out of bed.

'Get off!' I shout suddenly. I don't see the outburst coming myself.

Shocked, he stumbles backwards, his hands held out wide. 'Okay, okay.' He stares down at me, aghast. I catch a glimpse of him peripherally. He's concerned. 'Okay, I won't . . . touch you.' He maintains a softness in his voice. 'I'll make some salad. It'll be ready in fifteen minutes. Come down when you're ready. If you like.'

It's almost an hour before I have the courage to venture downstairs. As I approach the kitchen, I hear Paul's voice. It's short and sharp. 'Just tell her I'm unavailable. I don't know why, make something up. I'm busy with the case. I'm unavailable.'

When I enter, I don't make eye contact with Paul. I don't know what my eyes will give away if he sees into them; I'm not a good enough liar to conceal what I'm feeling.

There's a bowl of salad on the table. Next to it is some salad dressing. Paul is standing by the sink, drinking a Coke, no doubt with some whisky in it, and he's staring at his phone.

'Food's on the table,' he says.

Texting that bitch, I think, without going any further into the room. *Speaking to her, maybe.*

'I ate,' he says. 'Sorry, but you were up there for ages.'

I go to the table and sit down. I take a few mouthfuls of salad, slowly. It's dry, so I add some dressing. I can feel Paul's eyes drilling into my back.

Suddenly, I hear a thud. He's put his phone onto the counter with too much force. 'Listen, Alice,' he says loudly.

Despite the pull, I don't turn around. My stomach feels bloated, suddenly swollen, and bile rises from within. I drop the fork and can't hold it in any longer. Clutching my stomach, I spin round and rush towards where Paul's standing. It must be the look on my face, because he repels with horror, sidestepping as I aim for the sink. The sick starts to leave my mouth before I reach it, and the cupboard beneath it gets covered in puke. I lean into the sink, heaving, emptying myself.

I feel Paul's hand on my back, stroking, but the impact his touch has on me is like razors scraping. Tensing my shoulders, I rinse the sink, pull away and get some paper towels. On my knees, cleaning, I look up at Paul. He watches me as I wipe up the mess.

My body is light, my head too. Once I'm finished, I go back to the table. I don't eat, just lean my elbows against the hard wood.

Finally, Paul speaks up from afar. 'What is it?' he asks. 'What's the matter with you?'

I put my head in my hands. I can't help it — I start sobbing silently. *It's you, it's all because of you, you and her. And that man.*

What I did, what we did, and what he's doing now.

I can't hold it in any longer. I let out a long and pathetic wail. Paul is suddenly by my side, looking down at me again. Eventually, I strain my neck backwards and, seeing him, let out another shriek, directing the sound at him, my rage being expelled, only without any comprehensible words.

'Alice?' His face is full of disgust, or alarm. 'What is it?'

'You!' I blurt out.

'What do you mean?'

'You, you, you,' I repeat, and I swipe at him.

'Hey! What do you mean "me"?'

'You . . .' I'm confused. I don't know what to say. There's so much, I don't know where to start, how to say it. 'Why did you do it?'

'Do what?' he says through gritted teeth.

'Why did you . . . make me hide the body? And why . . .' I'm trying, but I can't say the words. 'Why did you do it?'

Why are you sleeping with her?

He crouches down beside the table, stroking my arm, repelling me, yet almost convincing me to leap into his arms.

The best-made liars are convincing . . .

'We had to do it, Alice,' he says softly. He strokes my hair, removing a strand from my face. 'It was us or him, remember.'

I close my eyes. 'I see him when I'm awake. I see him when I close my eyes.'

'Everything will be fine.'

'I can't sleep!' I stare at Paul intently, then I add, quietly, 'I see you, too.'

He eyes me suspiciously, then after a long pause he says, 'I did what had to be done.'

'That's not what I mean,' I say.

Paul's phone buzzes on the counter. Both our eyes glance at it. Without thinking, I dash to it. He follows me, too quickly, but I manage to reach it before him.

'Alice!'

'This!' I shout, holding it up high. There's guilt on his face.

'Alice—'

'Why—' It comes from nowhere, it hits me hard. I wince unexpectedly and snap forwards, dropping the phone onto the floor and clutching at my stomach. My stomach empties itself again, partly onto the floor and partly onto Paul's shoes and trousers.

As I go down, I hear him call my name, urgently, but he doesn't touch me. I'm on the floor on all fours, my gaze fixed on the tiles beneath me. I can't see Paul, but I can hear him. Sounds of movement, shuffling, breathing. Then something different: yes, a muffled sobbing.

I think Paul is weeping. I stay on my hands and knees, without looking up. Paul's phone lies next to me. I stretch to retrieve it, but my hand fails me.

There's a message on the phone. I know it's from her. I can tell.

I need to see it.

But I can't reach it.

Turning, Paul puts his hands to his face and walks out of the kitchen, his head bowed, his shoulders hunched forwards. He leaves the phone, and me, behind.

IO

Having been unable to locate or get in touch with Paul Reeve for three days, either at work or on his mobile, Detective Sergeant Katherine Wright arrived at his house without much expectation of success. Only this time, his car was in the driveway. She knocked on the door aggressively.

Paul Reeve opened the door. He was surprised to see Wright. 'Detective,' he said, trying to sound chirpy but ultimately failing to convince.

'If now's convenient,' she said, 'I'd like to speak to you. You haven't been returning my calls and you're a tricky man to track down in person.'

'I'm sorry.' He hesitated, glancing over his shoulder, then said quietly, 'My wife's not very well, everything's been a distraction, and I'm in court most days. Will it take long?'

'That depends on you,' she said tonelessly.

He stepped aside and led her through the lounge and into the dining room. 'A drink?' he offered.

She sat down. 'No, thank you.'

He remained standing, fixing himself a drink.

'You say your wife isn't well?'

'Yes, some kind of sick bug, I suspect.'

'Do give her my best.'

'I will, thank you.' He looked at her expectantly. 'Something tells me discussing my wife's health wasn't the reason you came here.'

'You'd be right.' She asked casually, 'How well do you know Tim Yardley and Lucy Sayles?'

'Um, I, well, I've met Lucy once or twice, several years ago now. And Tim, I know from my uni days. But we haven't seen each other in quite a while.'

'I met them recently.'

'I don't really see what they have to do with me, other than Tim also being a former colleague of Richard and Ethan's. You mentioned I might be in danger. Are you suggesting I might have something to fear from Tim and Lucy? Because if you are, I can categorically state that you're mis—'

'No, Mr Reeve, that's not what I'm saying.'

'I'm afraid, then, I don't see . . .'

'Tell me about your relationship with the three men.'

He did see. He had all along. 'I must apologise,' he said straight away, deciding to do what he should have done in the first place. 'I assume you're talking about Mike specifically.'

'Indeed, I am.'

'I should have said more the first time. I'm sorry I didn't.'

'I'm curious why you didn't. Sharing a flat must have meant you were pretty close?'

'We were friends, yes, but he kept himself to himself. But yes, I was likely closer to him than most.'

'So . . .'

'Well, initially you said Simon, I didn't think of Mike.'

'But you knew about the murders.'

He nodded. 'Yes, as I said I did. My wife . . . I was
. . . distracted. I wasn't thinking straight. I didn't want to
talk about him. I didn't want . . . anything to do with it.
Listen, I made a mistake. We knew each other, we shared
a flat for what was probably just over eighteen months. I
hadn't seen him since then and the only time I heard of
him in any detail since then was when I found out he'd
been killed.'

'But it was a conscious decision to omit those details.
You spoke quite clearly about Richard Dollard and Ethan
Fleming.'

'Okay, yes I did, I can't excuse that. As I said, it was a
mistake. I just don't . . . The truth is . . .' He paused and
took quite a long time to compose himself. 'The thing is,
Detective, many years ago Mike threatened to kill me, and
I didn't want to dig up old wounds. It was a long time ago
and I know he didn't mean anything by it. I was never
afraid for my safety. He was many things, but he wasn't
dangerous.'

'Of course, you understand how that potentially makes
you look?'

'Well, of course, but I assure you that wasn't my motiva-
tion for keeping quiet.'

'I'm afraid I'm not sure I believe that.'

'Believe what you will, but it was thirteen years ago,
Detective. Our lives moved on long, long ago.'

'And you've never had any contact from him, or been
in contact with him, since then?'

He shook his head firmly. 'Never.'

She believed him. There was a resoluteness about him; it was probably the only thing she was certain of about him.

'So there'd be no harm in recounting what happened to me now, then.'

Reeve emptied his glass and breathed deeply. He rubbed his face. 'Mike had a steady girlfriend. The long and the short of it is that I took her from him. *Stole her,* he said. He wasn't particularly pleased with me and I was too arrogant to give a shit. Which, of course, was a problem. I flaunted it, see, wanted him to really *know* what I'd done. I wasn't a good friend. Shortly after, in a drunken rage, he attacked me and said one day he'd kill me, that I should watch out. He grabbed his stuff and moved out.' He held up his hands. 'That was the last time I ever spoke to him.'

'Do you really believe he forgot and forgave?'

'No, I don't think many people would, but he certainly never did anything about it.'

'And what about you: did you forget and forgive?'

He leant on the table, bearing down over her. 'I'll answer that question and I'll also ignore the insinuation behind it.' She held his stare. He was a powerful man and wasn't used to being challenged. He also didn't like it. 'Yes, I forgot. And I didn't exactly have anything to forgive. After all, I was the one who stole the person he called the love of his life. He'd proposed to her shortly before it happened. They were young. He was foolish. And she was enamoured by his intelligence. But it wasn't enough to keep her away from me.'

'What became of her?'

'Her name is Alice. She's now my wife. So, you see, while I'm sorry for what I did, I can't regret it. Because if I hadn't done it, I wouldn't be spending every day with the woman I love. She's the most important person in my life, Detective. I trust her with my life.' Reeve felt a pang of regret, but he couldn't exactly work out what for.

When it was clear that was all he intended to say, Wright said, 'Is there anything else, or is that genuinely all of it?'

'Genuinely. And you have my apologies again.'

'Accepted. Tell me, when will your wife be home?'

'She's home now.'

'Might I be able to speak to her?'

'I don't see the need.' Paul Reeve sat down and shifted in the chair. Then he started speaking slowly. *Cautiously,* Wright thought. 'She's sick, like I said, some kind of vomiting bug. She's resting. But it's more than just that. This is an awkward time and has been for a while now. I'm dealing with some very sensitive issues with my wife. She's ill in another way as well, some form of . . . depression. It's become difficult to manage and we're seeking help. I'm afraid the day you came to see me before was a particularly challenging day in that regard, which I'm certain added to my lack of clarity when answering your questions. With medical help I'm hopeful, but we have a long journey ahead and she needs time. She needs to be left alone. No excitement.'

Wright nodded. 'I'm sorry,' she said.

'Me, too,' he said. 'Me, too.'

P

I can't concentrate.

Sitting at the bench, my mind keeps straying, often fixed on Alice's uncontrollable bouts of sickness, which have continued, or the anger that has started erupting from within her. And I'm afraid that Detective Wright might turn up again, that I didn't say enough to appease her.

And Belinda. I enjoyed my time with her, but away from work she keeps sending me messages and she's tried several times to initiate things when here. I've tried to resist and most of the time I've succeeded, but she's caught me at my weakest, at my unhappiest, and I've given in a few times.

It's all too much. Alcohol doesn't really help, yet I need it every evening. Often in the daytime, too. The trouble I could get into if I'm caught drinking while at work isn't worth contemplating. And to top that all off, I can't sleep properly.

My mind is all over the place, yet I'm expected to concentrate while the defence and prosecution barristers present complicated cases and cross-examine witnesses.

The content of the trial really is making things worse, too. I rued the day I met the defendants, Mitchell and Rosaline

Craven, both forty-two years old, who are suspected of killing twenty-one-year-old Lauren Moore. And I despair seeing them every day.

Craven became Moore's sugar daddy, a relationship sexually fulfilling for him, financially attractive to her, for over a year. His wife found out and took retribution into her own hands.

The part of the case that hits me the hardest: he helped her dispose of the body.

The similarities between their actions and what Alice and I did have pushed me to the edge of a precipice. I'm one step away from the cliff edge, teetering. The Cravens are here, sitting at the opposite end of the courtroom from me, behind thick protective glass and flanked by four guards, damned as far as I can tell, without a hope to spare them from a lengthy sentence, and all I can think of is, *it could be us up there.*

Alice brought a dead man into our marital bed and it could damn us.

Damn her for that. Damn her like this couple is damned. And damn her for the wreck she's turned me into.

I hear a humming, not a voice, and it's continuous. Before long, I realise the sound is coming from next to me. It's Jenny, my courtroom clerk. 'Hmm?' I say.

'It's been two hours. Don't you think the jury should have a break now?'

I glance at my watch, unnecessarily because Jenny is an impeccable timekeeper. 'Yes, of course,' I whisper to her. Then, unexpectedly cutting off the prosecution without realising what I'm doing, I address the room. 'We'll have a fifteen-minute break now. Let the jury take a breather.'

'Are you okay?' Jenny whispers, concerned.

I don't know how I look, but it can't be good. I nod, hoping to put her mind at rest.

'All rise,' Charles, the bailiff, says to the forty or so people in attendance.

Everyone stands, then I stand, bow, which they return, and exit, Jenny following me.

The door's green material cover reminds me of a psychiatric ward's wall padding, and it bears down on me, making me feel distinctly small. Jenny holds it open for me. When I'm on the other side, she calls from behind me, 'Are you sure you're all right? You don't seem yourself.'

'What do you mean?' I ask, trying to act nonchalantly, avoiding eye contact. 'Everything's fine.'

'You seem . . . distracted and uncomfortable. It doesn't look like you're following things properly.'

I hold my stomach. 'Just not feeling particularly well, that's all. But I'll be all right.'

'Do you want to cancel the rest of the day?'

'No,' I say, tapping her arm, 'I'll be fine. I just need a break.'

She smiles and nods understandingly, my cue to retire to my chambers, which is a short distance along the corridor. There, I grab my mobile from the desk drawer and collapse onto the sofa.

Another text message from Alice. *Will you be home on time tonight or not?* I sigh and drop the phone onto the floor.

The door opens and Belinda enters, creeping along the wall. She's playing one of her games.

'Belinda, I'm not feeling well.'

'Oh, don't be like that,' she says playfully. When she reaches the back of the sofa, she leans over it and reaches for my chest. 'Let me make you feel better.'

'Please stop.'

'Don't be like that,' she says, coming round and sitting next to me on the sofa.

'Please, Belinda—'

She cuts me off by kissing me on the lips, her tongue deep in my throat. I push her off. 'I said, please, really, I can't.' She stands above me, aghast, and I realise what I've done. She has the power to tell Alice. She has the power to make things even worse for me.

What I've done. The utter stupidity.

I have to keep her happy. 'I'm sorry, please, I just need a breather,' and I struggle up and kiss her on the cheek. But then, feeling sick, I do something that's completely against protocol. Fully dressed for court, I escape my chambers and head for the exit, where I emerge into the courtyard and suck in all the air I can.

The security guard, whose job is to man the gate at Warwick Square, which is known as the Lord Mayor's Entrance, a more discreet way of entering the building that's not open to the public, stares at me. I wave him off. 'It's okay,' I call, but it's a struggle. I see him pull out a mobile phone, so I turn away.

I need to think. I need to breathe. I need time.

I need to be anywhere but here, far away and alone. Free from Alice. Free from Belinda, free from the Cravens and their crime. Free from the lurking Detective Wright.

I need to escape what we've done.

A door bursts open and Jenny appears. 'Oh my God,' I hear her say as she jogs over. Bending over, I clutch my stomach. 'Jesus, you look like shit.'

My head's spinning. 'I think I'm going to be sick.'

'Get some help!' she shouts over to the security guard, who dashes into the building. 'Here.' She places a hand on the small of my back and leads me to the side of the building where there's a wall. 'Sit down.' She pulls off my wig.

'Oh no,' I say, 'I left it on.'

'It's okay,' she says reassuringly. 'You need to rest. It'll be all right.'

Charles, the bailiff, appears, the guard following him. He's holding a bottle of water.

'Thank you,' I say, taking the water. I gulp it down.

'Sip,' she says gently. 'Sip.'

After a few minutes, we head back inside. 'We continue in ten minutes,' I tell Jenny.

'Don't be silly. There's no shame in resting, you know.'

'I know.' I take a deep breath. 'Okay,' I add, realising I'm being foolish, 'we'll finish the morning session and I'll cancel this afternoon.' I look at my watch. 'There's only forty minutes left, so I'll find a way to hold on.'

She walks by my side, taking me by the arm, and we take the corridor slowly.

'All rise,' Charles says as I enter. I stumble towards to my chair. I look around the room, sweat all over my body, and sit down. Everyone in the room follows my lead. 'My apologies,' I say to everyone, coughing. 'I'm feeling decidedly unwell. As a result, we'll finish this morning's session, but this afternoon's session will be cancelled.'

The interview of a witness, a forensic specialist, begins, and I do my best to make notes on my laptop, but almost immediately my mind resumes wandering, my stomach churning.

I'm going to have to return home. I need to lie down and shut myself off. But I can just imagine what will happen when I get there. An angry, agitated Alice will be waiting for me. Some playful and inappropriate messages from Belinda will arrive. And Detective Wright will turn up on my doorstep. 'We've made a mistake,' she'll tell me. 'You're not in danger, Mr Reeve, you're a suspect.' The cuffs will be slapped on my wrists. And Alice will be there, but I can't tell whether she's watching the police cart me off or if she's taken away with me.

Jenny interrupts my thoughts again as 1 p.m. arrives. I don't speak, but Jenny says something, and then I hear Charles's voice call out, 'Be upstanding.'

Those assembled before me bow and I nod, making my way out. Jenny leads me to the door, taking my arm, and we exit. Leaning against a wall, I say, 'You were right, I need to rest. I'm sorry. And thank you. See you tomorrow.'

'See you tomorrow, My Lord.'

I spend almost an hour in my chambers, lying on the sofa. I must doze off, for I'm awoken by a knock on the door. *Christ, Belinda again*, I think. I ignore it, but there's more knocking and then a voice calls out my name. It belongs to John Fletcher-Smythe, my former mentor, so I have no choice but to let him in. As I stand, I feel decidedly better.

But I don't look better. 'Jesus, Paul, you look dreadful,' he says.

'Thanks,' I say, exhaling loudly. 'I think it might be food poisoning,' I pretend.

'Crikey. Well, I won't ask you to lunch then.'

'It's far more than just that, I'm afraid,' I say, not wanting to sound too melodramatic. 'I'm having some, erm, difficulties. Everything's piling up on me and I think my body's reacting badly.'

'What people don't realise is just how challenging this job is,' he says, helping himself to a seat. 'Yes, there's status and respect and the money and power, but it all comes with a level of responsibility that most people will never experience nor understand. Add to that a bit of dodgy tucker and you've got a devilish combination.'

I hesitate. I know that the opportunity to talk with a wise man whom I trust so deeply won't come around so often. 'Actually, John, could I ask for your advice? I could do with a helpful ear to chew on.'

'With a diet like that, no wonder you're ill,' he jokes.

I attempt a smile, but my stomach still hurts.

He says, 'Of course,' and indicates the sofa.

I move to it, but then say, 'Can I get you a drink?'

'Have never said no and won't start now.'

I make him a drink, my hand shaking, and automatically go to pour one for myself, but I stop. He sees my hesitation and adds, 'You know, if you already feel poorly, it can't make you much worse.' Shrugging, I pour myself a small one and sit down.

'How is dear Alice, then?' he asks.

I lean forward and play with my glass as he drinks from his.

He recognises I'm struggling to find a way to begin. 'Drink up, man,' he says, 'and that'll help the words flow.'

I do as he instructs. 'Jesus, John, I've made a huge mistake and don't know what to do.' I'm unsure of how much to say. I keep the focus on women. Maybe he can help me get beyond those messes; it won't be everything, but it'll be a start. 'I really think Alice might be losing her mind. She's become intensely paranoid and her behaviour . . . she's acting so bizarrely. She's not sleeping, then she's not getting up but staying in bed all day. And she's violently sick. It's some kind of depression, I don't know.'

'Has she seen a doctor?'

'No, God, no. She won't. And I can't help her. Nothing I do works. I took her to New York, for God's sake, and that just seemed to make things worse. She's not the woman I married, John, she's definitely not the same woman I fell in love with.'

'Are you in love with her?'

'How can I be?' I ask, shrugging my shoulders. 'I know how awful that sounds, but it's the truth.' She's left me with no choice. 'I don't know what to do or how to help her.'

'Well, normally major changes in behaviour stem from some kind of incident, perhaps of a traumatic nature. Has anything happened that might have triggered this change you're seeing in her?'

I close my eyes and shake my head, lying, even though inside I'm screaming, *Yes! She killed a man and we hid the fucking body!* Which means I know the cause, so it's the solution I need to discover. How to ask about a solution, which perhaps doesn't even exist, when the cause has to remain a secret.

'Think carefully. There must be something. Something must have happened to upset her. It's not rational to suddenly change your behaviour or the type of person you are.'

'It happened just like . . .' I click my fingers. 'That. I don't know why.'

'Deep breath, deep thought and look again. Explore. Be honest with yourself. You'll see the answer to the question if you seek it with honest intentions from the outset.'

'She's pushing me away, John.'

He crosses his legs and leans back. 'Pushing, or . . .'

I nod. 'Maybe I've pushed her.'

'Ah.' He gazes towards the corner of the room, then he looks back at me. 'Does *she* have a name?'

'How do you know?'

'If a woman's upset and the husband says there's no reason, that usually means there's a woman. The woman is, of course, always the reason.'

'But she can't possibly know?'

'*Can't possibly know* and *another woman* simply don't belong together.'

'So what's the solution?'

'Who is she?'

'Belinda, my secretary.'

'Oh, Paul, no. Not a secretary.'

'I know, it couldn't be any more clichéd—'

'And dangerous,' he cuts in. 'I mean, there isn't really a woman who isn't related to a man and is closer to him than his secretary. That will turn into a mess very quickly.'

'It is already. Belinda keeps bothering me for more.'

He raises his eyebrows. 'And you tell her to stop?'

I look away and mumble, 'Sometimes.' I pause while he shakes his head and thinks deeply. 'And one time when we were together I told her something ridiculous.'

'Which would be?'

'I told her something like I'd prefer my life to be like it was then all the time.'

'You mean life with her?'

I squint in pain. 'Yes.'

'Oh, you fool,' he says, wincing.

'It was a stupid throwaway comment. I'd had enough of Alice's odd behaviour. I was finally relaxed. It meant nothing.'

'To you, maybe, but to her . . .'

'I know, I know.'

'You've made a terrible mistake, Paul.'

'She keeps coming in here and she keeps sending me bloody messages. It's all cute and sounds innocent, but she's becoming intense.'

'How could Alice have found out?'

'I don't see how she could have, but . . .'

More forcefully: 'Is there evidence? Think carefully.'

'No. No, absolutely not. There's no evidence. I've been careful. It hasn't really been that often.'

He leans forward, his interest piqued. 'But you have a wife and you have a lover. The wife is suddenly behaving irrationally. You think the lover is a secret, but all secrets and lies eventually come out, Paul. Don't be naïve. You can't be sure of anything after the first lie. If she's suddenly irrational, that suggests something has changed. If you can think of nothing else, then perhaps this is it. Maybe she saw you together, saw one of the messages, or perhaps Belinda has said something to her.'

'No, no, no,' I say, shaking my head the whole time, but on the inside I'm worried that maybe he's right, that somehow Alice has found out about Belinda, even though I know there is a genuine, secret reason – *the traumatic event,* as John called it – that led to the change in Alice. Maybe this is something additional and it's pushed her over the edge. 'No. She can't possibly know.'

'Well, look into it some more. It might be worth it, just to be sure.'

'Yes,' I agree. 'I suppose I should.' I sip my drink. The alcohol aggravates my insides. The discomfort is piercing. 'I don't know how to get Belinda to calm down.'

'You have to tell her, Paul.'

'It's just so damned . . . difficult.'

'You're a grown-up, Paul, and, remember, you're her boss. She's the young one, the foolish one. You should never have crossed that boundary, but now you have, you have to re-establish the rules and remind her that you are in charge and if she values her job she's got to put some distance between the pair of you outside of work. You just have to be honest with her, in a polite way, a grateful way, even, but you also have to be firm about it. Make it clear to her that you aren't unsure. Make it clear to her that you're certain your fling can go no further and, most important, that you have no future together.'

I know he's talking sense and of course that's what I've

got to do. I have to be determined, I have to be firm and strong, I have to take back control of my life.

After I've thanked John and he's polished off a second drink, from which I abstain, I leave the Old Bailey and slowly make my way home. As I'm driving, my phone rings. I expect to see Alice's name pop up on the screen, but it says 'Belinda'. I don't answer, but I pull over into the first layby I come across. By the time I stop, a text message has arrived.

Are you OK, baby?

I make another foolish decision.

I type: *Belinda, please, no more. We've had a lovely time, but that's all it can ever be. I'm your boss, you're my employee. It was fun, but let's leave it at that. Please don't text me any more. I had to leave work because I came down ill, but I'll see you properly when I'm back in.*

I press 'send' and then stay where I am for a long time. I instantly regret what I've done. I'm all too aware of the problems Belinda could cause me.

But she's so young and attractive. And, right now, she's not Alice.

Nothing but regrets all round.

On the way home, I stop at a Hilton hotel and go into the bar. I need something to calm my nerves. I sip a whisky slowly, trying and failing to figure out what my next steps should be.

I waste about an hour and head home.

As I approach the entrance to my driveway, imagining the conversation I'm about to have with Alice, Belinda steps out from behind a tree and blocks my path. Shocked, I slam on the brakes. She stares at me through the windscreen. There's fury in her eyes.

The text message.

In an instant, she circles the car and is mouthing angrily at me through the driver's window.

Desperate to keep her quiet, I push open the door and whisper sharply, 'Jesus, will you keep your voice down.' I gaze towards the house to see if Alice is watching from a window. I can't see her, but that doesn't mean she's not there. 'Get in the car, will you.'

'No, no, I won't.'

'Belinda—'

'You used me. And you led me on. Just fun? You bastard!'

'Will you calm down?' I need her to quit this and leave.

'You men are all the same.'

'Look, I never said . . . I was just caught up in the moment. They were words, Belinda.'

'You lied to me.'

'How can it possibly ever be anything more than just sex? You work for me, for God's sake, and I'm married. It was relaxing and good, but that's it, surely. Surely you didn't expect more.'

'Married? You're married now? Well, if that's the only obstacle, let me see to that.' She turns and starts racing down the driveway.

'Belinda, no!' I almost yell, and I leap out of the car. Catching up with her, I grab her from behind.

She spins round and slaps me on the face. 'You're pathetic. You men all are. You've used me, too. Just like the others. Well, that's not good enough. It's not okay any more. I want to see your wife!'

She walks away from me, leaving me standing there. I
don't know how to react. She's halfway down the driveway
and I know she could ruin me. She could destroy my
marriage. A marriage I have to keep together. For the good
– and futures – of both of us. For reasons that no one but
Alice and I can understand.

She can't do this.

I stumble back to the car, trying to think of what to do.
I have only a matter of seconds.

I'm her boss, John said as much, and she's my employee,
and this is my life, and this is my fucking house, and she
just hit me. Who the hell does she think she is? She should
be listening to me right now.

I jump into the car and, knowing I have only seconds
left, yet without thinking clearly, I ram my foot against
the accelerator. The car lurches forwards and starts hurtling
down the driveway. I'm only metres from her when I
realise what I may subconsciously be about to do. She spins
round as she hears the car's tyres kicking up gravel. There's
a look of terror in her face. Our eyes lock as I'm almost
upon her, her life in my hands, and I grip the steering
wheel so tightly that my fingers could press through it. But
her deer-in-headlights daze makes me slam on the brakes.
She looks like a scared kid. The car skids to a halt just in
front of her. She staggers to the side. Even though I'm
frightened by my behaviour, I'm angry with her. Pressing
on the accelerator again, I open the window and snap, 'Do
as you're told and keep the fuck out of my life! Or find
yourself another job!' I don't look in the rear-view mirror
as I leave her behind and I don't look back as I get out

of the car, slam the door and storm towards the house. I only see her shrunken figure in the distance, her shoulders bowed as she walks away, as I shut the front door and lock her out of my life, I hope, permanently.

P

Alice wasn't downstairs when I came in, so I went into the kitchen and made myself a drink. Bourbon, neat. I wanted to feel its sting. I knocked it back, it hurt, and I poured another.

As I'm drinking, Alice walks in, stumbling. I think she's taken some of those stupid sleeping pills I know she's been sneaking recently. 'You were outside a long time,' she slurs.

I'm not in the mood for a pointless conversation, nor another confrontation, so I ignore her. She edges towards me, her hand gliding along the side unit. 'I said, you were outside for a long time,' more forcefully now but very slowly.

I turn to her. 'I was outside.'

'Don't you question me,' she says, suddenly animated and enraged.

'What are you talking about? How many of those pills have you taken, or are you just drunk again?'

'How dare you!' she mouths, closing the distance between us. 'You're the one holding a drink.'

'Listen, Alice, what is it you want from me? What do you want *today*? Because it sure as hell won't be the same as yesterday. And I bet tomorrow will be different.'

She sways violently. 'How dare you accuse me!'

'I'm not going to have a slanging match with you.'

'Go on,' she says, getting uncomfortably close. 'Hit me!'

'What are you talking about?' I try to walk around her, baffled by her, but she blocks my path. I use my arm to edge her aside. 'I need some time alone.'

She stumbles into my chest, grabbing at me. 'Some time alone? You're never here! Go on, abandon me again.'

I can't ignore that; I have to challenge her. 'I haven't abandoned you. I've been here all along, dealing with the same thing as you.' I stop. Then I see clearly. 'Only you've stopped trying. You've given up.' *I don't see a future for us any more.*

When I try to leave the room, she pulls at my clothing.

'This . . . this *thing* we call a marriage, I can't do it any longer,' I tell her. This time, I walk through her.

'No!' she screams, and she grabs me by the neck from behind. Her nails claw into my skin and she clings on. I wince and call out, 'Fuck! Stop it! Get off!' She's pressing on my windpipe, so I have no choice. I grab her wrist, spinning round, and she collides into the side unit, her back hitting it, and she crumples to the ground. She cries out, clutching her stomach, her face filled with agony.

I suffer at the sight of her. Horrified by what I've done, I kneel and reach out to her. 'Alice, are you okay?'

She wrenches a scream from deep within, something animalistic and desperate.

'Jesus, Alice?' This isn't normal, something's wrong. I run into the lounge and grab the telephone. Dialling 999, I charge back into the kitchen. Now Alice is lying prostrate on the floor. 'Alice?'

She doesn't answer.

I dive to floor level. 'I'm here,' I say as soothingly as I can while my nerves bubble over, rubbing her back. 'I'm here.'

The ambulance arrives within twenty minutes. The whole time, Alice is crying out and nothing I do helps. She's unable to say a word to me. All she can do is clutch her stomach.

The paramedics ask me questions, but I can't take in what they say. They work around me, regardless of me.

A writhing Alice is lifted onto a stretcher. The paramedics seem perplexed. I follow them out of the house and down the driveway as they carry her to the waiting ambulance. They lift her in and I'm just about to climb aboard when I hear Alice groan, 'No, I don't want him in here!'

Startled, I'm told by one of the paramedics that I can't board, that I'll have to follow in a separate vehicle if I want to go to the hospital. Obviously I want to. Above all, I want Alice to understand the words I was saying when she collapsed no longer mean anything. The concern I feel for her wellbeing has made me realise I can't let her go. Or lose her.

I grab my car keys, lock the front door and jump into the Outlander, accelerating quickly to catch up with the ambulance. But as I reach the end of the driveway, I can't see where it is, so I take what I think will be the quickest route to the hospital.

En route, I sweat and swear. I run a red light and almost get hit side on. By the time I'm halfway there, I'm out of breath and the panic is overwhelming. I'm worried about why Alice wouldn't let me travel with her in the ambulance. Worried that I may have lost her, when that's the last thing

I want. Worried also that she might say *anything*. I need her to know she means everything to me and we have to stay together. We can't survive without one another; our futures lie in each other's hands.

There's an ambulance in the emergency vehicle bay outside the hospital, its back doors open. Public parking is further along and to the right, so I find a space as fast as I can. Failing to pay, I run to the main hospital building and scan signs for the Accident and Emergency Department. I burst through some double doors. There's a reception desk about ten metres ahead and a lot of seating, most of it crammed with people. The corridor is all blue and grey. The whole building smells of disinfectant.

I run to the desk. A woman behind it is talking to a man. There's another woman behind her, looking through a filing cabinet. 'Excuse me,' I call to them. 'My wife?'

The woman at the filing cabinet turns around. 'Just wait in line, sir.'

'You don't understand,' I say with urgency. 'My wife, she's been brought in by ambulance and I've lost them. Where can I find her?'

'Follow me,' she says, animatedly dropping the papers and dashing out of a side door.

We move along a number of corridors, ending up in a larger space, this one filled with a huge reception desk and lots of people moving at pace.

'Your name, sir?'

'Paul Reeve.'

'And your wife?'

'Alice. Alice Reeve.'

She leans over the reception desk and speaks quickly to a woman, who nods in return. She turns back to me. 'Wait here. Someone will come for you.' She starts heading back to where we came from.

'Thank you,' I call after her, but I'm not sure if she hears me.

I shuffle and check my watch three times a minute, and soon five minutes have passed. I'm alone and feel useless. Eventually, unable to wait any longer, I go to the desk. 'Excuse me,' I call out when no one looks up. A woman with curly brown hair peers up. 'I'm waiting to see my wife, Alice Reeve. The receptionist from there' – I point behind me – 'brought me here and told me someone will come and get me.'

'It won't be long, sir. Just be patient. Why don't you take a seat over there?' She points down the corridor, to an alcove. 'Go there,' she says. 'It'll be fine. There's stuff to read. You won't be forgotten. Their first priority is to make sure she's all right.'

'Thank you,' I say. I start walking and say uncertainly, 'I'll be over there then.'

I get increasingly edgy as I wait for someone to come over. It feels like I'm waiting forever, that they may never arrive. To kill the time, I read every poster that's stuck on the wall or pinned to a board; I can't concentrate on an out-of-date magazine. I can't sit down. In all likelihood, it's only about fifteen minutes, but it's too long and my mind starts playing games with me. I wonder what she's saying and to whom, what she's telling them, what she's revealing.

What if this is the beginning of the end for us?

Finally, just as I'm about to start shouting in despair, footsteps approach. They belong to a man in his fifties, wearing a doctor's coat. I suddenly feel expectant, but then I'm hit by concern when I see there's a policeman following him.

'Mr Reeve,' the doctor says, not asking, but I nod my head nonetheless.

'I want to see my wife.' The look on his face tells me something's wrong. 'What's happening?'

He hesitates, stutters, making only a sound. The police officer steps forward and introduces himself. I don't absorb his name; my mind's in a haze. 'Your wife has made an accusation against you that means we can't let you see her at the moment. If she decides to press charges against you for assault, I suspect you won't see her for a while.'

'What do you mean *assault*?' I'm incredulous. 'She grabbed me. She just fell back when I tried to shake her off.'

'You'll have plenty of time to tell your side when you make your official statement, that is if she decides to take things further. At the moment, she's asked that you be kept away from her until she decides what to do next.'

'But that doesn't make any sense,' I say, now worried more than ever that she might ruin me. *What if she suddenly becomes vengeful and fanatical? What if my rejection of her has spurned within her a deep desire for revenge?*

I can almost picture my demise.

But it would also destroy her; surely she will see that. She can't possibly explain what happened in our house last October without implicating herself and if she implicates herself she'll ruin her own life.

I have to see Alice. I have to tell her I didn't mean it, that we can work things out, that I do want her. That we *can* figure out a way to make everything better again. 'I need to see my wife,' I say resolutely.

'Have you been drinking, sir?' He sniffs exaggeratedly.

'I had *one* drink. Regardless, I don't see how that has anything to do with this. I'm a judge, for God's sake. Do you know what that means? This is a terrible misunderstanding and you've got it all wrong. We had an argument, I tried to walk away, she grabbed hold of me and as I shook her off she fell. I didn't try to hurt her in the least. What happened doesn't matter.'

'In her condition, it most certainly does matter. You should have been careful, even though you and she might have been overcome with emotion.'

I'm silenced. I want to speak but can't. I open my mouth, but it's like there's a silencer on my voice box.

Her condition?

'Now, what I suggest, Mr Reeve, is that you go home and wait to hear either from us or from your wife. If she tells us she wishes to press charges, you'll find some officers on your doorstep and they'll want your statement. Or she'll call you and tell you it's okay and you can come here and see her. You just need to be patient and wait.'

My mind clouded, I say nothing else and drift towards a door. It might be the exit, I don't know.

The doctor calls after me. 'Your wife is going to be okay, she's just bruised and shaken up. She'll need no more than a day or two's monitoring.'

Little does he realise that's not the only thing I want to know.

When I get home, I sink onto the sofa with a bottle of Woodford Reserve in one hand and a glass in the other.

Her condition?

Alice pregnant? Impossible. We waited so long because of my career and then, when we eventually tried, the doctors said it couldn't happen for us.

We can't have children.

But what if they were wrong and Alice is pregnant? I might never be able to see my child. That's what could happen if I'm charged. Not only that, but Alice might tell the police about the man whose body we hid, and then she'd be rid of me forever; I could end up in prison, disbarred and without a family, without the child I thought I could never have.

I could be a father. The thought drifts around my head, swimming, like I'm floating. Euphoria, my dream come true.

It lasts until I see Alice emerging from shadows, standing in the way, blocking the door and the light beyond it, and the crib that's in there somewhere.

Guilt and loss strike fast. I drink heavily, hoping to bury them. *What if I never see Alice, or my child, again?* I'm over halfway through the bottle before the first tears arrive. I feel indelibly sorry for myself. There's nothing to suggest Alice will give me the chance to be the father I've always wanted to be. If she wanted me to be part of the child's life, surely she wouldn't have kept the pregnancy a secret and surely she wouldn't have told the police to keep me away from her.

A baby. A child.

I want to be a father.

Five years of trying unsuccessfully after I'd built up my career. IVF three times. And only failure and misery. Now an empty marriage crumbling.

I lie down, unable to remain upright, knowing that tomorrow a knock at the door could come. The police and it's over. *They know everything.*

Or there could be a different phone call altogether. A dreamy voice saying, 'Paul, I'm sorry, I made a stupid mistake, I want you here, right now.' And I could go to the hospital and we could embrace and we could say we're sorry and we could start all over again.

My vision is cloudy. On autopilot, I remove my mobile phone from my pocket and type words I can't see. *You're fired.*

I want to start all over again. I want to be a father. And that means I have to be a good husband.

I pray as I close my eyes, as I drift off into utter darkness.

P

It's almost lunchtime the next day before I manage to prise open my eyes. My head's pounding. The alcohol hasn't dulled my pain, only intensified it. I regret every mouthful.

I think of Alice. And I realise all I can do is wait.

I grab a glass of water and some Alka Selzer, hoping it'll work some magic. I want to think straight, but with each movement comes a sharp, piercing pain. I close my eyes, willing it to disappear, but it's dug in deep and immovable.

I lie back, stare at the ceiling and try to think. First, anger. Anger with myself, for how I've behaved, for all I've done. Also anger with Alice, for lying and keeping the largest secret imaginable from me. But who can blame her? I don't know how much she knows about what I've been up to, but the altercation I had with Belinda yesterday happened right under her nose, so it's possible she knows, or at least suspects, everything. And fury with that man, whoever he was, for tearing along the seams of our life.

And I imagine our child.

I will be a better husband. A better man.

I don't touch another drop for the rest of the day, but when neither a knock at the door nor a phone call arrive, I start to worry all over again. Shortly after 4 p.m., I call the hospital. I ask to be put through to the ward where Alice is. It's a long time before someone speaks on the other end of the line.

'All I'm allowed to say is she's recovering well.'

I hang up, frustrated that I'm not getting any further, but relieved I'm not in handcuffs, and surely that means there's still a chance for us. I have to wait.

I don't know how long I finally sleep for, it took ages to doze off, but I'm woken by a sound. There's the noise of a chain and a thud. It's the front door closing. I wait for Alice to appear at the top of the stairs. But when the figure emerges, it isn't her. It's him. Alice is lying by my side and he's coming for her. I have to help her, but my arms are strapped behind my back and my legs are chained to the floor. I'm helpless. Horrified and desperate to save her, I wrestle myself free, breaking metal with my bare hands, and I manage to move forwards, groggy and unbalanced, stumbling into the corridor.

Whereupon I come face to face with Alice.

For a moment, I suspect I'm still dreaming. She's like an apparition, a celestial being floating in the air. I murmur her name. Gliding like an angel, she moves to within inches of my face and then I feel her hands rubbing my shoulders, then stroking my face, and then she hugs me.

'Why?' I manage to say, clinging onto her hands, making sure she's real. I could ask so many questions.

'Why didn't you tell me?'

She looks me in the eye. 'I'm telling you now.'

A

'I'm pregnant,' I say.

'You really are?' Paul's smile is wider than I've ever seen it.

I nod my head. 'I really am.'

He kisses me and hugs me deeply and for a long time. 'That's . . . amazing!' Then he says, 'Thank you.'

'For what?'

'For coming back. For giving me a chance. For not turning me in.'

'Why would I do that?'

'Because I deserved your anger. They said you were refusing to see me.'

'I was. But I changed my mind.'

'I'm glad you did. You're going to let me be a father?'

'It looks like it.'

'A father next to a wonderful mother.'

'It was always meant to be that way,' I say.

He kisses me again.

That night, we're lying side by side in bed. At some point, Paul falls asleep, but I remain wide awake. I nestle my cheek below his shoulder blade. It feels bony.

I talk to myself, wondering if the words will reach him. 'Every day I think about what we've done and I feel sick. I was lost, but now I'm found. Now there's a child to think about. There's a reason to keep going. The problem was I didn't have a reason.'

His phone buzzes on his bedside unit. I reach over and read the message.

Why should I be surprised?

'But will it ever be reason enough for you, Paul? No, you can't be trusted. That means you're going to have to prove you're worthy of being my baby's daddy. You're going to have to show me. *Hubby*.'

Even without a child, I've always believed we have a future. Now, anything could be possible.

Of course, I could be very, very wrong.

11

Detective Constable Ryan Hillier, sitting at a desk in the incident room, was on the phone. 'Okay, thanks. That sounds like what we're looking for. Please send it through . . . Okay, checking now.' He brought the computer to life and clicked the mouse a couple of times. 'Yeah, got it. Thanks again.'

He leant back and looked over his shoulder, smiling.

Detective Sergeant Katherine Wright felt his eyes on her and peered up from the paperwork over which she was trawling. 'What is it?'

'One of our counterparts in Austria. They have a cold case that sounds promising.'

'Tell me more.'

'Forwarding the files to you now.'

'Give me the essence as I look.'

'Alexander Pavlik, wanted for fifteen years for a series of contract killings, including those of some very prominent figures. He was expensive, hence his ability to disappear into thin air, and highly effective, it seems. Military background, worked for the country's security forces. Weapon of choice, piano wire.'

'Piano wire,' Wright repeated, smiling for the first time in a long while.

Hillier nodded. 'Victims always garrotted – every single one, all twelve. Twelve victims over four years, and then he vanished. The last murder was unintentionally sloppy. His prints were discovered.'

'How so?'

'It seems he was interrupted and had to flee the scene. A glove came off in his struggle to get out. An international arrest warrant was issued after they thought he'd left the country, which they now believe was almost instantly. One confirmed sighting here in the UK almost a decade ago, but nothing since then. He's a ghost, doing and getting away with God knows what.'

'If it's him, I think it's safe to say we know exactly what he's been doing and getting away with,' she said. 'Until now.' Uplifted, she read some. 'Any murders here over the past ten years involving garrotting with piano wire, other than the three we know about?'

'Still nothing.'

'So he potentially comes here ten or so years ago and adopts a different method of killing until this latest spate, or he's remained dormant all these years and now he's come out of retirement.'

'Unless we're missing something. I mean, why after doing twelve with one method would he suddenly change? If he's had such success with it in the past, I mean. So maybe he has just been asleep and now he needs the money.'

'Unless he had a purpose in changing to something else.'

'How so?'

'Keep us off the scent, if he knew he was being looked for internationally. No piano wire means there's no easy link back to Austria. No link to the current arrest warrant. New identity, nothing to connect him to his past.'

'Perhaps, but then why suddenly return to using piano wire now?'

'No idea.' Wright opened a JPEG file. 'A headshot,' she said. On the screen in front of her was a photograph of Alexander Pavlik. It seemed to have been taken twenty years ago from his days in the Austrian army. 'Says here he made it to colonel and was highly respected and decorated.' She looked more closely at the image. Hair close-cropped, dark eyes, the army uniform from the shoulders up. She was particularly interested in his eyes. 'Look at the eyes. They're dead. You see that?'

Hillier pulled up the photo on his screen. 'Yeah, I see.'

'Nothing behind them.'

'He likely won't look anything like this today. This photo's probably all but useless, it's so old.'

'He probably won't, but his eyes will be the same.'

'He could be in disguise.'

'What's behind the eyes always remains the same, regardless. It'll be the same death stare, it lingers. You can't hide what's behind a person's eyes, that's the one thing they can't change or disguise. Let's get some computer-generated images ageing him by twenty years. Change of hair style, hair colour, facial hair, weight gain, stick on some glasses, you know the routine.'

'I'll get onto it.' He turned back to his computer.

'And Ryan?'

'Yes.'

'Good work.'

He smiled, pleased to receive a compliment. She went back to scanning the files on her computer screen. Hillier started to write an email requesting a variety of computer-generated images of someone who may or may not have been the ghost they were searching for.

P

When I wake up, Alice is still in bed. I put on some clothes, go downstairs and have breakfast. Afterwards, I head upstairs to kiss Alice goodbye. As I approach the bedroom, I hear water running in the bathroom.

'Alice?' I ask.

'I'm preparing a bath,' she says.

When she doesn't open the door, I say, 'I have to leave for work now.'

'Have a good day,' she says. 'I'm having a bath.' Her voice is oddly cold.

'Are you all right?'

'I'm preparing a bath,' she repeats.

I glance at my watch; I can't wait any longer. My eyes linger on the bathroom door – that awful place behind it, where Alice is right now – and I wonder whether we should actually put the house on the market after all, as Alice originally asked. Perhaps a fresh start, somewhere far from here, is what we need. A new child, a new home. I'll suggest it to Alice when I get back.

'See you later,' I say, and when she doesn't answer, I add, 'I love you, Alice.'

She doesn't reciprocate.

When I'm outside, I don't expect to feel relief, but that's precisely what comes over me. I feel like I've emerged from the recurrent black hole.

Traffic is surprisingly light and I get to work in good time. Tentatively, I put my head in Belinda's office. She isn't here; that's unusual because she's always here before I arrive. I find Jenny and ask, 'Has Belinda called? Do we know why she isn't here?' It's a null question because I know full well I told Belinda to get lost and that's likely why she hasn't come to work. I try to act surprised when Jenny tells me, 'No, not that I know of.'

As today's my first full day back at work after being off sick and there's a lot of work to do, I ask, 'Can you get someone to call her and find out where the hell she is? And if she can't be here today, can you get some kind of temp in to answer the phones and type up some documents for me? Nothing complicated, but someone literate, please.'

'Not a problem.'

I hand Jenny some documents I'd like put on the bench for my arrival in the courtroom. Once she's gone, I think about Belinda, who's usually so close to where I'm standing now, and wonder where she is and what she's feeling. *Does she hate me?*

I wonder if the incident outside the house was enough to remove her from my life for good. Then something distant comes to me, something hazy. A text message, perhaps. Drunk and angry. *What did I do?*

I open the messages section of my mobile, expecting to find a chain of messages she and I have shared over recent weeks. If I sent her a message, it should be the top one in the outbox.

But there's no record of any messages sent to her. None.

Strange, because I don't recall deleting them. Not that I completely remember sending anything to her, either. *I've been drinking too much.*

There's a knock on the door and Jenny pokes her head around it. 'We're ready for you,' she says.

I look down at the phone and wonder what could possibly have happened to the messages. I have no idea.

'My Lord?' Jenny says, using formality to get my attention.

I drop the phone into my pocket, put on my wig, pick up a file and head out.

To the sounds of, 'All rise,' I enter and walk along the dais to my seat behind the front bench. I stand, bow and look down at everyone present. All those eyes, they're all waiting to react to me, when I'm ready. There's an air of respect in a courtroom. I don't think it'll ever get old. Despite being uncertain about my messages to Belinda, being in here lifts me. I've earned this. This is where I belong.

I sit down. I find it hard to focus for the first ten minutes or so, but the prosecution's questioning of a forensic expert soon becomes so intricate that I have no choice but to force myself to follow the case that's being presented. Fairly soon, I'm fully immersed in it, and my external life becomes momentarily irrelevant.

The morning session flies by and I find myself engrossed in my work more than I have been for some time. It's uplifting and freeing. I want to take this fulfilled attitude home and channel it into my life with Alice.

I walk out of the courtroom for the lunch break and as soon as I enter my chambers there's a knock on the door. I open it. A young woman, likely in her mid-twenties, is standing there. Jenny is beside her. 'This is Collette Fisher,' she says. 'She'll be temping for you for the rest of the day.'

Collette holds out her hand and I take it.

'Have you been shown around?'

'Yes,' she says, revealing a brilliant white smile, which is in stark contrast to her long straight black hair and deep red lips.

Handing her a pile of notes, I say, 'If these could be typed up in the first instance, that would be great.'

'Can I get you a drink,' she asks, 'or anything else?'

She's swaying on the spot. The movement makes her look young, immature. She reminds me of Belinda. I shake the thought away. 'No, thank you. Nothing.'

She leaves and I turn to Jenny. 'Did, um, did anyone manage to get hold of Belinda?'

'No, no answer on either number we have for her. She lives alone, but there's a next of kin, so we called that number – it belongs to her sister – and she's said she'll do her best to reach her. We're waiting for her to get back to us.'

'Okay, well, Collette seems . . .' I struggle for an appropriate word. 'Nice.'

'I'm sure she'll work out just fine for you,' Jenny says, with a knowing smile. 'You have a nice lunch now,' she adds and leaves.

I search through my phone messages again. Not a single one to or from Belinda. That doesn't make any sense. *Where the hell have they gone?*

A

I haven't been here for eight years, but I've come back. I stand at the end of the path, arching my neck so that I can see the top of the building.

Eight long years. During that time, I've been through so much. I didn't think of this place during that time, through all those struggles, and it's plainly obvious to me that this place didn't think about me.

Nobody here helped me. He didn't offer me anything.

Yet now I'm back. I needed reassurance but had no idea where I could get it from, so I left the house and walked. Walked miles. My feet brought me here. Something automatic.

I take a tentative step forwards and keep stepping until I reach the large wooden door. I press my hand against it, think back to all the times I walked in here without hesitation, proudly and happily, feeling like each visit offered me something, feeling more whole each time I left.

I push and the door opens. There's a wide-open space before me, then another set of double doors. I haven't been in here for eight years, but everything about the place is familiar. It hasn't changed.

Not everything changes.

Emerging through the next set of doors, I find myself in a vast space, rows of wooden benches before me, only one grey-haired head in the distance, facing away from me. She doesn't turn towards me, even though I'm certain she can hear my footsteps as I move towards a bench; concentration comes naturally here.

Sitting down, I remove my coat and stretch my shoulders, staring at the cross that sits on the wall behind the altar. On the cross, there's the figure of a man, his head lowered, his body defeated. He's nailed to the cross and there's nothing he can do to get off it. He won't even try to.

I feel like I should talk to him but am without words. I search for them, but they are too deeply hidden to be found. So I sit in silence, absorbing the atmosphere, empty, cold, holy. Not at all unsettling, though, actually peaceful.

Footsteps approach behind me, but I don't acknowledge them. After a few moments, a lullaby voice hums, 'Are you here for confession, my dear?'

I turn around. The priest is a plump Irishman in his sixties. He has a kind, pudgy face. He wasn't the priest when I used to come here with my parents every Sunday.

'I'm sorry,' I say, 'I don't know you.'

'I'm just a pair of ears to listen and a pair of hands to reconnect you with God, dear.' He smiles wistfully. 'You don't need to know me.'

Reconnect?

'But I'm . . . disconnected,' I say.

'Then join me.' He stretches a welcoming arm towards the small confession room that's next to the vestry.

As if instinctively, my body stands. I leave my coat where it is and float into the room. It's the same as it always was, white-walled and a white partition separating two seats, a gauzed window in the middle of it. I can't see the priest clearly; he's already sitting on his side of the partition, leaving only his shadow in view. I kneel on the stoop on my side.

'When you're ready,' he says, sensing my reluctance. 'Take your time.'

'Bless me, Father, for I have sinned,' I say, as if eight years have evaporated in an instant. 'It's been . . . eight years since my last confession.'

He breathes in deeply. 'Then speak and let God help you.'

I need to know what to do. I have to be sure I'm right.

P

Lunch is over before it began and the afternoon session goes to plan. Court is adjourned till tomorrow.

I get undressed in my chambers and pack my bag. As I'm locking the door, Jenny appears. 'Are you happy for Collette to come back tomorrow if we don't hear from Belinda?'

'She's been fine, so yes. Still no news on Belinda?'

'We heard from her sister. She can't get hold of her. I'd say she's a write-off, at least for the time being. I'll ask Collette to come in tomorrow regardless. That way, she'll be here when you arrive and there'll be no delay if Belinda doesn't show up.'

'Perhaps make it for the rest of the week, just in case. Let's cover all bases. And keep in touch with Belinda's sister. As soon as she hears from her, I want to know about it.'

I drive home during rush hour, so it takes almost ninety minutes to get there. I'm preoccupied the whole way. Although I know Belinda won't return to work, I can't imagine where she's disappeared to; she should surely be in contact with her sister. I know they're close.

As I pull into the driveway, I hit the brakes.

The house is completely dark. The front door – it's open. Alice's car is in the driveway.

A chill hits me.

It's happening again.

I edge the car forwards and get out.

'Alice?' I call into the pitch-black, stepping inside. 'No,' I murmur, the parallels to that night flooding over me.

I switch on the hallway lights and call her name again, despairing at the sound of my own voice. I don't want to go further in, but I have no choice.

I quickly check in each of the downstairs rooms, all of which are empty. *This can't be.*

I dash upstairs and come to the bedroom door. This is where it all began. *Can it be happening all over again?* I push open the door, half expecting to see Alice in silhouette, sitting on the bed. I put the light on straightaway.

She's not here.

So the bathroom. I brace myself as I stand in front of the door. My heart pounding, I push it. I step into the room slowly and, horrified, see the bath. It's filled with water. I walk to it and look down. 'No,' I gasp. Sitting at the bottom of it, like a heavy rock on a riverbed, is my letter opener.

'Alice,' I mouth, clueless.

I pull out my phone. No message from her. No missed call. I dial her number, unable to take my eyes off that water. 'Answer,' I urge. It rings and rings. 'Answer, Alice.' Then the voicemail connects. 'Alice,' I say, speaking after the beep, 'I'm home. Where are you? Do you want me to come to you? Tell me. Please.'

Pulling myself away from the bath, I head downstairs, confused. I don't know what to do. The emptiness of the house is overpowering and it feels like it's been empty for a long time. It doesn't feel like my home any more.

I redial. Voicemail again. 'Alice, is everything all right?' I ask, my voice more urgent. 'Let me know where you are.'

I'm lost. It's gone 8 p.m. and I'm here, home alone, without a clue. I call Amanda. I can think of no one else. She answers on the second ring. 'No, haven't seen or heard from her, not for a few days,' she tells me.

'Are you certain you don't know where she could be?'

'She's probably just out shopping or something. I wouldn't worry.'

'You know that's not true. It's night-time and she lost her love for shopping when we got back from New York, you know that. Her car's still here, Amanda.'

'Oh God,' she says, 'I don't know, Paul. I really don't. I'm sorry. Are you all right? I'll tell Laurence. He can help.'

'No, don't say anything. I'll sort it out. It'll be all right.' And silence. 'I'll be in touch.'

As I ring off, my stomach is in knots.

All I can do is stare at my phone. I'm helpless again, at a loss. Feeling like this is alien to me; inside I'm screaming.

Weak, now pathetic again, I head for the kitchen. I need a drink.

But no, I tell myself, fighting. *Alcohol has done enough damage these past few weeks. I need to keep a clear head.*

I sit on the sofa, waiting, mobile in one hand, landline phone in the other. Waiting and waiting. My anxiety continues to build. Two hours pass. It's gone ten o'clock when I dial Alice's number again. Now I can't keep the panic from my voice, it's like a spillage. *What if she doesn't come back?* Now I believe that's a real possibility. 'Alice, where are you? What's going on? Are you all right? Please, tell me you're all right. Please God, call back, Alice, I beg you.'

My hands are trembling. I pull myself up and stumble into the kitchen. *Fuck it,* I think. I pull a beer out of the fridge, open it and down it. It's not enough, so I get a bottle of Woodford Reserve from the dining room. Although I remember where the last bottle got me, I don't care – I can't help myself.

I need to be numb. I take a glass from the cabinet and fill it, knocking back its contents. Then another, which is when I start to feel the alcohol. *That's right – that's what I want.* Then another, and I can't stop, and I've lost count by the time I make it to the sofa, a much lighter bottle in my hand, the glass abandoned on the dining-room table.

'Where are you, Alice?' I call to the ceiling. 'Where the fuck are you?'

P

I sit up suddenly, feeling like an earthquake is striking inside my head. I shut my eyes, press tightly, and open them again. Slowly, they adjust to the early morning light. It's quarter past seven. Picking up my phone, I glance at the screen. No contact from Alice. 'Shit,' I groan.

I hear a noise. Some kind of rustling in the hallway.

I drag myself off the sofa and stagger out of the lounge, reaching for the wall to steady myself.

On the floor next to the front door is an envelope. I pick it up, blood rushing to my head as I bend. It's some time before I make my way back up.

The exterior of the envelope is blank: no name, no address, no stamp, no postmark. I peel it open and pull out a single sheet of A4 paper. On it are two lines of typed text.

One body. One married couple. One secret.
One very big mistake.

My instinct is to swivel round, someone must be in here, I'm being watched. I'm feel like I'm going to vomit. I'm being swept along by a wave of paranoia.

'What the fuck!' I say, my heart erupting.

I glance up at the front door. That noise. I zoom in on the letterbox. It must have been the sound of the letter being pushed through it. I open the door and step outside, the letter still in my hand. I try to scan the area but see nobody and nothing that's out of place.

There must be someone here. The letter only just came through the letterbox.

I move down the driveway as quickly as I can, which is slowly, each step poking a hole in my head. Scanning the trees and bushes, I see nothing. I reach the end of the driveway and look left and right, near and far. Empty cars and nothing else. I walk over to the side of the driveway and peer through the trees into next door's property. Near his house is our neighbour, Bob. He's washing his car. I struggle along the fence and reach a point that's parallel to him.

He's not close, but I call out, 'Hello, Bob,' trying to sound calm yet feeling anything but.

'Morning, Paul,' he calls back, sounding chirpy.

'Did you see or hear anyone delivering something a moment ago?'

'No, sorry. Haven't been out long and concentrating too much on this new baby.' He steps back and holds out his arms proudly, as if showing off a landscape painting he's just finished after days of effort. 'Maserati,' he boasts.

I give him the thumbs up as I feign interest. 'Must come over for a spin one day.'

'Any time, Paul. Any time.'

253

My eyes continue searching. 'Anyway, have a good one.'

As I'm walking back into the house, I hear his satisfied voice saying, 'Oh I will, I will.'

I shut the door and stand, dumbstruck, on the inside, staring at the words on the piece of paper.

Someone knows. Someone knows everything.

Someone's playing games with us, threatening us. And then, despite the pain that's racketing around my head, I'm struck by the real possibility: what if Alice's disappearance is linked to this letter? What if she's been taken by whoever wrote this?

What if the dead man's accomplice has struck after all?

My shaking hand drops the piece of paper onto the floor. I go into the lounge as quickly as my body will take me there, pick up my phone and, although I know it's futile, call Alice again. This time, there's not even a connection to voicemail. The number just rings and rings and rings and eventually cuts off. I cry out in frustration.

I'm stuck. The only thing I know is I can't go to court today. I can't go anywhere.

I dial Belinda's number before I realise she's disappeared, too, and probably isn't my secretary any more anyway. Then I realise I don't know how to reach Collette.

Sunken and deflated, I fall onto the armchair and ring Jenny. 'Sorry, we're going to have to cancel. I've come down with a horrific sick bug. I don't think I fully shifted the last one and it's hit me twice as hard.'

'Oh no. I'm sorry, Paul. Shall I have Collette call you when she gets in?'

'No, no. Just ask her to continue typing up the documents from yesterday. I'm going to try to sleep it off and hopefully be back on Monday.' I say this knowing how unlikely that is. I have to find Alice and figure out who the hell sent this letter. Nothing else matters.

Feeling like an invalid, I ring Amanda again. 'She still hasn't come home,' I say, unable to conceal my worry. 'Are you certain you haven't heard anything?'

'Nothing, no. This doesn't sound like her at all.' The concern in her voice is genuine. I'm almost annoyed she isn't in on an obscene joke with Alice.

'No. No, it isn't like her. Is there anyone else you can think of who she might be with?'

'I don't know. I'm sorry.'

'Anyone, I don't know, a man, even. I don't care at this point. I won't be mad even if there is someone else, I just need to find her.'

'Alice isn't like that, Paul. I think you know that.'

'I know she isn't,' I say, realising she's not like me at all.

I scroll through the contacts list on my phone and ring everyone I consider our friend. No one's heard from her, most of them for weeks or months, since Alice fell into her depression. Since that night.

Then, desperate, I call everyone who knows her, even those with the tiniest connection, but come to nothing but dead ends. I log onto Facebook to check when her last post was: more than a month ago. I click on her Friends list in the hope I'll spot someone I haven't thought of. They quickly become a blur. I'm getting nowhere, apart from more frustrated and disappointed. More paranoid.

No, there's only one option left. There's only one other place she could have gone to. Even though deep down I know it's the unlikeliest place on earth.

I've got to head for the one place I thought I'd never return to. I have no choice.

P

I arrive outside number 3 Mortimer Drive. I haven't been here for eight years. Remaining in the car, I stare at the front door. Only a gate and small path separate me from them.

Alice's parents have lived here forever, just twelve miles from our home. Alice grew up in this house. Her bedroom was behind the upstairs window on the far left. Yet she hasn't stepped foot inside it, as far as I'm aware, since one March evening eight years ago when her relationship with her parents fell apart. When they did to her what she called the ultimate betrayal, after which she vowed never to forgive them.

Alice struggles to forgive.

Yet here I am, considering that she's actually come back here. They probably blame me for the decisions she made that evening. I'm probably completely unwelcome, yet I have to knock on that door because I'm only left with questions, not answers.

I gingerly make my way to the front door, passing through the gate, stepping over the line that has marked their home as a foreign territory for all these years. I clear my throat and knock. A chain rattles on the other side of the door and then a surprised face, the heavily aged image of Alice's father, Arthur.

'Paul,' he says, sounding as surprised as his face suggests.

'Mr Morton,' I say, deciding formality is the best approach.

'Arthur, you know it's Arthur,' he says softly.

I nod. 'Arthur.'

'Come in,' he says, stepping back. The hallway is narrower than I remember, and I stand awkwardly close to him when we're inside. The air in the house is stale.

'Can I get you a drink?' he asks.

'No, thank you. I, er, I won't keep you long, I just need to ask whether you've seen Alice.'

'Seen her, when?'

'Yesterday, today. Sometime recently.'

He shakes his head. 'No, we haven't.'

'Are you certain your wife hasn't?'

'She would have told me. Why? What is this about?'

'She's gone missing,' I concede. It's the first time I've used the word 'missing' and I bear its heavy weight; my knees start to buckle.

Arthur Morton reaches out to me. 'Are you okay, Paul?'

I hold up an open palm. 'Just a little overwhelmed, that's all. I thought maybe she'd come here. She hasn't been feeling herself.'

'Well, she hasn't.' A pause, thoughtful perhaps. 'Goodness me.' He breathes deeply. 'I really don't know what to say. I don't think I can do anything to help. Can I fix you that drink at least?'

'No, no, thank you. I'd best be on my way.' I turn towards the door.

'It's taken a lot of courage for you to come here,' he says to my back. I hesitate. 'Very brave, especially on your own.'

'I had no choice,' I say, without turning back.

'I'm glad you did,' he says quietly. Now I turn and I see standing in front of me a shrunken man, not the man I remember at all. Propped on his forehead, just underneath his thin white hair, is a pair of glasses he didn't need the last time I saw him. His cheeks have sunken in on themselves. His back is stooped. His eyes are sad.

'You know, perhaps I will have—'

The sound of fast footsteps interrupts me. I look up and see Daphne Morton thundering down the stairs. 'You've got a nerve,' she says, 'coming here after all this time. Some nerve indeed.'

'Darling,' Arthur speaks up before I can figure out what to say, 'Alice has gone missing. Paul has come to ask for our help.'

'*Our* help?' she scoffs. 'That's rich. I haven't heard you asking for help for eight years. What, finally pushed her away, have you? I always knew you would.' She's so close her spittle lands on my cheek. 'I always said to Arthur, that one's trouble, you watch, and look at you here now.'

'I just needed to check whether she was here, that's all,' I say, keen to leave.

She raises her voice. 'And what in that tiny brain of yours makes you think she'd ever set foot in this house again? You heard what she said, didn't you? *You're dead to me,* that's what she said. In front of you! WE ARE DEAD! And you, brainwasher, it was you who took her from us.'

'Mrs Morton, you're very much mistaken—'

'Dead, we are! And as corpses can't speak, we have nothing else to say to you.'

There's a moment of silence. 'I'm sorry,' I say, breaking it, and I step towards the door. I don't intend to argue. They've been through enough and I don't blame her for reacting this way.

They've suffered enough. Now it's my turn.

'Thank you, Arthur,' I say softly, and he nods. 'And I'm sorry,' I say to his wife, a woman full of bitterness and anger, who scoffs again and steps forward, grabbing hold of the door and slamming it shut.

P

By the time I return home, hoping to find Alice but unsurprised when I don't, I realise I'm close to having only one option left. Although calling the police will invite even greater risk into our lives, I'm not sure I have any alternatives left.

Too many lies, too many secrets. Now everything is in jeopardy, just when things seemed like they'd been sorted, when I thought our future had been mapped out.

I start on another bottle of bourbon. After more drinks than I can count and with darkness shrouding over the house, I ring Belinda's mobile, with absolutely no idea why, other than being enveloped by a need to do so. I want to give her a piece of my mind. She slapped me. She could be the reason Alice has disappeared. She doesn't answer. Then I call Alice. After the seventh or eighth ring, knowing the voicemail will fail to pick up again, I start talking as if she's on the other end. 'Why have you left me? What have I done to deserve this?' I wait for a response that's not forthcoming. 'Too much. I've done too fucking much.' I start sobbing. 'I'm sorry for everything. I'm sorry for what

I've been and who I am. I promised you. I promised, and I failed.' The ringing ends and the line goes dead, but I don't stop. 'Were you taken? Are you hurt? Has somebody got you somewhere?'

I visualise a man breaking into our house. He's sneaking up the stairs. I'm fast asleep in the bedroom and Alice is in the bathroom. He grabs her from behind, placing his hand over her mouth, and drags her along the corridor, down the stairs. Maybe he hits her. Maybe he kills her right here and now, snapping her neck like a dry twig. Then he lugs her lifeless body outside and into the back of a waiting van. He drives off into the darkness.

I know who he is and I know where he's taking her. I know the exact spot.

He drops her body on the wet earth and starts digging, the rain falling relentlessly.

'Alice!' I call out, my eyes springing open. My trousers are wet and I look down to find my glass of Woodford on its side on my lap. 'Shit,' I say, dabbing at a large wet patch. I pull off my trousers and sit back down, something rustling under me as I do so. Reaching behind my back, I pull out a piece of paper.

The letter. I read the words over.

One body. One married couple. One secret.
One very big mistake.

So many fucking mistakes.

I try to breathe deeply, horrified by the dream and the reality to which I've reawakened. Through my cloudy mind comes one thought. *Alice's disappearance and this letter have to be connected. They must be.*

Dizzy, I stagger upstairs and find a fresh pair of trousers. I've consumed far too much to drive, but I must go there; it's drawing me like a magnet.

I get into the car, press the 'start' button and clutch hold of the steering wheel. I need to do this carefully. I shake my head, futilely trying to clear away the fumes of alcohol. The driveway doesn't look straight and I instantly regret my decision.

I drive slowly, but not too slowly that I might draw attention to myself. The whole way, I try to keep my concentration on the road, and it's a struggle.

The twenty-minute journey takes just over half an hour and I'm sweating profusely by the time I get there. I park and I'm about to make my way into the nearest entrance to the woods when I suddenly realise how vulnerable I am. Drunk, or at least half drunk, and without anything to defend myself should I encounter any danger.

I remember there's a jack in the car boot, so I grab it. It's heavy and awkward to carry, and with my balance already impaired my progress is impeded, but it makes me feel safer.

I struggle along the mud paths, amid the trees and bushes. Finally, I stop several metres from the spot. Peering round a tree, I try to see if anyone else is here. I can't see anything in this darkness and the night is silent.

Cautiously, I move forwards and stand upon his grave. Could Alice be here, somewhere? *Could she be down there?* The only sound is the breeze in the cool night's air. I get on my knees, trying to see if the ground has recently been disturbed. It doesn't feel like it. I reach into my pocket for a torch, but I forgot to bring one. So I listen. All I can hear is my heavy breathing.

Now that I'm here, I'm lost again. I'm in the dark in more ways than one. 'Why did you have to come into our lives?' I whisper to the ground. 'You've ruined me.'

I'm not sure who I'm talking to. I don't even care. I smack the jack against the ground and leave it lying upon his grave. 'I hope you rot in hell.'

P

I wake up groggy to the sound of my mobile phone ringing. I answer, 'Yes?' in great anticipation.

I hear sounds but don't take in the initial words. The voice, though, is not Alice's, but it is familiar.

'Yes, you are coming to court today, or yes, you are still ill?'

I realise it's Jenny and steal a glance at my watch.

'What day is it?' I mumble.

'Monday. You said you'd try to be back by today.'

By now, my watch's hands are coming into focus. Twenty to ten.

'Did you say Monday?' *Christ, where did the weekend go?*

'Yes, My Lord, it's Monday.'

'Oh God, sorry Jenny, I've been so ill, you've just woken me. I feel horrendous. So sick. I think it might be some kind of food poisoning. We're going to have to cancel today.'

'By we, you mean me?' She doesn't sound pleased.

'I'm sorry, and please pass on my apologies. I will do everything to be in good health to return tomorrow. I'll try to be in touch by the end of the day to tell you for sure.'

As I'm speaking, there's a noise in the distance. It's familiar, but my swimming head doesn't fully acknowledge it. It quickens my pulse, whatever it is.

Rustling. From the hallway. A light, floating contact, a sliding sound.

Then I realise: something coming through the letterbox.

Hanging up the phone, I drag myself into the hallway. There's an envelope lying next to the front door. This time, I don't pick it up, but rather burst outside. Out of breath, I lean forwards, my hands on my thighs, my neck twisted awkwardly so that I can scan the area while catching my breath.

Not a soul anywhere.

'Who are you?' I say to myself.

Deflated and frustrated, I slam the door. I bend down and pick up the envelope. It's blank, just like the last one. I remove a single sheet of paper and read the words, once again typed text.

I have proof. I know who you killed. And I know what you did with the body.
Both of you.

The words are simple, but the tone is more threatening than the last one. 'Oh God!' I screw it up in desperation and anger. *Who's doing this?*

It's only when I return to the lounge and pick up my phone that I see there's an unread text message. It was sent at 7.30 a.m. by Jenny. *'Haven't heard from Belinda. Will check in with her sister today.'*

I dial the office. Collette answers. 'Collette, it's Paul.'

'Oh gosh, Paul, I've heard all about it. You poor thing, how are you?'

'Awful,' I say bluntly. 'In absolute hell. Now listen, I need you to get the phone number of Belinda's sister. Belinda Adams is . . . was . . . my secretary. Ask Jenny, she'll find it for you. And as soon as you have it, call me back. My number's—'

'I can see your number on the caller ID.'

'Okay, get back to me quickly.'

After Collette calls back with the number, I ring Esther Adams. I've met her once or twice over the years, but beyond a few words shared, I know little about her.

'Esther, this is Paul Reeve. Belinda works for me. We've met a few times.'

There's silence for a moment. Eventually, she says, 'Yes, I remember.' Her voice has a suspicious lilt to it.

'I'm looking for her. She hasn't turned up to work for five days now. We can't reach her.'

'Like I said to your colleague, I haven't seen Belinda and she hasn't told me where she is. I sent her a text message and she responded late last night saying she's fine but nothing else. I'm afraid there's nothing more I can tell you.'

'Well, at least you've heard from her, thank God,' I say, relieved. Then I add, because it feels necessary, 'I guess we can stop worrying then.'

'You were worrying?' she asks sarcastically.

I'm taken aback. 'Of course I was.'

'Yet you waited five days to call me personally.'

I clear my throat. 'I've not been very well. In fact, I'm ill at home as we speak. I'm sorry. If I could handle it differently, I would.'

'Well, like I told your colleague, I'm sure Belinda will be in touch when, or if, she wishes to.'

She cuts off the call before I can say anything else.

Thinking about Belinda makes me realise: she disappeared right before the first letter arrived. She was furious with me. She was threatening. I almost ran her down. What if this is all to get back at me? What if she had been spying on Alice and me? What if she saw us dumping the body? What if she knows what we did? Belinda writing the letter would make sense. She's always been overly friendly. She came on to me.

What if Belinda has somehow got Alice?

It sounds ridiculous, I know, but everything fits. Finding my wife may mean finding Belinda first.

'Collette,' I say before she speaks, 'can you check on Belinda's HR file and see if Esther Adams' address is listed?'

'Where would I find that? Jenny got the phone number for me.'

Electronic copies of all personnel documents are kept on the computer system. I tell Collette how to locate the relevant folder.

'Are you okay, Paul? You sound kind of anxious.'

'Food poisoning,' I tell her. 'It's awful. I'll be fine.'

I hear some clicking and then she says, 'Yes, got it. Esther Adams, sister.'

'And the address, somewhere in Cambridge if I'm not mistaken?'

'Yes.' Collette reads it to me and I write it down.

'Thanks, that's helpful. Look, I'm not feeling any better. I'll confirm by the end of the day, but I suspect we'll have to cancel court tomorrow. I'll let you know, though.'

Cambridge is about an hour and a quarter away and I use the GPS map on my mobile phone to navigate the quickest route. Gloucester Square is just a stone's throw from the city centre. Esther Adams lives in a terraced townhouse in a surprisingly quiet street, given its proximity to the busy centre. I knock on the front door, the majority of which is a very large opaque and colourful window pane. There's no answer. There's a buzzer on the left-hand side, so I hold it down for a few seconds longer than would be viewed as polite by those living inside.

I think about calling Esther Adams' mobile, but I want to catch her off-guard, so I decide my best move would be to wait and surprise her when she returns. I position the Outlander on the opposite side of the road, sit in the driver's seat and wait.

Two hours later, as 1 p.m. approaches, my bladder's uncomfortably full and I'm thinking about finding a loo when I see a figure approaching. When I see she's heading for the house, I spring out of the car and leap across the road. I reach it at the same time as her.

She comes to a sudden stop when she sees me standing in front of her, first alarmed, but then she eyes me with recognition. 'Mr Reeve,' she says, her head cocked to the side.

'Ms Adams,' I reply, relieved, 'I need your help.'

'I've told you everything I know.' She aims a key at the door lock and steps away from me.

'Please, just five minutes.' She hesitates. 'I beg you, I'm worried. Five minutes and then I'll leave. You have my word.'

She nods without looking at me. 'Come in, then.'

'Thank you.'

'Can I get you anything?' she asks as she hangs her coat on a rack and places her handbag on the staircase post.

I scan the corridor and a nearby dining room, whose door is wide open, for any sign of Belinda. Shoes, coat, handbag. 'Thank you but no. I promised I would be out of your hair in five minutes and I intend to keep my word. But I could do with using the loo really quickly if you don't mind.'

'Door under the stairs,' she says.

When I come out, Esther Adams is in the kitchen, which is through a door to the right of the toilet.

'You have a nice home,' I say, hoping to put her at ease.

'I love Cambridge,' she says. 'It's expensive to live here, but it's a lovely house and a great place.' She indicates that I should sit down as she does. 'But when I think of what I could live in if I were to move. Some kind of manor house in the country, a life of luxury, I expect. Still, I couldn't bring myself to sell it.'

I smile.

'Now, why are you here? I thought you said you were ill.'

'I am, but I'm more worried than ill. There's still been no contact from Belinda and since day one we haven't been able to reach her by telephone. We haven't heard a single word from her, but you have. We're worried.' She doesn't say anything but stares at me inquisitively. 'Okay, *I* am,' I concede.

'Aren't you kind of important now? Sounds a bit strange, someone in your position travelling all this way just because a secretary hasn't shown up for work. They're replaceable, aren't they?'

I'm in two minds as to how much to say. Perhaps she'll answer questions just as quickly as she makes statements, so I ask her, 'What has Belinda told you about me?'

'We're close,' she says, 'so take from that what you will.'

I smile awkwardly. Rubbing my temple, I say, 'So you know about her and me?'

'I know everything, Mr Reeve.' The words sound sinister, so I don't tell her to call me Paul. 'She believed you, you know, when you said you wanted to be with her.'

'It wasn't like that. It was a one-time flip comment. I promised her nothing.'

'You don't need to excuse yourself with me. I understand what you were doing. Belinda's young and attractive, very attractive, and . . . incredibly naïve. I told her several times to stop living in fantasyland – I guess I tried to help you in that regard – but she wouldn't see it. She was blinded. You're a powerful man, Mr Reeve, and it seems you have an eye for young ladies and you take advantage of those who aren't headstrong enough to realise what reality is actually in front of them. You want them, you don't want to be with them. They just don't realise it.'

I want to say something in defence of myself, which she can intuit, so she holds up a hand and continues, 'I'm not insulting you and I'm certainly not criticising you. I understand you, so I'm just stating a fact. There are many men like you, you're hardly unique. It comes with power, which comes with position. But Belinda didn't understand you for what you are, as I do. She doesn't understand the baser instincts of men. The last time we spoke she told me what you did and said. I told her not to be surprised. She'd pinned you into a corner and there's only one way out of a predicament like that. You had to fight and hurt her. You were vicious and nasty because you had to scare her off. But she's been hurt by so many men.'

'I need to speak to her.'

'Uh, uh,' she says, shaking her head definitively. 'I don't know where she is, but even if I did I wouldn't tell you. You've caused her enough pain. Now it's time to leave her alone. Find a new secretary. She said she needed time. If she wants to speak to you or see you again, she'll get in touch in the future, but I hope she won't. If she has any sense she won't.'

Here she leans forwards, taps the table. 'Isn't this some kind of blessing in disguise for you, Paul? Aren't you still married? I mean, if she doesn't come back to work and isn't part of your life any longer, you can carry on pretending to your wife that life's just swell. Isn't that grand?'

I don't know how much to tell her, but I can't leave it at that. 'I need to speak to her,' I say again, slowly and clearly. 'It's really important.'

'You told her to get lost and now you're surprised she doesn't want to talk. Give me a break.'

'My wife's gone missing,' I say simply.

She frowns. 'And?'

I can't say anything about the letters. 'And I want to know if Belinda . . .'

'What, that Belinda might have ratted you out? Oh, poor you. You'll have to forgive me if I have no sympathy for you whatsoever. If she's told your wife and your wife's done a runner, that's what you deserve. You've treated Belinda like shit. You're responsible for whatever's happened.'

She's not seeing it. That's not what's happened.

'I was wondering whether Belinda might be . . . with Alice.'

'*With?*' She laughs wildly. 'What are you suggesting?'

'Okay, taken.'

'My little sister? What, you think Belinda has kidnapped your wife? Oh, come on, Paul, don't be so ridiculous. Your wife's more than likely found out about your fling and bolted. I know I would. No, I can assure you, what's happened is this: Belinda has taken herself off because she can't bear the sight of you, not because she's done anything wrong. She's run away before, it's not the first time, always over a man. She never learns. But kidnap? I've never heard anything so preposterous in my life.'

'I know it sounds ridiculous—'

'That's because it is. I'm afraid you're going to have to look a little more closely at yourself to explain this mess, and if your wife is ever stupid enough to come back, well, I suggest you thank your lucky stars and change everything about yourself to stop her from running away again. *If* you're that lucky, that is. Now, you said something about five minutes?'

I can tell I won't get any further with Esther Adams, so I stand up and thank her for seeing me. She shows me to the front door. From the doorstep, I say, 'If you hear from Belinda—'

'I won't,' she says and she closes the door.

I get back in the car, defeated again. Now I'm really anxious. Anxious about what is happening – and will happen – to Alice. Scared, more than anything, for the safety of our unborn child. I cry for my child I believed I would have, the child I once thought I would never have, the child I desperately want to have.

I cry for the child, and for the woman carrying it.

P

As soon as I got back from Cambridge, I ignored the urge to drink and collapsed into bed.

Having an early night has served me well. I've woken up a little before half-past seven, alert but quickly realising I didn't call Jenny to cancel today's court sessions.

I pick up my phone and send her a text message: *Still horribly unwell. Going to the doctor. Please cancel next few days and I'll try to be back by end of week. Give sincere apologies to all.*

This can't go on indefinitely; I know I'll have to return to court soon, regardless of whether Alice turns up or not. I can't keep up this pretence for much longer, and the longer I leave it the more in jeopardy my new job could be.

Coffee, I think. I get up, my phone in hand, and head to the kitchen. As I walk past the front door, my peripheral vision spots something white on the floor.

Another envelope.

My body instinctively slouches, as if I've been punched. No sound today, and I'm up early, so who knows how long it's been lying there.

I don't bother opening the front door. I take the envelope into the kitchen. There, I place my mobile phone on the counter top and open the letter, carefully as usual.

Contained within it, the same as both previous occasions: a folded piece of A4 paper. But there is something on this letter that wasn't on the others. A red smear, as if made by a paintbrush, diagonally across the page, swiped from a higher to lower point. I know what it is instantly, before I've read a word of the typed black ink over which it trails.

Blood.

Say hello to your wife. £100,000 for her safe return.
(And the babies.) Or more blood.
You have 24 hours.

My hands tremble as if I'm neurasthenic and I feel woozy. I'm clutching hold of the piece of paper, but the trembling turns the words into a blur. The only thing that remains distinct is the blood.

My wife's blood. The blood that keeps our baby alive.

I can't help my wife and child. This person, whoever it is, Belinda, whomever, holds all the cards. At a loss, I want to pay, right now, I want to be able to tell them, whoever they are, that I will hand over however much money they want, that they mustn't hurt Alice and they must leave my baby alone. The cash means nothing; they can have it all.

But I can't tell them because all I have is this piece of paper.

I don't calm down for a long time. It takes a seat at the dining-room table and a stiff drink to get close to that point.

The early morning drink makes me think over things more clearly. What if I hand over the money and they don't give Alice and the baby back? There are no guarantees. What then?

Maybe I should negotiate. But how can you negotiate with someone who is a ghost, someone who sees everything but cannot be seen at all?

As my mind swims in circles, I'm startled by the vibration of my mobile phone. I pick it up, not paying attention to the caller ID. 'Alice?' I say hopelessly.

'Paul, are you okay?' It's Jenny. When I don't answer, and I'm certain all she can hear is me choking back tears, she says again, 'Paul, are you all right? I'm really worried about you. Is everything okay?'

I want to be convincing, but I really don't know how to be any more. I can't lie. My ability has been diminished. 'It's awful,' I manage to say. 'I just can't. I'm sorry.'

'Paul . . .'

'I need more time. I'll be okay. Please just hang in there for me.'

'I will. Paul, can I help you?'

'I'm going to the doctor today. Things will be okay.'

I end the call and scream. My eyes are closed, but when I open them the words on the letter slowly come into focus. *Those words.*

I zoom in. '*And the babies*,' I read, curiously.

I reach forwards, suddenly enlivened and pulling the letter closer to my eyes. '*And the babies*,' I read aloud again. 'And the fucking babies. *Babies*.' I turn in a circle and look all around me. 'The bitch.'

One of Belinda's habits – or flaws, as I saw it – was her grammar. Her errors were daily. Most of these were because of her confusion about the apostrophe. She often mistakenly used a plural noun when an apostrophe was needed to show possession.

So it has to be her.

Now I know what I have to do. I don't want to do it because I understand the danger it will bring into my life, but I cannot find Belinda alone, and her sister won't help me, even though I think she may know where Belinda is.

I'll have to be careful, and if I get caught out, I'll have to lie better than I've ever lied in my whole life.

This is a kidnapping. And I know who the kidnapper is.

I go to the shelf in the kitchen from which I pick up a business card. I stare at the name on it. I have no choice.

Detective Sergeant Katherine Wright.

12

Detective Sergeant Katherine Wright picked up Paul Reeve's voicemail near the end of the day. His words were fairly cryptic, asking for help, saying he was struggling, something about his wife, something about his fears. But the word *kidnapping* couldn't have been clearer.

The following morning, she stood at his front door and knocked.

He opened it very quickly. 'Thank you for coming so soon,' he said, a mixture of urgency and relief in his voice. 'Come in.'

She took a seat on the armchair, while he sat on the sofa. 'What can I do for you?'

Paul Reeve clasped his hands together. 'My wife has gone missing.'

'Quantify *gone missing*.'

He sighed. 'I haven't seen her, or heard from her, in a week. I have absolutely no idea where she is. One moment she was here, and we were happy, then when I got back from work she was gone without a trace. Her car's outside and hasn't moved. She's not answering her mobile. The first couple of times I called, her voicemail kicked in. Now it just rings and rings and cuts off. I've called everyone we know and they all say they haven't heard from her. I have no reason to doubt them.'

'Why did you call me?'

'You're a face and name I know, and I'm in the dark. It was all I could think to do. I'm scared, Detective, scared for my wife and the baby she's carrying.'

'She's pregnant?'

He nodded his head.

'You didn't tell me that when we last spoke.'

'That's because I didn't know then.'

'Her illness.'

'The sickness part, yes. But I was telling you the truth. My wife hasn't been well, she has some kind of depression, too. Now I feel completely and utterly helpless, and for someone in my line of work that's a very scary and unusual predicament to be in. I called you because I need your help. I can't find Alice alone, so I need you to help me find her.'

'There are protocols I should follow in missing persons cases, Mr Reeve. I'm sure you know that.'

'There's more,' he said urgently, sensing that Wright was going to pass him on to an anonymous task force assigned to missing persons and wash her hands of his request.

She cocked her head. 'Yes?'

He stood up and went over to the mantelpiece above the fireplace, retrieving a sheet of paper. 'I received this letter,' he said, stepping back and handing it to her. She took it from him.

'When did you get this?'

'Yesterday morning. I was trying to deal with this on my own, but the letter made me realise I had no option but to seek help. That's why I called you.'

'How did you receive it?'

'Someone put it through the letterbox. It was there when I woke up.'

'What time was that?'

'About half seven.'

'And you didn't hear anything or see anyone?'

'No, nothing.'

He wouldn't reveal the rustling sound of previous letter drops. In fact, he wouldn't mention the other letters at all – they contained incriminating evidence. Receiving today's letter had to be an isolated occurrence.

More lies were necessary.

'Do you have any idea who might have written this?'

He stretched his shoulders. 'Actually, yes.' Here was where a little truth was required. He knew he would make himself look like a scumbag by speaking honestly about his relationship with Belinda, but it was a price he was willing to pay if it meant that Alice would be returned to him, that is if Belinda was holding Alice against her will.

'My secretary, who has also recently disappeared. Well, her sister says she's gone off for some alone time. But she's a secretary who recently got angry with me. The thing is, she and I had a short affair and she disappeared after I told her in no uncertain terms it was over. But you need to know I love my wife, she's my whole life. I'm a stupid idiot, I know, for getting involved with someone so young. But it happened and I can't change that. The last time I saw her,

I upset her when I said I wouldn't leave Alice and she got angry with me. I think she threatened me.

'You think?' Wright looked unimpressed.

'I've been drinking rather too much recently, trying to deal with all the . . . pressure. Alice's illness. The booze has skewed my memory.' He added reassuringly, 'I've stopped now. I won't touch a drop again, I swear, but she was certainly angry enough to retaliate, I think.'

'So this woman, who may or may not have threatened you, may or may not have kidnapped your wife, is that what you're saying?' The tone of Wright's voice suggested she wasn't convinced.

'Okay, so there was that last argument we had, but look.' He stepped towards Wright and placed his finger on the word 'babies' that was written in the letter. 'The misused plural. Not using an apostrophe but instead using a plural noun. It was a common error of Belinda's.' He let out a constrained laugh. 'It's all I have and it might seem like I'm stretching it, but with everything else it makes perfect sense to me. Belinda has Alice. She must have her. Help me find Belinda and I think we'll find Alice.'

'It sounds very far-fetched to me,' Wright said. 'Or at least you have no concrete evidence, nothing more than a gut instinct and a common grammatical error.' She could see that he was about to plead with her. Sighing, she held out her hand and said, 'You mentioned that Belinda has a sister?'

'Yes.'

'How do I get hold of her?' Paul told Wright her phone number and address in Cambridge. 'I can drop her a line. I'll see if it gets me anywhere, but I can't promise anything.'

Paul stepped awkwardly close to her. 'Thank you,' he said.

'It'll probably lead nowhere, so don't get your hopes up,' she said. 'If I don't get anywhere in the next twenty-four hours or so, you'll have to lodge an official missing persons report. Like I said, I'm supposed to follow procedures.'

Relieved, he smiled, but he knew there wasn't much time left and was worried. He had to find Alice and Belinda soon.

'Why didn't you report your wife missing sooner?'

'I foolishly thought I could handle this myself.'

'Yes,' she said, 'foolish.'

'No more secrets,' he said.

'There'd better not be.'

'You have my word, Detective. And please give me yours – please, keep me updated.'

'I will.'

He realised that by revealing the truth about his relationship with Belinda he'd put himself – and potentially Alice – in danger. But it was the only option he saw. He was banking on Wright keeping in contact with him and he hoped she'd lead him to Belinda. He needed to talk to her as soon as she was located; he was sure he could convince her to keep quiet, but more importantly he needed to find his wife.

Paul assumed silencing her, and getting Alice back, would require money, lots of it, but he was prepared to pay all that was necessary.

He was prepared to do anything. But he'd set in motion Detective Wright's involvement and there was nothing he could do about that now, other than try to use it to his advantage. And hopefully reach Belinda – and Alice – before Wright could learn more than she needed to know.

P

'Is there any news?' I ask Detective Sergeant Wright, even though she only left me two hours ago. I hope I come across as a husband desperately eager to track down his wife, not as someone desperately eager to keep a secret.

'I've just arrived in Cambridge,' she says through a sigh. 'Look, Mr Reeve, you need to give me space to work if I'm to use the time wisely. Twenty-four hours will go by very quickly, believe me. I meant it when I said I'll call you if something comes up. Just keep your phone close to you and be patient.'

I apologise and urge her to keep in touch, even though I'm already worrying I've involved the police too quickly.

Perhaps I should be in Cambridge or close by, just in case. My indecisiveness is frustrating, so I decide to be impulsive. I pack a bag and lock up the house. As I'm walking towards the Outlander, I can see something white on the windscreen, held in place by the windscreen wiper. I narrow my eyes.

It's an envelope. I remove it, scanning all around me. As usual, I don't see anyone, but I wonder whether there's someone nearby who can see me. Perhaps Belinda is hiding.

I open it. Lines of typed bold text.

£100,000 in a bag. Deposit in bin behind public toilets next to lake. St Albans park.
5 p.m. TODAY.

My instinctive response is to call Detective Wright, but then I remember where she is. But thinking about it, this could actually allay my concerns; I have the chance to get Alice back, while hopefully locating Belinda, while Detective Wright is out of the way. There couldn't be a better time for all this to end.

Maybe it will end today.

I drive into London to a safety deposit box I keep in Finchley Road. Aside from investing in property, I keep a lot of my wealth in cash in boxes like this one, most of them in London. I'm paranoid about keeping all my wealth tied up in bank accounts. Besides, I obtained some of my wealth without paying the required tax, so it's safer to hide it in places like this.

I remove the exact amount demanded in the ransom note, £100,000, and return the box to its slot. Then I rush back to St Albans. I have about an hour to spare before making the ransom drop, so I decide to position myself early.

After parking, I pull out my phone. I have a missed call from Detective Wright. For a moment, I consider returning her call, but I decide not to. There may be no more cause for her involvement in just over an hour's time. Calling her back can wait until I know more.

I cross the small bridge and enter the lake area. The bin is on the left side, behind a concrete block of public toilets. It's an old wooden bin with curved and damaged side beams and I see why it's been chosen: it's concealed by the building on one side and a row of bushes on the other.

I sit on a bench about three quarters of the way around the lake. It's not far from the toilets and even though the bin is out of view I can see the approach to where it is; anyone heading towards it will be visible.

No one goes near the bin, from what I can make out, during the time I'm waiting for 5 p.m. to arrive. When the time comes, I move towards the bin, the bag in my right hand. My plan is to deposit it in the bin, keep walking without looking back, cross the bridge and then find a way back over the river while remaining out of view.

After casually dropping the bag in it and crossing the bridge, I double back on myself, dropping down the river bank. The water looks only ankle deep, and there are lots of large pebbles on the river basin.

I take a large step off the bank and into the water. Rushing to get through it as fast as possible, I slip on the pebbles, landing on my knees and falling forwards. My knee scrapes along the basin, my trousers tearing. I wince in pain.

Dragging my injured leg, I pull myself to the other side. Soaked, I catch my breath on the bank. As I rise, I see I've become a spectacle, with onlookers staring at my rather ludicrous attempt to cross the river.

Regardless, I rush up the bank, dropping shortly before I reach the top and lie on my stomach, peering over the hill's peak. From here, I have a view of the bin. I hope I haven't missed anything.

I scan every person who's within reasonable distance of it. Nobody looks suspect. As I wait, no one approaches. The lower half of my body is uncomfortable, but I'm determined to wait this out. I try to check the time on my watch, but the screen is cracked and its hands aren't moving. Worried my phone might also be damaged, I grab it from my trouser pocket. It's working, but I have another missed call from Detective Wright. 'Shit,' I say to myself.

I try to block Detective Wright from my mind and refocus. Belinda, or whoever it is, has got to be here somewhere. I try to visualise her in a disguise of some kind. A hat perhaps, a head scarf, sunglasses, or maybe she's dyed her hair or cut it short.

I start zooming in on faces, hoping to spot a single feature that reminds me of her, and when I have no success I start to feel desperate. 'Come on,' I whisper. 'You've got to be here somewhere. Where are you? It has to be you.'

After another fifteen minutes pass, doubts start to fill my mind. *What if I'm wrong? What if it's not Belinda and I've been searching for the wrong person and have missed the real person? What if someone's made it to the bin and nabbed the cash?*

I don't know how much longer to wait; I feel like I'm wasting my time. Lying here soaking wet, I feel like a prize fool.

Suddenly, I see someone, a male, approaching the bin, and then lurking by it. I'm sure he takes a quick glance inside it, and then he's moving his head round in a semi-circle, scanning the area. He doesn't go right up to the bin, but he's near it for several minutes, shuffling around, and then he gradually moves closer to it. Then he makes a fast move: he spins round, ducks his head low into his shoulders and leans over the bin.

Without thinking, I scramble to my feet and run down the other side of hill. I charge through the bushes, scratching my legs but without losing momentum. I'm metres away and he's still there, his head dipped low, his shoulders hunched over. I reach out and grab him by the scruff of the neck, pulling him backwards. He spins round, alarmed, giving off a pathetic whine, and I find I'm facing a kid, perhaps fourteen years old, a cigarette in his mouth. His lips open wide, the cigarette drops to the ground.

The bag is still in the bin. Realising I've interrupted a kid having a sneaky fag, I say as intently as I can, 'No smoking at your age,' and push him aside. Reaching into the bin, I grab the bag and take it back to my car, angered at the waste of time this has turned out to be.

Perhaps that was the point all along. An attempt to torture me, playing tricks on my mind. *Here, have your wife and child back. Actually, no, I've changed my mind, you can't.* I can only imagine what the next letter will say.

I drive home, utterly dejected. I thought I had worked it out. I thought I'd be able to pay Belinda, or reason with her, or scare her, and get Alice back and then we'd be able to get on with our life. I was wrong.

As I pull into the driveway, my phone rings. Detective Wright is calling again. 'Goddamn it.' I can't answer it. I have no excuses to explain why I've been unavailable all day and my ability to lie seems to lie far off.

I press 'ignore'. I merely want to pick up a bottle and drown my sorrows again. It's the only source of comfort I have. Lose all consciousness of what has become my life. I laugh, wistfully. How things were different so recently. How life was great. Then that first lie and the others that followed. Too many lies and everything crumbled.

As I step into the house and take off my sodden shoes, I see how filthy my trousers are. Before I drink myself into oblivion, I want to clean myself of the remnants of my time in the park. As I approach the bathroom, I stare at the door. *I want to experience it. I want to feel her right now. I want to feel what she felt.*

I want to understand *her.*

This godforsaken room. I enter it and start filling the bath with water, like she did. I stand over it, staring at its enamel shell, unable to deny my own stupidity and misery.

When the bath is half filled, I pour in some bubble bath. Standing still as the monotonous sound of water fills the room, I look at the bath and its surroundings, now so clear of blood. The bathtub, the tiles, the shower curtain. All of it covered in blood only months ago, now the memory of that night the only thing that connects me with that time. Yet it's a memory that's impossible to erase.

I'm staring at the bath and shower curtain. Steam fills the air. The sound of the water trickling into the bath. I'm preparing to wash. There's music in the background. It dulls out all other sounds. He sneaks in, emerging through the steam, the shower curtain drawn. He pulls it aside and then sharp, piercing heat ripples through him as the blade is thrust into his neck again and again and again, his body collapsing into the bath.

As my imagination relives the part of the night I didn't experience, the warmth of two hands presses onto my shoulder blades. I think, *He's here, he's returned, he's come for me,* but then I realise that's impossible, he's dead. My heart skipping a beat, I turn around, bracing myself for the worst, but instead I'm met by a familiar face.

Alice.

She takes my hands in her hands and says softly, 'You came to make the drop, you wanted me back.' Then she brings her lips to mine, delicately.

I want to speak, but the words don't come. I'm stunned.

She can read my mind. She understands I want to know why.

When she draws back, she says, 'I had to know whether you really wanted me back. Whether you loved me. I had to know you deserved to be my baby's father. Above all, I had to be sure we meant more to you than your secretary.'

'You do,' I manage to say, but that's all I can manage.

'You wouldn't want the bath to overflow,' she says casually. 'Perhaps you ought to turn off the tap.'

A

Paul didn't want to be parents for the first five years of our marriage. His career was the most important thing to him and, rightly or wrongly, I chose to support him.

Things changed on our fifth wedding anniversary. We were in Paris to celebrate, staying at a beautiful five-star hotel; Paul's career was booming. On the second night, we had dinner at the Eiffel Tower, he made a toast, to a future of success and one blessed with children. We went back to our hotel, the Grand Hôtel du Palais Royal, a stunning place on Rue de Valois, where we made love. And it really was making love; every gesture, every kiss, every movement was filled with care and attention and tenderness. He loved me deeply and I loved him. Perhaps it was our intense love that convinced us a child would be a natural result.

Therefore, nothing could protect me from the shock when weeks later I took a pregnancy test, with Paul sitting expectantly on the bed, and we received a single blue line, a negative reading. Having to walk out of the bathroom and stand in front of Paul, whose smile was wall to wall, and tell him no, it hasn't worked, we're not pregnant, was one of the hardest things I've ever done. He was crushed, he couldn't conceal his disappointment. He said the right words, that it didn't matter, that we still had time, but I could see the truth in his eyes. He was hurt.

I felt like I'd let him down, or at the very least like I'd done something to cause us to fail. In my eyes, it was a failure. We had – or *I* had – failed to do something that was completely natural. Women were supposed to get pregnant.

That's what my mother told me when I tried to get comfort from her. She blamed me, blamed us, and I haven't been able to forgive her since. My father, too cowardly to stand up to her and protect me, just nodded along as she ranted about the sanctity of marriage and what only *true love* can deliver, at a time when I just wanted her to hug me. And Paul, frustrated because we couldn't conceive, didn't hold back his opinions about them.

He whispered in my ear and I haven't seen them since.

We tried repeatedly for the next three years, disappointment every time. And then, finally, my eyes were lit up by a blue cross that confirmed it had actually happened. I had fallen pregnant. We were both delighted; I've never seen Paul happier. Each test, for three years, he'd sat on the bed, waiting, hopeful, defeated each time.

We were only allowed to share the joy for two short months, though, when at a scan the midwife discovered an ectopic pregnancy. I still remember her words. 'I'm afraid there's no option but to terminate.' Our hearts sank. I was crushed, I fell in on myself, and so did Paul, the light that made us shine extinguished and so suddenly and without warning.

We didn't try to conceive again for the rest of that year. The pain wasn't something I could overcome. Paul wanted to keep trying, but I couldn't do it, and I know I frustrated him. But it was my body and he couldn't possibly understand what it was like to know someone was growing inside you, only to be told that little person was going to be taken away.

I don't remember the conversation we had that led to us eventually trying again, but over a year and a half, I managed to get pregnant on two further occasions, each time with the same result: ectopic pregnancy, no choice but to terminate.

It wasn't going to happen for us, we both reluctantly acknowledged.

IVF was an option, but Paul wasn't keen. Adoption too. He wanted the child to be *his own*, whatever that meant. Over time, conversations about children dried up, and then children, we decided independently of one another, wouldn't happen for us.

So when I discovered I was pregnant, our baby conceived while we were in New York, I was delighted, shocked and, if I'm honest, scared. I discovered early on that the pregnancy wasn't ectopic, but I found the prospect of telling Paul about the conception worrying. Day after day, thinking about what we'd done, the man I'd killed and the body we'd hidden, I struggled to open up to him. Morning sickness started playing havoc with me. And then when I found out Paul was having an affair, that was it.

He told that detective I was unstable. When I overheard their conversation, rarely have I been madder. And the day he pushed me and I fell, at that moment, I was petrified for my baby's life. I thought for a time that I could do it alone. But after a night's sleep, during which I dreamed about our earlier years together, the happiness, how we both wanted a child, I changed my mind. I couldn't press charges. Paul had wanted to be a father for a decade and I couldn't deny him that.

As it turns out, he found out about the pregnancy from the doctor at the hospital, but I could see the delight in his eyes when I returned home. I believed the things he told me, the promises he made, that he was desperate to take care of us, that he loved me.

But . . . then I saw the text message he sent last week. That changed everything. It brought home exactly what he had been doing. I'd seen them at the hotel, but the message showed it was much more than that.

The words are etched in my memory: *Belinda, please, no more. We've had a lovely time, but that's all it can ever be. I'm your boss, you're my employee. It was fun, but let's leave it at that. Please don't text me any more. I had to leave work because I came down ill, but I'll see you properly when I'm back in.*

No, he didn't deserve this child.

So he had to prove how much he wanted it. He would have to win me, and our baby, back.

I decided we'd play a game, with my rules. He'd have to convince me to return to him. If he took one wrong step, that would be it, he'd never hear from me again.

He had only one chance.

He's passed the first part, but that's not the end. Now the game will get interesting.

A

I've encouraged Paul into the bath and he's sitting there, peering up at me like a puppy, as I'm perched on its edge.

'Alice, are you sure you're okay?'

'Never been better,' I say chirpily.

'I'm sorry,' he says.

'I think you are.' I pick up a bottle of body wash and a sponge. I squeeze the bottle and let the liquid drizzle along Paul's chest. I start stroking his body with the sponge. 'Did you know that when you went to the Waldorf, I was there?' His eyes answer me. 'I came to meet you. I foolishly wanted to be with my husband. You didn't see me, but I saw you, and the way you walked holding her was not the way a man normally walks with his secretary. I don't want denials and I don't want confessions. *I know everything.*'

'I've been so fucking stupid.'

'You used her, Paul. You used me, too.'

He sits up. 'God, I'm sorry. I need you, Alice. You're my life.'

I smile and nod. 'You've taken the first step in proving that. But there's still one more step to take. A very big step.

You're going to have to prove it to your ill wife. Isn't that what you said about me to Detective Wright?'

'I just needed an excuse to get her to back off. I was trying to get her to feel sorry for me.' There's panic in his voice.

'But not for me.'

'I've been a selfish bastard. I'm sorry.'

'I'm scared, Paul.'

'Scared of what?'

'Scared you're lying to me again. That you'll give in to her if she comes back.'

He grips the sides of the bath. 'I won't. You have my word.'

'Your word hasn't meant very much for a long time.'

'I mean it this time,' he says slowly. 'Besides, she won't come back.'

'How do you know?'

'Trust me, I know.'

'How do you know?'

'I just know.'

'Man's intuition?' I laugh.

'She definitely won't be back.'

'There's only one way to know *definitely*.'

'What do you mean?'

'I need you to be certain.'

'Alice—'

I lean forwards and whisper, 'I want you to kill her.'

13

Detective Sergeant Katherine Wright knocked on the front door. She was frustrated that she hadn't been able to reach Paul Reeve by telephone.

When there wasn't an answer, she knocked a further three times, progressively louder, believing he was in because his car was in the driveway.

He eventually opened the door, a dressing gown wrapped around his body, which was dripping wet. He looked flustered. 'Oh, Detective. I'm sorry.' He stepped aside, stumbling awkwardly, and said, 'Come in. Let me dry myself properly. I was in the shower. Take a seat in the kitchen and I'll be a couple of minutes.' He watched her go into the kitchen and, as he was about to return upstairs, he caught sight of Alice's jacket on the coatrack. Her beige jacket. He thought back: had he said she was wearing it when he first called Wright to ask for her help?

He couldn't remember. He hoped Wright hadn't seen it. Snatching it off the rack, he quickly took it with him upstairs.

When he entered the bedroom, Alice appeared from behind the door and said, 'What's she doing here?'

'She's been calling me all day and . . .' He drifted, was thinking.

'And what?' she snapped in a whisper.

'And I ignored her, all right. Your damn ransom drop distracted me.'

'Why is she here? Why are you even in touch with her?'

He pushed the bedroom door shut, dropped her jacket on the bed and spun round towards her. 'Because I thought you'd been kidnapped and no matter what I tried, I couldn't get anywhere in finding you. I called her when I felt I had no alternative. There was no choice.'

'Oh, you had a choice, Paul, and you made a very bad one.'

'I know that now.' He was thinking. 'If you hadn't run away . . .'

Alice shook her head. 'Don't you dare. Look, this needn't be a problem. Just remain calm, speak to her and find a way to get her out of here quickly, and we'll work it out afterwards. She thinks I've disappeared. As far as she should be concerned when she leaves here today, I'm still missing. Do you get that? Don't tell her I've come back. Nothing has changed since you last spoke to her. Is that clear?'

'I understand,' he snapped, 'but it's just another lie to keep up with.'

She grabbed his dressing gown sleeve. 'We still have a lot to do and can't let her ruin things. Hear her out, act concerned, and watch her leave. We're going to have a baby, remember. You, a father. That can still happen. Getting rid of her is just an extra step in that journey. If she asks, tell her you have no idea where I am and then let her go on wasting time looking for me. I'll reappear eventually with a straightforward explanation, pre-natal depression perhaps, but only when it's convenient to us. Everything will work out fine, you need to hold it together.'

He went back downstairs and was suddenly struck by the scent of perfume. Was it from where he'd come or was it where he was going? It was the smell of Alice, it had returned to the house.

He glanced into the kitchen. Did Detective Wright look like she suspected something? Had she noticed? He wasn't sure.

He entered and offered her a drink, which she declined, so he sat opposite her at the kitchen table. He couldn't recognise a glint of suspicion in her eyes.

'I met with Esther Adams,' she began. 'Since you went to see her, she hasn't been able to get hold of her sister. That's within twenty-four hours. She says that's really out of character, that they're very close, and even though Belinda has done a disappearing act before she always kept in phone contact. She's especially worried as the last couple of times she's tried calling, the phone has been switched off and she says that's never happened before. Have you heard from her?'

'Not at all. But when I saw Esther Adams she wasn't worried about her sister at all. What, you turn up and suddenly she's singing a different tune? She told me Belinda is an adult and will decide when to come and when to go.'

'She's changed her mind, then.'

'I only saw her on Monday. That isn't exactly long.'

'How long before you started worrying about Alice when you couldn't find her?'

'Instantly.' He held up a hand. 'Okay, point taken.'

'And speaking of your wife, have you heard from her?'

There was a slight hesitation. 'No.'

'And you have no idea where either of them is?'

'I called you for help, remember.' She frowned. 'Sorry, that came out all wrong. It's just so frustrating, this not knowing. No, I don't have a clue.' Then he added, 'And I am really worried.'

'Do you still think they're together, that Alice has been taken against her will?'

'Well, the letter, you've seen the letter.'

'Esther Adams said the last time they spoke, Belinda told her you tried to run her over with your car.'

Paul Reeve rubbed his face with his hand and looked pained. A gust of air escaped his mouth involuntarily. He didn't know whether to lie or tell the truth, but he couldn't conceal his shock. He didn't want to incriminate himself; he wanted Wright out of the way and, besides, he had nothing to do with Belinda's disappearance, if indeed that was what it was. Yes, one small act of stupidity with the car, but he had stopped himself and merely scared her; he would never have actually hit her, he thought.

'That's, um, a bit of an exaggeration,' he finally said. 'She stood in my way as I was coming down the driveway. I stopped and then I drove around her when she wouldn't move. She was here threatening me, she was furious, and I told her to get lost.'

'Why was she angry?'

'She had this fantasy that I would leave my wife for her. She said she would tell Alice about us.'

'That could be considered a good motive for getting rid of someone, couldn't it? I mean, if it was presented in a court of law.'

'That's not what happened. I know how it sounds, but I've done nothing to Belinda. I can't even find my wife, for God's sake. I called you to help me, not accuse me.'

'Precisely.' A creaking sound from upstairs. She paused. 'According to Esther Adams, Belinda told her she was in love with you.'

'In love? That's ridiculous. I was her rebound – did Esther Adams tell you that?' Wright remained silent. Paul scoffed, 'She was not in love with me. She wanted to make herself feel better after her boyfriend tossed her aside. She probably just saw my wealth and position and thought they were appealing.'

'That would suggest she was very materialistic.'

'Is there anything else a young woman can be?' He forced his eyes together, realising how wrong that was. 'I'm sorry, I shouldn't have said that. It's the pressure. I'm finding this all really difficult to deal with.'

'Of course,' she said, the tone of her voice lifting, 'your wealth.'

'What do you mean?'

'Do you have a pre-nuptial agreement with your wife, Mr Reeve?'

'No,' he said, involuntarily.

'Why not?'

'We love each other. That's a ridiculous question.' Then more forcefully, 'I didn't need to call you, but I did. Please don't ever forget that. If I was involved in the disappearance of either of them, I'd be mad to have called you. I strongly believe that if you find Belinda you'll find Alice. That's what I'm asking for your help with, nothing else.'

'I understand that.'

'I have done nothing wrong, other than cheat on the woman who means everything to me. Please make this about her.' He paused. 'My wife needs your help.'

'I'll give you one more day. In twenty-four hours, I want you to officially log a missing persons enquiry about Alice. You'll have had forty-eight hours of my time.' She stood up. 'But that is all.'

'Thank you,' he said.

As they walked towards the front door, Paul saw a pair of Alice's shoes on top of the shoe cupboard. They were muddy and the mud looked fresh. His gaze froze on them.

Wright added, 'And Paul?'

'Yes,' he said, quickly shifting his attention away from the shoes.

She faced him from the doorway. He thought he saw her quickly glimpse towards the top of the staircase. 'Keep your phone on you at all times.'

P

I remain facing the front door for some time. It's only when I hear Alice calling me from upstairs that I snap out of it. Although she showed no sign of seeing them, I'm worried that Detective Wright might have spotted Alice's jacket or shoes. And whether she smelt a woman's perfume other than her own. She definitely heard the noise Alice made upstairs.

This is too much. I'm struggling to keep up with all the lies. So many lies, and where are they getting me?

Alice calls out again.

'I'm coming!' I respond, glancing hopefully at the shoes. I decide not to mention it to Alice.

'And?' she asks when I get back upstairs.

I can't look at her. What she's suggested . . . 'You made a bloody noise. I think she heard it. Oh, and she seems to think I've got something to do with both of you disappearing. It would have been easier to tell her the truth. Now God knows what she thinks about me.'

'I'll turn up soon.'

'And that's not all. It seems that Belinda has actually gone missing.'

'You had nothing to do with that, did you?'

I want you to kill her. It's pure madness. The thought sickens me.

'Why does that not worry you?' I snap. 'You turn up now and she might think I got rid of Belinda.'

She frowns at me, questioningly. 'Did you have anything to do with it?'

'No, nothing at all.'

'Then I'd hardly call it a disappearance and we needn't be worried. She's probably off somewhere licking her wounds. After you almost ran her down, and given your text message, I'd hardly call you her favourite person. But I know women, Paul, and there's none easier to manipulate than a needy woman. That's what she sounds like to me.'

'She's just young and naïve.'

'Do what I say and she'll come running back.'

'I don't want her to come running back.'

'I haven't changed my mind, Paul, and I won't. She *will* come back. She has to, because you still have one last hurdle to jump to prove yourself.'

I walk into the en suite. I don't want to be with her right now. Even though I've just bathed, I feel dirty. I jump into the shower and put my head under its powerful stream. 'Can I?' I ask myself, squeezing my eyes shut.

'Of course you can.' Two arms wrap around my body from behind and I feel Alice's naked skin press against my back. 'You can do *anything* if you put your mind to it.'

A

'Here's how it has to be done. You're going to send her a message and in it you're going to invite her for a meal. *Here*. I'm missing, remember, so you'll have the house all to yourself. You regret what you said, you've changed your mind, blah, blah, blah. Maybe I won't come back. Maybe it's time for you to start a new life. You'll wine and dine her, and then with it all going swimmingly, you'll kill her.'

I can see his Adam's apple move up and down as he swallows deeply. 'How exactly?'

'You're going to bring her up here, celebrate the reunion properly and get into bed. And it's while you're in bed that you're going to strangle her.'

I walk towards the built-in wardrobes. With my back to him, I say, 'And I'm going to be in here, *watching*.' Then I turn around and stare at him. 'Prove to me we're more important to you than she is.'

'You are,' he says, shaking his head, 'but, Alice, I can't do that, you know I can't.'

'If you want to be a father, you will.'

'But—'

'This special place, this bed, where we tried so many times, unsuccessfully, to conceive a child that I could carry to term. Now it's the place that's going to make you a father forever.'

He tries, 'And how do you propose I get her here? I haven't been able to reach her. I don't even know where she is.'

'Where's your phone?'

He hands it to me.

I take it from him and type the right words. Handing it back to him, I say, 'Send it to her.'

'That easy?'

I nod. 'That easy.'

He takes the phone from me and reads what I've written. Then he stares at the screen. I see hesitation in his eyes, but I don't need to say anything else. After a few moments, he looks from the screen to me and, without looking back, he presses 'send'. Our eyes lock.

'Has this been your plan all along?' he asks.

'Not *all* along.' I may be smiling.

'You manipulated me?'

'How so?'

'*One hundred thousand pounds for her safe return. And the babies.*'

'Oh, you mean the reluctant apostrophe. Well done for spotting it. I wasn't convinced you would.' After a pause, I add, 'I just used what you told me, Paul.'

'You tricked me.'

'You complained about her writing a lot. It just seemed appropriate.'

'Her disappearing has complicated things a bit.'

'Don't worry,' I say, 'it may actually help us. After all, if she's already missing, she won't be unexpectedly missed when she's dead.'

'If she falls for the message.'

'Oh, I think we'll hear from her soon. Very soon.'

14

Detective Constable Ryan Hillier stood in the conference side room, off the main incident room. The blinds were open, permitting the day's dismal light to enter.

Hillier had divided the conference desk into three sections, displaying within each a range of documents and photographs. A laptop was on the table next to where he stood, the screensaver with the force's insignia on display.

On the far side of the room was the portable whiteboard with points of similarity listed on it. Written on the board in capitalised black ink were the words METHOD, PROFESSION and UNIVERSITY. Under each, in smaller writing, further details were presented, and stuck on the board were ten-by-eight colour photographs of each murder scene. At the top of the board was the suspect's headshot, the only one they'd managed to obtain, from his army days, with the name ALEXANDER PAVLIK written underneath it.

Hillier was checking for anything he may have missed, while his colleagues continued sifting through new files and information as it came in. He was designating sheets of paper from a large pile to appropriate places on the desk.

Anything he deemed unhelpful was piled on one of the leather wheelie chairs.

A woman with curly brown hair poked her head in. 'More files,' she said.

'Thanks, Steph.'

She placed them on a small side table that was next to the door and left.

Hillier's neck hurt and he was tired. He was fed up of all the trawling and feeling like he wasn't getting anywhere. Still, he'd been a detective long enough to know that patience was the main characteristic needed for someone in his job. That, and the ability to survive without much sleep.

The answers are here somewhere, he thought, or hoped.

He continued scanning the pages in his hand, deciding where each sheet belonged. One he was looking through was a log of emails sent and received, listed with email title and recipient, which had been taken from Simon Michael Ryman's personal computer. Its encryption software had resulted in a delay in retrieving it.

An email title caught Hillier's attention: *Letter of application*. He picked up the phone and asked the computer team to forward him the complete email. It arrived almost immediately and he opened it on the laptop.

He read the letter and his attention was drawn to lines about the major challenge of the role and how, despite his relative youth, he believed he had the experience to be effective in the job. He called his potential acceptance for the role *historic*, his enthusiasm for the opportunity palpable.

Hillier recalled the conversation he'd had with Karen Dollard, Richard Dollard's sister, about his excitement over a ground-breaking job opportunity. A major step up, a big challenge, something that hadn't ever happened before.

He located his notes from that meeting and scanned through them. 'No,' he said. 'No.' He put his finger on Karen Dollard's phone number, which was written at the top of the sheet, and keyed it into his mobile phone.

He apologised for interrupting her day.

'Not at all. Happy to help.'

'You mentioned your brother was excited about a job opportunity, something he'd described to you as a major step.'

'What about it?'

'Do you know what the job was?'

'Absolutely,' she said, and she told him the job title. The acceleration of adrenaline inside him was automatic. 'And I can go one better than that. I can tell you the name of the person who was responsible for setting up the job interviews.'

His ears ringing, he thanked her and hung up. 'Jesus,' he mouthed, looking at the name Karen Dollard had just told him on his computer screen; the recipient of Simon Michael Ryman's email.

He started to scan through the email log taken from Ethan Fleming's account for the name Alma Patrick, but he couldn't locate it. 'Sod this,' he said, and he quickly googled her place of work. He dialled the number he found and asked to be put through to her.

'HR, Alma Patrick,' she answered.

Hillier introduced himself and explained he was working on an active murder investigation, hopeful that she could

– and would be willing to – help him. He told her the vacancy for which both Richard Dollard and Simon Michael Ryman had applied and asked, 'Did someone by the name of Ethan Fleming also apply?'

She said she was happy to help, but that she'd need some time to search the application records. Hillier held for what felt like a lifetime, but eventually Alma Patrick returned, apologetically. 'Yes, he did,' she said chirpily.

'I don't suppose I could get a complete list of who applied for the position?' he asked.

'To go that far, I'm afraid you'd need a warrant because of data protection laws.'

Of course, he already knew this, but his eagerness to speed things along had made him ask. 'I'll get one. In the meantime, if you could prep it for me, I'd appreciate it. I'll be in touch very soon,' he said and thanked her.

He walked over to the whiteboard, drew arrows from PROFESSION under each victim's name towards the space below, where he wrote in large capital letters, APPLICATION FOR CIRCUIT JUDGE.

P

Just say when. x.

The response arrived really fast. I'm stunned by how right Alice was.

'Told you,' she says, peering over my shoulder, an awkward grin on her face.

'When should I say?' I ask, full of doubt and uncertainty.

'Tonight,' she says. 'Nine p.m.'

'Alice, you can't be serious.'

'I'm deadly serious.'

I breathe deeply.

'Tell her,' she encourages.

'Alice—'

'Tell her,' this time a little more forcefully.

I feel like a puppet on a string.

She sees my reluctance. 'We need each other, Paul. *If* we're to survive. We both told a lie and we have to keep it secret. No one can get in our way of complete happiness. Because our complete happiness is our complete safety from that truth ever being discovered.'

I know exactly what she's suggesting.

Tonight, 9 o'clock.

Belinda's response is almost instantaneous: *xxx*.

'We've got a lot to do, we'd better prepare,' Alice says, bringing her hands together. 'Starting with this. A *dry* run.' She takes me by the hands and faces me. 'I'm her.'

'What?'

'Let's pretend. Pretend I'm her. That way, later won't be your first time and you won't mess things up.'

'I already said I'll do it, isn't that enough?'

'There have been enough mistakes already, Paul.' She frowns and then places her hands on my chest. 'We've just had a lovely meal. I've remembered how charismatic you are and why I fell for you in the first place.' She brings her lips close to mine and lets them linger. 'You've brought me up here into your bedroom where we're going to reconcile. It's going to be so special. The perfect end to the perfect evening.' She suddenly kisses me, intensely. I try to resist, but she presses deeper.

'Lie me down,' she instructs, and I lower her onto the bed. 'Now, on top of me.'

I lie atop her. She places her arms around my neck and pulls me closer to her. 'When you're here and I'm clearly enjoying it, that's when you're going to do it.' She takes one of my hands and places it on her neck. 'Squeeze,' she orders, and tentatively I do as she instructs. 'More.' I respond. Then she taps my other hand, which I move so that both my hands are on her neck. 'More,' she mouths. I squeeze.

She starts to make a noise that's somewhere between a pleasurable sigh and a horrified rasping. *I could end everything now*, I think. She starts to struggle, grabbing my wrists, her body writhing beneath me, and I realise I could remove the source of all the problems I'm currently experiencing, *maybe Alice never came back*, and the option is tempting, I could do it, end it now, but that would mean my baby as well. I lower my eyes and see her stomach.

My child is growing in there.

At the thought of our child, I scramble off her. 'What is this?' I shriek, looking at my hands. 'What kind of fucking game are you making me play?'

Gasping for air, she says, 'You felt it, didn't you? I knew you had it in you. Don't tell me that wasn't a thrill.'

I hold my up hands, as if I'm facing the police. 'What is wrong with you?'

'I'm ill, remember, I'm fucking depressed. And you cheated on me!'

'But I told you I love you.'

'You slept with someone else!'

'It's over, she meant nothing.'

Alice laughs. There's something sinister in its sound. *This isn't my wife.*

'Something's happened to you.'

She looks at me steadily. '*You* did.'

Then she leaves me sitting on the bed. I fall back and stare at the ceiling; I don't want to see anything else.

P

I open the front door and Belinda steps in, as if emerging from a thick mist. I give her room, eyeing her up and down. She's wearing a sleek thigh-length black dress with thin shoulder straps. Her hair is glossy and her scent travels past me. It's a sweet smell I've missed.

Once inside, without saying a word, she turns around and kisses me, pressing me up against the cloakroom door. The softness of her youthful lips gives me a jump start.

'I'm so pleased you asked me here,' she says and kisses me again.

'You look . . . stunning.' The compliment is real.

'Something smells good,' she says.

'Come in.'

I lead her into the lounge and tell her to make herself comfortable. Returning with a bottle of white wine and two glasses, I pour each of us a healthy serving. 'Here's to us,' I say, handing her a glass.

She stands up and faces me. 'To us.'

Our first glasses finished, I serve the meal. We sit at the dining table and eat slowly. If she's nervous, she doesn't appear to be.

315

I don't bring up the past week. Initially, I speak of the mundane, of the everyday. Then, as things start to feel more natural, I focus on topics I know she's interested in.

After the third glass, my mind becomes a little hazy. I'm not used to drinking wine. Belinda touches my hand, telling me how wonderful the meal was. Then she kisses me again. She guides me into the lounge and towards the settee. 'Not here,' I say. 'Upstairs.'

Looking round the bedroom before entering it, Belinda exhales. 'Oh, Paul,' she says, noticing the effort that's gone into preparing it: flowers in vases, rose petals on the bed, candles lit.

I lift her and place her on the bed, kissing her from head to toe. I climb on top of her. She enjoys it immediately. It's not long before I lift one hand and place it on her neck, apply some pressure, and then I bring my other hand into position.

Both hands there, thinking, waiting, I can't do it. I can't end her life, her youth, her vitality.

Mistaking my pause for tiredness, Belinda rolls us over, sitting astride me. She calls out my name, I incorrectly believe in pleasure. Before I know what's happening, what I initially mistake for spittle sprays into my eyes, which close instinctively, and I take my hands off her body and rub my eyes, now feeling a stream of liquid running across my chest, and I clear my eyes, open them, and look at my hands to see blood, and then I look at Belinda and there's a confused expression on her face, blood spraying from her neck, covering the bed like a tap fills a bath, and there's a vacant look on her face and her body finally topples forwards. Before she lands on me, I catch a glimpse of Alice, behind where Belinda was, with some kind of wire in her hands. Her eyes speak of rage, but then there's only darkness and I can't see anything because Belinda has fallen on top of me, and there are no more sounds.

P

'I do need your help, you know.'

I awake from dreaming about Belinda's death to the sudden sound of Alice's sharp voice.

'Come on, we haven't much time.'

She leaves the room. I'm still lying on the bed, facing the ceiling. *She killed her. And she did it so easily.*

It only takes a moment. It doesn't need much thought.

I sit up, grab my phone and check the time. 5.15 p.m.

Not long now. I don't want to do it, but I must acknowledge the temptation; with Belinda out of the way, things would be easier. And I know Alice wouldn't hesitate, so why should I?

Because of who I am and what I stand for.

Which is what, exactly?

I slow-cook a curry and Alice selects what she assures me is the right wine to complement it. I clean the downstairs of the house while she prepares the bedroom. I don't go in there while she's doing it, but when she calls that it's ready I head upstairs to see what she's done. Fresh sheets have been laid and there are three scented candles in the room, all lit. Anything suggesting Alice, my missing wife, has been hidden.

I stare at the place where it's supposed to happen, the bed, and sense I've let things go too far, but I confess that permanently removing Belinda from the equation isn't something I can fully disregard. After all, just like with the dream, I'd wake up tomorrow and it would be a completely new day. Each new day brings a new opportunity.

I just don't know for certain. I'm running out of time and haven't come up with a plan either way. Whatever I choose to do, I have to do it with absolute confidence. I have to succeed in making our future brighter.

Alice stands back to look at her handiwork. 'Beautiful, isn't it?' she asks.

Side by side, I turn to face her. 'You're enjoying this, aren't you?' I'm appalled at what she has become. And now I'm worried about what I may become.

'No, Paul, I'm just doing what's necessary. Cleaning up your mess.'

'By causing another?'

'And what would that be exactly?'

'You're asking me to create another crime scene right on top of the one we've already covered up.'

'I wouldn't worry about that. After all, you're so meticulous in covering your tracks, isn't that right, Paul? You're the perfect liar. Just look how successful you were the last time we were here together. I followed your every expert word without hesitation. And I haven't been able to forget it, not even for a moment, since then. Not forgetting how your meticulous cover-up skills have only got sharper in the time that's passed.'

'You're punishing me.'

'No, Paul, you punished me. That night and then ever since. Tonight, you're going to make things right.'

'By killing in cold blood?'

'You should know what it feels like.'

'Oh, I know, believe me, I already know all too well.'

She steps close to me. I edge gingerly backwards. Something in her eyes unroots me. She says quietly, menacingly, 'You have no idea.'

'I hid a fucking body for you! I did everything I could *for you.*'

'*Everything?*' she says in mock horror.

'Yes, Alice, everything. I committed a crime for you. Me, a fucking judge! I have lied and lied for you and it's got me deeper and deeper into this mess.'

'Everything we did that night we did because you said to! You're the expert, remember. *You* told *me* what to do!'

'I didn't tell you to kill someone!' I say and instantly regret it.

Her face becomes ashen, her voice weak. 'That's right, I killed a man. I killed a man, Paul, and I have to live with that. What did you do by comparison?'

'I could have lost everything, Alice. Everything we've worked for.'

'And I did lose everything.'

I hesitate, then I say hoarsely, 'So much more than I ever felt possible.'

'And you're about to lose me. Do as I say, or it's over.' She takes me delicately by the lapel of the jacket. 'Refuse me and I won't lie any more.'

'What are you saying, that you'll go to the police if I won't do it? Because if you are, this sick, twisted thing between us—'

'I'm saying . . .' She pauses. 'Life can't be any other way. Do it, or you'll live to regret every decision you've ever made.'

I breathe in deeply. 'It's not too late, Alice.'

'It was too late a long time ago, Paul.'

Yes, I think. *It was.* I guess an ending like this was always inevitable.

'Now, just make sure you cough as you bring her up the stairs. I'll be ready for you.' She stares deep into my eyes. 'Both of you.'

A

She arrives on time like an eager whore.

Actually, I'm not being fair on her. He could have said no, after all. That's why he has to do this – he has to realise the error of *his* ways. She's superfluous.

The front door opens. I remain in the bedroom, so I only hear muffled voices, but they start low and fairly quickly become higher pitched and more animated.

The sounds of a good time being had, I think.

I'm curious to see whether he'll go through with it. I'm not sure he has it in him, but I know how much the baby means to him and I've used that as great leverage, and there's one other way I could ruin his life. I don't see how he has much choice.

So, yes, it is punishment. I just needed him to believe there was more to it than that. There isn't. I hate what he's done to me. First, that night when he made me dig a muddy hole and bury a corpse, and then when he slept with her while I was at home suffering because of *that night*. The night when I did everything he told me to do.

About an hour into the evening, I can't hear their voices any more – they're probably in the dining room – so I creep along the corridor and stand at the top of the stairs. I'm there for a long time, I don't know how long, I lose track. I see him and her together as vividly as if I were in the room with them.

The most striking sound is their laughter. It has a repetitive beat-like quality. His sounds genuine, even though he's supposed to be pretending. If he's enjoying himself . . .

When there's finally movement in the living room, I return to the bedroom, checking to make sure everything looks perfect. I open and gaze into the walk-in wardrobe, my seat for the finale. I've cleared it, so there's plenty of room.

An approaching cough catches my attention. Then another. It's coming from the bottom of the staircase.

I step towards the wardrobe, but then I hesitate. The coughs have stopped and I can't hear any footsteps coming upstairs. I listen more closely.

No, nothing, just silence.

I turn towards where they are. All I'm faced with is an empty corridor.

He's not coming.

Deflated, I creep out of the bedroom, along the corridor and towards the staircase. When I reach the top, I position myself so that I can listen but not be seen.

'Paul, are you okay?' she asks, concern in her voice.

Eyeing around the wall, I see them. He's in front of her, kneeling on the stairs, his body hunched forwards. She behind him, standing upright. Their hands are still connected, his reaching back to hold onto her.

322

'Fine,' he mumbles, but he doesn't move. *He can't do it.*

'Come on, baby,' she says, placing her hands on his shoulders, rubbing. She tries to encourage him up.

As he gets up, he coughs and starts moving forward.

I step into view.

They freeze, Belinda giving off a small gasp. Paul's eyes fix on mine, silently pleading with me, then he mouths, 'What are you doing?'

Belinda speaks up first. 'What the fuck is this?' She glances quickly between Paul and me.

He turns to her and reaches out. 'Belinda, I can explain.'

She swipes at his hand. 'Don't you fucking touch me. What kind of sick game are you playing? What the fuck is she doing here?' She's shrieking at full volume now, out of control.

'It's not what it seems—'

She slaps him and storms down the stairs. When she grabs her coat from the rack, she says, 'You son of a bitch, you called me here, for what?'

Paul has charged after her. 'Belinda, don't—'

He looks like a pathetic, forlorn schoolboy. I almost laugh, taking a couple of steps down so that I can watch their final moments together.

'You're sick,' she says. 'Sick.' And she pushes him out of the way and opens the front door, escaping to her freedom.

Leaving the front door open, he comes back to the staircase. After a couple of steps, he stops, looking up at me. We stare at one another, several metres between us, trying to read each other's minds.

I can tell he wants to go back to that October night. He wants to pick up the phone and call the police. He wants to see me arrested for the crime he now regrets helping me conceal. But I can also tell he's worried about what I might do next. He knows that if the police come knocking, I won't go down alone. That's the way it will always be.

There's a mixture of anger and pain in his eyes. He's sorry for what he's let happen, yet he knows he's trapped. I don't know what my eyes reveal, but I'm sure I'm unable to hide the bitterness and disappointment I feel. Disappointment for so many things, but especially for what must come next. I truly hoped we'd have a future together.

'Alice—' he says, but he isn't able to finish.

I throw myself down the stairs, my body tumbling against each step and the wall, stopping only when I collide with his legs. Landing, I catch sight of the horrified expression on his face and hear him shout Belinda's name. After that, there's no more sound and only darkness.

P

'Belinda!' I shout. Then I shout Alice's name. She's lying prostrate at the bottom of the stairs. Instinctively, I turn her over, even though the moment I move her I realise it's a mistake. Our eyes meet momentarily, but there's nothing behind hers, she's vacant. 'Oh, Christ,' I say, trying to identify a pulse on her neck. 'What the fuck – what did you do? What the hell—'

Belinda gasps behind me. 'Paul—'

I spin around. 'Belinda, it's not . . . she fell . . . threw herself, God. Oh my God!'

She's trying to work out what to do. Her thoughts are impeded by the alcohol she's consumed and she's not sure whether to continue showing me her anger.

'Help me,' I say as I cling onto my wife. 'Call an ambulance.'

She thinks for a moment, then runs into the lounge. I hear her voice. She's speaking with urgency, urging whoever it is on the other end to make sure they hurry.

As she returns and crouches down by my side, I say, 'Thank you.'

'Fuck you,' she says without looking at me and then she takes control, pushing me out of the way and putting Alice into the recovery position.

15

Detective Constable Ryan Hillier was meeting with Jesus College alumni who had studied with Richard Dollard, Ethan Fleming and Simon Michael Ryman, and others whose names had been linked to the cases. For each visit, he was armed with a collection of photographs, all very natural-looking, but all computer-generated images of Alexander Pavlik. His task was to see if any of them had any memory of ever encountering Pavlik; he wanted to find the killer, but he also wanted to know whether there might have been more intended victims.

Now he was at Laurence Sanders' office. Impressed, he remembered how Wright had described it as palatial and he couldn't disagree.

'None of them look familiar,' Sanders said after briefly scanning through the dozen or so shots.

'Are you certain? No one from your past? From your Cambridge days, perhaps, even though you were at a different college, just imagine him younger? No one following you around in the months before their deaths?'

'No,' he said. 'I've never seen him before in my life.' He

leant back in his chair. 'Should I be worried, Detective? Are you suggesting there's still some kind of danger?' He didn't look concerned.

'I don't know. You all need to remain vigilant, that's all I can recommend.'

'Have you warned my friend, Paul Reeve? He studied with two of them and shared a property with Mike.'

'Mr Reeve has been spoken to, yes.'

'And he knows to keep his eyes peeled?'

'I think so, yes.'

Sanders stood up and started to make his way around his desk. 'Well, if that's all—'

'Yes, indeed. Thanks for your time.'

Sanders placed his hand softly on Hillier's back and led him to the door. 'You know,' he giggled to himself, 'it's all very sad now, but I found it most amusing last year when they all went for that same promotion.'

Hillier stopped. 'Who?'

'Richard, Ethan, Mike and Paul. I mean, who'd have thought it all those years ago when we were studying. Once best friends, then bitter rivals for that Circuit Judge position.'

'They all applied for that job?'

'Absolutely.' Now he clapped his hands together. 'I know he's dead, but Mike, even though he was the youngest, was probably pissed off when he lost out. He was ultra-competitive and I bet he thought he had it in the bag. Paul's a deserving winner, though. There's no one more suitable for it than him.'

'Did they all know the others had applied?'

'I've no idea, although I suspect so. After all, I knew.'

'How did you find out?'

'Paul told me. Oh, it must have been eight, nine months ago.'

When Hillier left the building, he called Wright. 'The three of them,' he said, excitedly, 'they all applied for the job that ultimately went to Paul Reeve.'

'Go and collect the list of applicants in the morning,' she said, not missing a beat. 'I'll chase the warrant application first thing, God knows what's delayed it, and I'll tell them to send it straight through to you at the Court's HR office. Wait there for it. Let me know when you've got the names.'

P

Belinda waited with me for the ambulance to arrive. She also travelled with us to the hospital. She said she wanted to make sure Alice was stabilised successfully.

'Thank you,' I said to her, appearing in the waiting area of Accident and Emergency.

She glared at me, nodded her head as if she were satisfied and then turned around and walked off, leaving me standing there, deservedly alone, feeling like a complete fool. Now I know I'll never see her again.

Alice regained consciousness almost as soon as we arrived at the hospital a little after 1 a.m., but she was exhausted and has been drifting in and out of sleep since then. She's sleeping right now, even though it's several hours later. I decide to use the opportunity to have a breather and a strong coffee.

Oh God, to be able to turn back the clock to last October and make everything happen differently. To somehow just make it all go away.

I return to the ward about twenty minutes later and kneel by the side of Alice's bed. The early morning sunshine is piercing through the ineffectual blinds, partly illuminating her. She looks so peaceful. I take her hand in mine and tell her I love her. 'I'm sorry, Alice. I'm so sorry.'

When I feel like I can no longer keep my eyes open, I stand up, kiss Alice on the forehead and sit on the solitary chair in the room. Leaning my head back, I close my eyes.

16

'I'm here,' Hillier told Wright. 'Got it.'

'Excellent,' Wright said. 'And listen, I've just had contact from the Cyber team. Paul Reeve's name keeps cropping up. Apparently he's been buying Bitcoins, the online currency.'

'I know nothing about Bitcoin.'

'I didn't, either. It seems he's been buying them through something called CoinJoin, a service that links users who want to make similar payments and allows them to pay together, mixing their Bitcoins and making it harder to identify them. It's basically a way of laundering money online and doing it very, very anonymously.'

'What money, though? What exactly has Paul Reeve been laundering?'

'We don't know yet, but there's plenty of money. And twenty-four hours prior to each of the three murders, they've identified transactions from an account linked to Paul Reeve's email address to an account linked to an individual called Brian Clarke.'

'Who's Brian Clarke?'

'We don't know yet, but there are three repetitions of his name. We're running him through all our databases.'

As soon as the call with Hillier was over, Wright called Philip Moorse, who led the Cyber team. 'Can you tell me anything else, Phil?'

'Yeah, it's coming in slowly. The Bitcoin account, it seems, is linked to a Bank of Scotland account that's solely in the name of Paul Reeve. No withdrawals have ever been made from that account, only transfers. The money gets moved from Bitcoin account to Bitcoin account and then we lose track of it and it disappears, likely abroad. But the Gmail address used to activate the Bitcoin account is active and is also under the name of Paul Reeve. That email address is used to sign in to access the online Bank of Scotland account and then that money gets moved. We've followed it to several accounts and then we lose track of it when it goes abroad.'

'Can you track the final destination of the money? I want to know where it's going.'

'We're trying. That part is more difficult and will take time, if we can get there.'

'How long?'

'How long's a piece of string?'

Wright thanked Moorse and hung up. An email alert on her computer screen caught her attention. Opening it, she read the message:

SUBJECT: Re: Brian Clarke.
Assuming it's not CLARK but WITH an 'e'. 37 Brian Clarkes on our databases. 4 currently serving prison terms. 29 others

with files containing photos. Other 4 only last known contact details/next of kin (see attached) but no photos. See 2nd attached document for collection of images currently on record for 33 in total.

She opened the file containing the images first and began scrolling through them. The first dozen: all white, various ages, every hair colour. She kept scrolling, the computer working frustratingly slowly. One black man amid the next five. Then she paused when she saw the eighteenth image.

She grabbed the phone.

'Hillier.'

'Ryan, do you have it?'

'Just waiting for Alma Patrick. Shouldn't be long.'

'I've got a photo of Brian Clarke. He was arrested five years ago for assault in Birmingham. Unshaven, hair close-cropped. He looks different, but it's definitely him. I see it in his eyes, like I said we'd be able to. Dead eyes.'

'What, Clarke *is* Pavlik?'

'Yes,' Wright said eagerly. 'Brian Clarke is Alexander Pavlik, no question about it.'

'You're telling me Paul Reeve sent money to Alexander Pavlik?'

'That's what it looks like.'

'Get those documents from Alma Patrick and confirm exactly who applied for that job. I'm going to pay a visit to Paul Reeve's house just as soon as I get a final update from Moorse, see if he finds out anything else that connects Reeve to Pavlik. All goes well, we'll be done at the same time and you can meet me at Paul Reeve's house.'

334

Hillier stood impatiently in the reception area of the office in Bishop's Court, where the HR department of the Central Criminal Court was based. 'Will it be much longer?' he asked the receptionist.

'Let me check.' As she picked up the phone, a door opened and Alma Patrick entered.

'Sorry to keep you,' she said, handing over a five-page list. 'The contact details of each applicant are listed next to each name. It was a popular vacancy, as you'll see. Seventy-eight applicants.'

Hillier thanked her. 'Do you mind if I sit while I go through this?' he asked, indicating some seats that circled a table towards the other side of the reception area.

'Please.'

They shook hands and Alma Patrick left Hillier to it. After sitting down, he started to trace his way through the names using his index finger. He saw the names Ethan Fleming, Richard Dollard and Simon Michael Ryman. And he came across the name Paul Reeve.

'Got you,' he said, tapping it. He pulled out his phone and called DS Wright. She didn't pick up, was probably on her way to Paul Reeve's house, so he left her a voicemail. 'Katherine, just to confirm, Reeve is on the list, and so are they all. It's indisputable. They all applied for the job and Reeve got it.'

Having shuffled the pages neatly together, Hillier was about to fold them up, but some words caught his eye. He paused, certain he was mistaken. He looked more closely.

What the hell is going on here? he thought, no longer understanding anything.

P

I dream of different times. Before I even knew Alice. All the girls I'd been with and how my intelligence and looks appealed to so many. And of when Alice and I met. She was my flatmate's new girlfriend and he brought her to a party. Not long after meeting her, I vomited over a wall she was standing next to, chatting to friends. She helped me when I tripped over, and at that moment I knew I had to have her.

So I took her. From Mike.

I dream of our first date, a meal and film. Of how young we were, and how much we had to say to one other and about each other, and how much promise we shared and the hope we had for the future.

How times have changed so very much.

'Mr Reeve.' Dream or reality, I'm not sure.

Someone's tapping my arm. I slowly open my eyes, desperate to remain in my past.

Startled, I find Detective Wright standing above me.

'Oh, Detective,' I say, shifting into a more upright position. 'I'm sorry, you've caught me . . . I was asleep . . . You've come by at a difficult time.'

'Is everything okay?' she asks.

'My wife had a fall. It was nasty.'

'You've got some explaining to do.'

Coming to more fully, I ask, 'How did you know I was here?'

'Your neighbour, Bob, he said he watched you, your wife and another young woman get into an ambulance in the early hours.'

'Belinda,' I say softly.

Her eyes widen. 'You were with Belinda?'

'She's fine, Detective. You have nothing to worry about. She came to dinner.' I grimace, realising how ludicrous that sounds.

'Dinner?' she asks, surprised.

'My wife . . .' I say. 'My wife invited her.'

'Your wife?'

'Yes. Hard to believe, isn't it. I can hardly believe it myself.' I feel overpowered by the sequence of events that I've endured and remain quiet for a time. Detective Wright scans the room. 'Forgive me, I'm so exhausted, I'm worried I'm not being very coherent. But what I've told you is true. My wife and Belinda have both returned and I was wrong, there was no great mystery. They just left separately and . . . returned. Thankfully. So I'm afraid, or rather I'm pleased to say, that means I won't need to trouble you any more.' I lean back, my body eager to return to sleep.

'Well, this is certainly not what I expected to find, Mr Reeve, and we will discuss all that later, but right now I'm actually here an another matter.'

'Oh, yes?'

'Have you ever heard of Bitcoin, Mr Reeve?'

I try to conceal my surprise. 'Sorry?' I say, sitting forward.

'You heard me.' Slowly, she repeats, '*Bitcoin.*'

'What are you talking about?' *This doesn't make any sense.*

She stands up. 'The timing might be inconvenient with your wife here, but I think we need to discuss things further at the station.'

'Look, Detective, I really have no idea what you're talking about or what you're suggesting.' I remain seated while she looms over me. 'I haven't done anything wrong.'

Then she leaps into it, breathlessly: 'I want to know why there's a Bitcoin account with your name on it that's linked to a man named Brian Clarke whose real name is Alexander Pavlik, the man whom I suspect killed Richard Dollard, Ethan Fleming and Simon Michael Ryman. Or Mike, of course, as you know him.'

I spring up. 'It's what?'

'An Eastern European hitman named Alexander Pavlik who goes by the alias Brian Clarke. You paid him close to £10,000 on three separate occasions, twenty-four hours before each of the men were killed.'

I shake my head, my body quivering, my voice stuttering. 'I . . . I . . . I did no such thing.'

'The account's in your name, Mr Reeve, and they were three competitors for the job you got.'

'Yes, but—'

'The job you *desperately wanted.* You'd kill for it, I believe your wife said. Perhaps, after all, that's what you did.'

'But . . . I didn't. What is this? They were my friends.'

'Even Simon Michael Ryman?'

'But . . . he threatened . . . me.'

'The money will prove it. We can track the money, you know.'

'There's no such thing. There's only . . . an account . . . it's just an unused account . . . we share it for the rentals . . .' My voice sounds off. 'We hide the income . . . from the taxman . . . It's not possible.' I stand, holding my hands in the air.

I've been betrayed.

'Mr Reeve, I'd like you—'

The sound of Alice stirring in the bed interrupts us. Her eyes open and she sees Detective Wright first. Then she twists her neck and sees me. Detective Wright and I both look back at her.

Alice's eyes fix on me. Then, suddenly, she starts writhing on the bed and cries out, 'Did you? Did you push me?'

Detective Wright and I move towards her. A nearby nurse dashes to the bedside, taking Alice by the hand. 'Pushed you where, dear?'

'The stairs! Oh God, did you, Paul? He pushed me down the stairs. I think. I don't know. Did you try to hurt me, Paul?'

'Alice, no,' I mouth, shaking my head.

'He pushed you down the stairs?' Detective Wright asks, stepping even closer to her.

'I . . . Alice . . . don't,' I manage to say, edging backwards.

'Are you sure, Alice?' Detective Wright says, reaching out to her.

'I think he may—'

339

As Detective Wright turns back to face me, I lunge at her, push hard, and she falls into Alice's bed and then onto the floor, knocking over a monitor. It crashes to the floor.

I start running, out of Alice's room, then along the corridor, and I keep turning corners, without looking back, until I come to a staircase. I charge down it and emerge on the ground floor. Running, I turn each corner I come across, desperately trying to read signs but failing because I'm moving too quickly.

I have no choice.

Eventually, I arrive at the main entrance, but as I do so the lift doors open and I see Detective Wright emerging, nursing her elbow, scanning every direction. I don't know if she sees me; I lunge through the nearest door, finding myself in a large store room, but it's one without another door. There's a window, it's small, but I think I might be able to fit through it. It won't open, no matter how much pressure I apply, so I take off my jacket, wrap it around my fist and punch it several times. The glass cracks, then shatters. I push my hand through, clearing the sharp edges that remain.

I scramble through the gap and find myself in a yard behind the catering area. There are bins and carts of deliveries everywhere. Stumbling through them, I emerge into a courtyard that's connected to a small road. I move along it as quickly as I can and find myself on a main road. The hospital is behind me and to the far right.

Realising I don't have my car nearby – I came in the ambulance with Alice and Belinda – I'm grateful when I spot a taxi rank nearby. I jog to it, affording myself one glance back as I get in the first car in line, and give the driver my home address.

I need my car. I have to get to London.

P

The taxi drops me off at the end of my driveway. I'm desperately worried that Detective Wright might have got here before me, or maybe she's requested support and other officers are here waiting for me. Finding a way along the driveway through the bushes and trees that line it, I carefully check for any signs of life.

All seems quiet.

Relieved, but also desperate to get out of here, I emerge from the bushes. As I do so, my eyes meet Bob's. He's in his driveway, polishing his car, and he can't disguise his surprise at seeing me dishevelled and muddied.

'Hello, Paul,' he says.

'Afternoon, Bob,' I answer, without slowing my pace to the front door.

'A police officer was here looking for you this morning. I said I saw you going off last night in an ambulance. Is your wife all right? I was worried. Is there anything we can do?'

'All okay, Bob, thank you for being concerned.'

'A little accident?'

'Yes, she tripped and fell down the stairs.'

'Oh, gosh, I hope she's all right.'

'She's going to be fine. Thanks, Bob,' and I step up to the front door, unlock it and grab my car keys. Immediately, I leave the house, locking it. Bob says something else, but I don't hear what and get into the car.

I accelerate and head down the driveway quickly. At the end of the driveway, another car appears. I swerve to avoid it and end up on some grass and bushes. The car's big wheels easily get me over them.

The driver of the other car looks official. A police officer. I speed to the end of the road and enter a heavy stream of traffic, weaving in and out of vehicles and taking corners at dangerous speeds, hoping he hasn't been able to turn around with me still in sight. The Outlander's CVP groans under my acceleration. I can't let anything or anyone stop me. I can't believe what's happened. I can't believe I didn't see it coming.

I'm soon on the M1 and heading towards London.

As I drive, I keep checking the rear-view mirror. No sign of police, but I won't relax. Now is the point when I need to be careful and draw as little attention to myself as possible; I have to get there. No doubt my licence plate and vehicle description have been circulated. I'm a wanted man. I'm finished, yet getting to London still gives me purpose.

I make it to Brent Cross and head west on the A406, then towards Finchley Road. The traffic is heavier here, which is a blessing in disguise. My car becomes surrounded, making it difficult for anyone to see the licence plate from anything other than up close.

After almost half an hour, I turn left onto Euston Road, pass King's Cross Station and make my way along City Road, the traffic still heavy. The whole way, I keep glancing in the mirrors and turning my head left and right.

At the Old Street roundabout, I turn onto Great Eastern Street and it's at that moment when blue flashing lights appear a few cars behind me. They're followed by another car that's driving at speed. I recognise it as the car I almost careered into at the end of my driveway. Instinctively, I accelerate, swerving in and out of traffic, making the cars on the other side of the road veer into kerbs or onto pavements. Pedestrians leap out of the way. I'm so close, I can't give up now. So long as I don't get blocked from the other side, I should get there.

I turn sharply onto Curtain Road and hit the gas with the force of my body. When I reach my target, I slam on the brakes, the car skidding to a halt, smacking into the kerb and mounting the pavement. I leap out and run. Police sirens fill the air all around me. I see officers climbing out of cars as I barge my way through the revolving doors and scramble to the lift. When I see a queue of people by the lifts, I leap into the stairwell and climb, two steps at a time.

By the time I reach the tenth floor, I'm gasping for breath. I jog to the lifts, pressing the call button and hoping the police won't be in the lift when it arrives. I step to the side as its arrival is sounded and cautiously peer in. There are several people in it, but no police. I hit the button marking the twenty-third floor.

When the lift arrives, I walk at speed past the reception desk, ignoring the woman behind it who calls out, 'Can I help you, sir?'

344

I shoulder-barge through the office's double doors. A young couple sits with their backs to me, but they spin round at the sound of my entrance, and Laurence Sanders, who's on his feet and pointing at what could be a map on his desk, peers up from it.

'Paul,' he says, forcing a smile and trying to conceal his surprise.

Covered in sweat and breathing heavily, I say, stepping forwards, 'You set me up.'

He laughs awkwardly. 'Paul, I don't know what you mean.'

'The Bitcoin account. You only put it in my name and you used it. You used it to hire a man to kill Richard and Ethan and Mike. And me, you sent him after me, you son of a bitch.'

He looks uneasily at the couple in front of him as I step closer. He laughs again, shaking his head. 'Paul, that's insane.' Then he says to the couple, 'I'm sorry, my friend, Paul, isn't very well.' Then to me: 'You're obviously not well, Paul. Why don't you take the weight off your feet, relax for a while?'

'Fuck you, Laurence, you've ruined my life!'

At the sound of my raised voice, the woman squeals, the man sheltering her, taking her from her seat and retreating to the side of the office, where they crouch.

'You sent him for me. Why, Laurence? Why? For some stupid, fucking promotion. All because of some job? Because you were jealous, you didn't think you had what it takes to be chosen over us?'

I hear a commotion nearby and realise I only have seconds left. I look over my shoulder and see the three police officers running towards the office. I dive over the desk and grab Laurence by the hair. My foot gets caught, giving him time to react, and he strikes me on the back of the neck. Pain reverberates down my spine. I scramble off and we grab each other by the throats. He hits me in the stomach, knocking the wind out of me, and attempts a second strike, but I manage to pull my body away so that he misses me and I bring up my knee, hard and sharp, connecting with his face. He reels backwards, the back of his head colliding with a framed picture on the wall behind his desk. It falls to the ground, the glass smashing. I grab him by the throat, squeezing. 'You set me up!'

He manages to grab a shard of glass and slashes at me, catching my cheek. I fall backwards and he gets up, lunging at me, shard of glass outstretched, but I manage to catch hold of his hand. We fall onto the desk, him on top of me, the shard of glass getting closer and closer to my face, my hand desperately trying to hold him off. I'm failing. The glass is only centimetres from my throat. I feel it pin-prick my skin.

Someone leaps over the desk, a knee colliding with the top of my head, everything goes dizzy, and all three of us fall in a heap to the floor. Clutching my head, I sit up and see the man from my driveway atop Sanders, holding him by wrists twisted behind his back. The pounding in my head intensifies and my bearings go, my body drifting against the wall and sliding down to the floor. I end up in a mass next to Sanders. He's been handcuffed.

My eyes close. Everything's over.

A

Waking up in the hospital to find Paul and Detective Wright in the room, I knew what had happened to me – I remembered falling – but I couldn't picture it happening. I couldn't see Paul, whether he had his hands on me, whether he was above me or below me. I didn't know if he'd done it to me, or if I'd slipped, but he was there, he was close, I could sense it. Since Detective Wright chased after him, I've been lying here, trying to see it clearly, trying to relive what happened last night, but I'm still as confused as I was when I woke up.

The most important thing – I was desperate to hear about the wellbeing of my child, and I was so relieved to learn that he or she is okay. *Thank God.*

I need to be here for my child. Being here, the fear that I may have lost my child, makes me understand that more than ever before. Whatever's happened, I have to find a way through this. My child is my priority.

Once Detective Wright had gone, another officer arrived and told me, after I badgered him, that Paul is suspected of hiring a hitman to have his former university colleagues killed. When Paul told me he'd kill for that job, I didn't believe he meant it for a single moment.

Of course, after thinking about what else that implied, I came to the horrifying conclusion: that same man ended up in my home. Which means Paul wanted to have me killed as well, most likely so that he could start a new life with his secretary. She probably wasn't deluded or lying, after all.

I can imagine what went through his mind when he walked into the house last October and found me alive in the bedroom after he'd prepared himself to discover a corpse. He must have been so disappointed, but to appear so convincingly surprised as he did, and able to decide what to do with the dead body so spontaneously, showed great skill. He is a wonderful liar.

First one lie and then another. Telling lies was as easy for him as turning the pages of a book.

So what do I do? Self-preservation is all I can think of, it's what's necessary to guarantee my baby's safety, but how can I ensure it? One word from Paul, and the hitman's body can be found. And if they dig up the body, even though we were careful, who's to say there won't be some of my DNA on it.

Paul has got me trapped, although for all intents and purposes I've got him trapped, too. Because I can implicate him in the same way he can me.

He will be selfish and try to save himself, I know that. Which means I have to bring him down first. Strike, I tell myself, *before he has the chance to strike at me.*

He hid the body. He told me what to do. He forced me to help him; he did it so that I'd be silenced. He's hurt me before – an ambulance took me, the police kept him away from me — and I just knew he would do it again, maybe even worse, if I didn't obey him. There are records. Just take a look at them and you'll see. He's a menace, a danger to me. Detective Wright has had her suspicions all along. So I had no choice. I had to remain silent while he did those awful things, afraid he'd do even more awful things to me. And then yesterday, knowing the police were closing in on him, he threw me down the stairs.

Even though I'm not certain he did.

I can make it sound convincing. It may be the only way to guarantee my safety and a future with my child.

At best, I could negotiate some kind of plea deal. At worst, I'll be sentenced for a lesser crime.

No, I've suffered enough. Now it's his turn. It's time I end this.

17

'Your child will be fine.'

'Thank Christ.' Paul Reeve leant on the table. 'Oh, thank Christ.'

'Now tell me about Laurence Sanders.'

Paul Reeve sat up. 'He's been my best friend for years.'

He sat facing Detective Sergeant Katherine Wright and Detective Constable Ryan Hillier in a stale interrogation room at Charing Cross Police Station.

'He and I have been business partners for over five years. We own twelve properties together. Sometimes we buy, do up and sell. We're landlords who share a property portfolio. It was something we discussed back at university and when we started earning good money, within just a couple of years of working for law firms, because it really can happen that quickly, we had enough money to start doing it. We built it up over several years and now we do very well from it.'

'So that's where Bitcoin comes from, is that what you're saying?' Wright asked.

'Yes. Bitcoin was Laurence's idea. He told me he'd heard about the Silk Road and the Dark Web and how Bitcoin was untraceable. With our salaries, by the time the portfolio got going, well into the hundreds of thousands, he said if we could deal with some of the rental fees through Bitcoin we could make it untraceable to avoid hefty taxes. On what we were already earning, we'd be looking at forty-five per cent of everything we got from the properties. He said he'd sort it, to leave it to him. I mean, I knew there was an account, but I had no idea he'd set it up through my name alone. I just signed what he asked me to. I trusted him; he's been my closest friend for close to two decades.'

'What happens to the money in Bitcoin?' Wright asked, making notes as Paul answered.

'He has a way to filter it through several accounts, I don't know how or where, I never asked and was never much interested, I just did it for the cash, which he eventually gave me after it went through whatever processes were necessary. At least, that's what he told me. Much of it, though, has been used to pay for renovations on the properties. We've never bought new-build. All our properties have been old and decrepit and he's done them up. I put money in, but he does or arranges all the work. I'm not good at things like that and I was never much interested; my career in law was always my priority. All that was his forte, but now I understand why he was so keen. He wanted to set me up. I swear I had nothing to do with the deaths of Richard, Ethan and Mike. And I haven't sent a penny to this Brian Clarke you mention. I don't know anyone called Brian Clarke or Alexander Pavlik, either. I haven't sent a penny to anyone. Laurence has always controlled the portfolio finances.'

'And what about your wife and Belinda Adams?'

'Like I told you earlier, they've both come back. I don't know why it happened the way it did, it just did. It really is a coincidence. Horrible timing, if I'm honest.'

'Did you push your wife down the stairs?'

He looked at her levelly. 'No.'

'And you've never put a hand on your wife before?'

'No.' He instantly saw where she was going with her questioning, so he jumped in, 'Well, okay, she was recently taken to hospital because of a misunderstanding. I was trying to leave the kitchen, she was holding onto me and I shrugged her off. She fell. I never assaulted her. It was an accident.'

'But she was hurt?'

He said clearly, 'She was fine.'

'So she's lying then?'

'Yes,' he said, without hesitation.

'Why?'

'I honestly can't say.' He didn't know how much to say. He was worried she'd reveal what they'd done, but he didn't believe she'd sacrifice herself or risk losing the child by incriminating herself. And he couldn't see how she could reveal what had happened without incriminating herself. 'I don't know, she just is.' He knew it was an unsatisfactory answer, but he couldn't say more.

For now.

'Why was Belinda Adams at your house last night?'

Paul Reeve sniffed. 'I'm sorry,' he said, 'but the answer isn't going to impress you.' He cleared his throat and looked uncomfortable. 'The truth is, my wife told me to invite her.'

'Your wife?' Both detectives smirked.

'I wasn't lying when I said to you a while ago that my wife is ill. She's irrational and yesterday was another example of that when she told me to invite Belinda to dinner. As irrational as throwing herself down the stairs afterwards.'

'Was it dinner for three?' Hillier asked sarcastically.

'This isn't funny to me,' Paul said sternly. 'Look, Alice wanted Belinda to be happy to hear from me and then she wanted to surprise Belinda.'

'Why?' Wright asked.

'She wanted to shock her, I think. She wanted Belinda to be out of my life forever and I guess she believed that turning up unannounced in the middle of the dinner would be enough to make Belinda stay away in future.'

'You expect me to believe that?'

'It's the truth. Not much of what Alice has been doing or saying over the past few months has made much sense. I'm afraid that's just the way it is.'

Wright stood up. 'We'll see.'

'Am I going to be able to see Alice?'

'No.'

Wright and Hillier left the room. 'Find out how we're doing with getting Sanders' computers seized.'

'Warrant request's in, I believe. If it's been issued, a team may be executing it right now.'

'I want some time with Alice Reeve. Find out about the warrant and then come and let me know.'

18

'Do you mind if we speak here? I know the conditions aren't ideal.'

They were in the hospital ward. Alice's room had been cleared of other patients so that Detective Wright could talk to her in private.

'Did your husband push you down the stairs last night?'

Yes.

Now that she had the opportunity to say it, to sound firm and resolute, something made her hesitate. She didn't know what. Some kind of misguided loyalty. Something about the life she and Paul had shared together, the love that they had once upon a time felt. She didn't want anything to stop her. She didn't want it, whatever it was, to be there.

Her head hurt. Everything was a blur, and it was only getting worse.

'I think so,' she said eventually.

Detective Wright paused to give Alice Reeve time to say more. She didn't.

Wright chose to move on. 'And was Belinda Adams in your home at the time?'

'No,' Alice said. 'Yes. Well, not exactly.' She knew she couldn't deny Belinda's presence; checking would be too easy for the detective. 'She had just left. I wanted to get rid of her. I surprised them and then when she'd gone he got angry with me.' There was a pause and then she added, 'That was when I fell down the stairs.'

'Fell or were thrown?'

She reached up to her head and pinched the skin between her fingers. 'Pushed.'

'Are you certain?'

'Everything is . . .' She sobbed silently. 'He was having an affair, Detective, and he was angry with me. I'm the innocent wife and he's a serial liar who's been lying for God knows how long.'

'I see.'

'Do you know about his affair?'

'Yes. So let's start with that. How did you find out about it?'

'It must have been . . . one day in April. I went to the Old Bailey to surprise Paul and they came out. I followed them to a hotel where . . . well, you know. Where I knew.'

'What made you follow them?'

'I just had a feeling. For some time, I thought that something wasn't right. I didn't know what exactly, but . . . I think a woman just knows.'

'Yes, you'd be surprised how often I've heard that.'

Alice reached her hand out to Detective Wright. Wright took it. 'Detective, did my husband send that man to kill his colleagues?'

'That's what I'm trying to find out.'

Wright's phone buzzed and she glanced down at its screen. 'Apologies, I must take this. I'll be back as soon as I can. You take it easy and rest.' She stepped outside to answer Hillier's call. Hillier had remained at the station.

'The warrant came through,' Hillier said. 'Sanders' computers and personal mobile phone, his business phone too, have been seized and they're on their way here now.'

'Great.'

'That's not all. A call has come through from Sanders' firm. He wasn't brought in for questioning, it seems. Instead, he was being spoken to at the office. Aside from having a fight, there wasn't anything concrete to bring him in for apart from Paul Reeve's accusations and, besides, it seems his boss is chummy with DI Lange, so someone decided it would be best to deal with him in a civilised way – i.e. not at the station. Anyway, after news of the computer and phone seizures were sent to his office, one of the secretaries found him in his office bathroom. He hanged himself.'

P

Detective Wright is sitting opposite me again, her colleague, the man who wrestled Laurence off me, next to her. She must see the expectation on my face because she asks, 'What would you like to say?'

I've decided to come clean and explain everything. There have been too many lies – so many I can't keep up – and it's time to say the truth. Life as I knew it is over anyway. I can't be a judge any more. I doubt I have a wife. And I fear I've lost my unborn child. Everything that's ever meant anything to me is gone. Now I need to try to get the best deal I can to help me cope with the misery that's to come.

I open my mouth, but then the sight of a heavily pregnant Alice, some months in the future, comes into my mind.

She's carrying your child. You can still have a child. Confess everything and you'll lose that chance.

But that would mean lying and I'm tired of lying.

I sit up straight and cross my arms. 'I want to tell you the truth, Detective. Right from the start. I want to tell you everything. And I ask you – no, I plead with you – please go easy on my wife, go easy on Alice. She's pregnant, she shouldn't have to deal with all this. I've caused it. It's my fault, and my fault alone.'

Wright settles in her seat as if she's making herself comfortable. 'If she's done nothing wrong, she'll be taken care of. Now, what do you want to tell me?'

'I want to start in October last year. The night of October the second, to be precise. I want to start with the man I now know is called Alexander Pavlik.'

A

Detective Wright's phone rang over three hours ago and she left me mid-conversation and hasn't been back since. I'd normally be angry at being kept waiting for so long, but the stay has given me time to think about my options, and I've decided: I'm willing to accept whatever punishment comes my way, but I think the truth needs to be spoken. If in the process Paul gets hurt, then so be it; he sent someone to kill me and I'll never be able to forgive that.

In fact, I realise that with our life assurance he'd have profited quite nicely from my death. This may not have been about a secretary, after all; it could have been about money. Who knows, and at this point who cares.

I've lost my life anyway – the visions of that man plague me and I doubt I'll ever be free from them – and even if I am free and with child, things will never be normal again. But I hope there's a way I'll be allowed to be this little one's mother. I've always wanted to be a mummy.

'I'm so sorry,' Detective Wright says, finally re-entering. 'I had to go back to London, to the station. I had to see your husband. I didn't want to keep you waiting so long, but it was unavoidable. I wanted to be the one to talk to you, not someone else.'

'I am a lost woman, Detective. Being kept waiting, especially as I lie here with nothing to do but think and realise all I've lost, is the least of my worries. The life I knew has gone.' I feel tears building up in my eyes.

Detective Wright smiles. '"She has to live," your husband has just told me. "My child must live. So I've got to tell you the truth."'

I cock my head. 'What are you saying?'

'You don't need to lie any more, Alice. You needn't try to protect him. Your husband has explained everything. He's confessed to killing Alexander Pavlik and concealing his body. And we have the evidence from Laurence Sanders' computers to prove that it was him, not Paul, who made payments to Pavlik before the murders of Richard Dollard, Ethan Fleming and Simon Michael Ryman. We also have communication between Sanders and Pavlik. And the fact that Sanders has taken his own life is, I think, a major indicator of guilt on his part. You see, Alice, your husband was set up and was also targeted just like his former colleagues.'

'By Laurence?'

'Yes. Laurence Sanders also applied for the Circuit Judge vacancy. He tried to kill off the four men he believed were his fiercest competition. He succeeded in having three of them eliminated, but your husband was a lucky man to be able to fight off his attacker the way he did. Paul was foolish not to report it and to then take things into his own hands. And he was foolish to ask you to lie for him to cover up what he'd done. He couldn't risk the promotion, he said.'

'I can't believe it,' I say. Startled, I have to play along. I don't think she's trying to trick me. 'It was awful. Burying the body did him damage. He wasn't the same after it.'

'It changed you, too, he said, keeping it secret all this time. He's seen the effect it's had on you and he's sorry. He regrets putting all that pressure on you. He says he wishes he'd reacted differently, then maybe things could have been better for you. So he wants things to be better for you now.'

'Now I'm pregnant?' I say, the tears drifting down my cheeks.

She nods. 'Now you're pregnant.'

'Paul?' I ask, completely confused, completely thankful.

'Yes,' she says simply. 'Sometimes those closest to us can be capable of doing things we never thought possible.'

'Paul,' I repeat, dream-like.

He's done this for me.

She smiles and gently takes my hand, squeezing reassuringly. 'Yes.'

For us.

A

I've been bailed and I'm facing a charge of attempting to pervert the course of justice. Detective Wright says there's a good chance I'll be given probation, which means I'll be allowed to be a mummy. One dream can come true, despite everything that has changed.

All because of Paul and his selflessness. He had told one more lie – for me.

For us.

Two months have passed and not a single day has gone by without feelings of gratitude overwhelming me. I owe a great debt to my husband, a man who's far braver than I ever knew. My husband, who I still love.

My bump is starting to show, so I've decided to take that bump on a journey.

Wherever I go, as soon as people see the bump, they're ever so helpful and ever so nice. Today is no exception. I'm not kept long in the waiting area and quickly ushered along a couple of corridors to a room that's closed off by dull metal double doors. The guard, a tall, muscular man with close-cropped hair, opens them for me and I enter, thanking him. A row of chairs is behind a white table that stretches the length of the room. Some kind of glass or plastic divides it from the other side, which is identical in layout.

Paul, in a faded blue shirt, is sitting in one of those chairs.

I hesitate momentarily at the edge of the room, staring at my husband, the man to whom I owe everything.

Everything.

A slight pressure on the small of my back encourages me forwards. 'Go ahead,' the guard whispers.

I take a deep breath and walk to the table. Pulling out the chair, I stand so that my thighs touch the table edge. Paul eyes me up and down, taking an extra-long look at my mid-section, and he smiles and stands slowly. We face one another, divided by a piece of glass. I know what he has done for me, the freedom his selflessness has given me and our child. I place my hand on the glass and he does the same. Our hands connect, but we don't touch. We can't.

As our hands are together, he brings his second hand towards the glass and places it lower down. I see what he wants to do – I understand him better than anyone else, after all. I lean forwards but can't get close enough, so I struggle onto the table, on my knees.

I press my belly against the glass and his hand rests on the other side of it. He has his hand on our child but doesn't touch it. Even though they're not touching, I can see from his eyes that he feels his child. I know his child feels him, too. He bends forwards and rests the side of his head against the glass, where our baby is.

No, this won't be my last visit.

Despite the physical barrier between us, I feel closer to Paul now than I ever have before.

28 November

19

Detective Constable Ryan Hillier was standing in the Great Hall, gazing up at the dome, admiring the blue mosaics, when he felt a tap on his shoulder.

Turning around, his smile beamed. 'Katie,' he said. He was now the second person who called her that.

'Ryan.'

Although he thought momentarily about hugging her, they shook hands. 'Has it already been six months?' he asked.

'Five and a half,' she said. 'I couldn't miss this day.'

'I know how you feel. I'll be here every day I possibly can, too. Should be a long one, though.'

Dozens of people streamed past them, others milling around and waiting for the same thing as them.

'How have you found your time off?'

'The sabbatical?' she asked in a mocking tone. He nodded. 'Oh, it's been . . . interesting.' She smiled. 'I'm not sure I feel much rested, if I'm honest, but the break can't have done any harm. I think it's just solidified the notion that this job is for me despite what I may have started thinking.'

'So you are coming back?' he asked keenly.

She shrugged. 'What else would I do?'

'I'm glad,' he said softly, thinking the darkness in her eyes had brightened a touch, and he rubbed her arm soothingly with his hand. Her head turned, her eyes landing on it.

The doors to Court Number One opened from the inside.

'It's time,' she said.

Hillier stepped back and smiled widely. 'After you, ma'am.'

She exhaled the edge of a laugh. 'After me, indeed.'

Smiles on their faces, they headed towards the entrance to the courtroom.

'So what do you make of what's going to happen?' he asked.

'It's a concrete case, I can't see anything going wrong. There shouldn't be any surprises. I think Paul Reeve is going away for a long time.'

'And the wife?'

Wright stopped for a moment and looked at him. 'I think she's got a very good husband. Or at least, he's a good husband now. I don't know how long it took, but he finally thought of her. He finally did the right thing.'

They resumed walking. 'You know,' she added, 'the baby must be nearly due. She never thought she'd be a mother. Imagine that, trying and trying and then finally accepting there's no hope, that it's over.' She nodded slightly and smiled. 'Only to be surprised out of the blue.'

Court Number One at the Old Bailey is saved for prolific cases, mostly murders and terrorism, or those that catch and don't let go of the public's attention. The press had a field day reporting on the arrest of Circuit Judge Paul Reeve, and the opening of the trial was no exception: a packed Court Number One, standing room only in the public gallery. Paul Reeve, whom the press had heralded so positively just over a year ago, was to stand trial for one count of manslaughter, preventing the lawful burial of a body and perverting the course of justice.

Detective Sergeant Katherine Wright would be a key witness in the trial. She sat with Detective Constable Ryan Hillier in the guest seats at the far side of the court room.

A commotion rose as Paul Reeve was brought in, flanked by three attendants, and settled in the defendant's dock at the far end of the courtroom, opposite the judge's podium. There was a long distance between where the defendant and the judge sat, about fifteen metres, making Paul realise just how far he had travelled from where he once was.

'All rise,' the bailiff called.

Everyone, including Paul, stood. As Judge John Fletcher-Smythe walked in, along the dais before sitting down upon his throne, Paul bowed his head, in shame this time, not in reverence, nor as part of procedure.

'Be seated,' his former mentor, friend and drinking buddy said.

As Paul sat down on the uncomfortable wooden chair, his body defeated but his mind buoyed by the news that his child would likely have at least one of her parents in her everyday life, he rested his head against the wall behind him. That was when his eyes met the eyes fifteen metres opposite.

For a moment, but only for a moment, Paul thought there was a glance of recognition in his former mentor's eyes — he almost wanted to smile at John — but as quickly as the familiarity may have been there, it was gone and instead Paul faced the serious, business-like glare that belonged to Judge John Fletcher-Smythe, the man who could, and probably would, determine a lengthy sentence as the most appropriate punishment for the crimes the man seated before him had committed.

John Fletcher-Smythe called out, 'Bring in the jury.'

This was the beginning.

A side door opened. Seven women and five men entered, sitting in the two rows of jury seats to the judge's near right and Paul's far left.

A door closing high up to the right of the room caught Paul's attention. He turned towards it. A few additional members of the public had been allowed to squeeze into the public gallery. One was taking the only reserved seat up there.

She sat in the centre of the front row, almost at full term now. It was three weeks before their miracle would arrive. She appeared to be healthy, radiant and completely ready to be a mother.

Looking up at her, he wondered how many years it would be until he could stand next to her again as a free man, until he could be a real husband and father. How many years would it be till his child could get to know her father properly? Ten years? Fifteen? That sounded about right for his sins and crimes.

Paul smiled at Alice. He was a broken man but one forever changed for the better. He would not regret his final decision.

She smiled back at him, a woman forever grateful, a wife forever in love. She would wait for him.

And, at that moment, as they watched each other with understanding, admiration and appreciation, they both knew they had done the right thing.

Acknowledgements

My sincere thanks and appreciation to everyone at Orion who has worked on *The First Lie*. Particular thanks must go to my editor, Emad Akhtar, without whom *The First Lie* wouldn't exist: thank you for doing things a different way, for having faith that I could pull this off even after draft one went in a 'slightly different direction', and for showing me how wonderful the publishing experience can be. Here's to Spam Folders and Good Timing!

I hope readers will forgive me for taking some creative liberties with the legal details and procedures in this novel. All creative decisions were taken solely in the name of entertainment.